SWALLOWED BY THE BEAST

Swallowed by the Beast

Swallowed by the Beast

Swallowed by the Beast

Contents

Cleanliness is Next to . . .
Robert Tozer

The heavily chlorinated water splashed up and stung one of her eyes. She paused in her work to fiercely rub and dig at it. She prayed for a little relief. Finding none, she continued on as she always did, *"fighting the good fight"* against the endless dirt and filth. She tried to think of a time when she wasn't toiling, trying to keep her home, as her mother used to put it, *"spic-and-span"*.

She caught a glimpse of herself in the door's mirror. She wasn't that old but the years of conscientious work had begun to take its toll. She noticed that her tired eyes had suddenly become even more withdrawn and sunken. Her hands were weathered and beaten. And her face! Her face seemed so weary, and it was now etched in a permanent scowl that would frighten children. Even that polite young man down at the grocery store, the one who always packed the brown paper bags so neatly, had given her a fearful glance like she was a witch or something. He wouldn't even make eye contact, favoring to divert his eyes to the floor instead.

This transformation of her physical features apparently didn't stop there. Lately, she swore that her personality had become afflicted too. An example of this was made clear to her just this morning when her neighbor's dogs—which happened to be the friendliest dogs in the world—shied away from her, with one letting out a small growl as she made her way back to her apartment not twenty minutes ago.

She paused again to stretch out the length of her back, hoping that the bones would somehow snap themselves back into a semblance of comfort. But her hope was in vain, and she sighed heavily before once again tending to her work. She visibly brightened when she remembered her parents' words, and she repeated them aloud, *"Cleanliness is next to godliness."*

Her father, the strict, small-town preacher who seemed to give more sermons around the home than at the church, and her mother, the frail, nervous housewife who had to have everything perfect and *"just so"* had relentlessly drilled that saying into her.

She paused a final time and leaned over the tub to see the fruition of her hard-fought efforts. From underneath the water her daughter's large, bulging eyes stared lifelessly out toward her. Tiny air bubbles were caught on her long lashes and the pupils were rife with fright and terror. Her gaze was directed toward her mother, but continued on past and got lost somewhere in the darkness of the ceiling.

Her mother said in a sickeningly sweet voice, "There, there, buttercup, God will absolve you of your sins now. I don't know darling. Where did you first go wrong? My fourteen-year-old baby girl enjoyed going to parties, getting drunk, getting . . . *pregnant."* Her voice suddenly turned severe and mean, and she snapped, "God frowns on bastard children, you know!" Then she resumed her saccharine tone of voice. "But everything's all alright now, buttercup. Mama has cleansed you and made you one with The Lord again. I'd imagine there'll be quite the homecoming what with your older sister up there and all. Tell her I love her, and that I still forgive her of her sins as well."

Like an automaton, she rose off the bathroom floor and began the process of removing her daughter's body from the tub and preparing it for burial. Her work was interrupted when the front door opened and a young, lively voice sang out, "Hi, Mom! Can't talk now! I've been invited to the biggest party of the year! And can you believe that Roy, the captain of the football team, invited me? Me!! I still don't believe it! Don't wait up for me! Bye, Mom!"

Her mother's words echoed cold and menacingly down the hall after her.

"*Stay clean!*"

Maggot
Arnaldo Lopez Jr.

Topo grabbed the corpse roughly by the shoulder and turned it on its side. The blood, already drying in the apartment's oppressive heat, made a ripping sound as the body was separated from the cheap plastic cover on the couch. Viscous strands of it still connected the dead man to his furniture as Topo inserted a dirty forefinger into one of the sixteen knife wounds he'd helped inflict and explored until he scraped a rib. He grunted in satisfaction.

New York City in the summer of 1988 was plagued by record-breaking heat...and homicides. Newspaper headlines featured the triple-digit numbers of the temperature alongside the quadruple-digit number of murders as if trumpeting the daily results of a macabre contest. While scientists and other talking heads blamed the rise in temperature on Global Warming and El Nino, police blamed the rise in violence on that summer's two most readily available commodities. The heat, and crack cocaine.

In the tiny tenement apartment where Topo and his accomplice stood, covered in an old man's gore, the air felt almost as thick and sticky as the blood that now decorated the walls and cheap, sparse furniture. A screenless window stood wide open, torn gray curtains hanging limply on either side, but no soft breeze disturbed or stirred them. The only things that stirred in the relentless heat of that summer—were the flies.

One of those flies, a fat, hairy specimen, buzzed close by and landed on Topo's hand. He shook it off and let the body of his girlfriend's uncle roll softly to the floor. Topo looked up and glared at his blood-spattered co-conspirator, her own knife still held loosely in her hand and stepped over the body towards her. A fly, bloated with eggs, flew lazily onto the corpse and disappeared into one of the brownish-red wounds in its back.

Topo planted himself in front of his girlfriend and stared down at her. Even though he was barely eighteen years old, he towered more than a foot above his sixteen-year-old "main squeeze". She kept her eyes on the body of her dead uncle on the floor, her young/old face expressionless. Topo placed a large, knobby hand on her head and twisted his fingers into the tight curls of her hair. Suddenly, he yanked her head back, forcing her to look at him. Sharon yelped in pain and dropped her knife.

"I thought you said your uncle had a lot of money on him, Sharon," Topo hissed.

"H—he did, I mean he does," Sharon replied. "I—I mean he's supposed to. Today's Thursday, and he always gets paid on Thursdays."

Sharon flinched, expecting Topo to strike her at any moment. She wouldn't blame him either. They'd planned to kill her uncle and use his money to buy crack cocaine. Then after using some themselves, they would turn the apartment into their own crack den and make more money—more money than they ever imagined. She rolled her eyes and looked again at her uncle's corpse. Now the whole plan may be ruined because there wasn't any money. Sharon didn't understand it...what happened to the money?

Sharon's large eyes widened even more at the sight of the large number of flies that were congregating near the wounds on her dead uncle's body, she saw that some of them were actually entering the nasty gouges in his flesh.

A fly landed on Sharon's face and she quickly brushed it away. Suddenly the sight of the corpse and its flies was replaced by a kaleidoscope of stars as Topo struck her in the face with his big, bony fist. The force of the blow knocked her backward; leaving a few strands of her hair trapped in Topo's other fist. She fell against a small ornate table, breaking it. The carefully positioned collection of small statuettes, incense burners, and candles, along with a tiny basket of ripening fruit, fell to the floor. Sharon laid there not moving, dazed. Topo stomped to where she was, fanning a cloud of flies out of the air before him, and prodded her in the ribs with his foot.

"Don't you ever raise a hand to me bitch," he yelled. Topo knew Sharon's gesture had been harmless, but he liked to assert his power over her. "You even think of raising your hand to me again and I'll kill you!"

Sharon moaned and pulled herself up onto the plastic-sheeted couch. Blood, like a bright red tear, trickled down toward her mouth from a cut high up on her rapidly swelling cheek. Her eye, now partially closed, didn't see the fly that buzzed toward her face, and her cheek, painfully numb from the blow it'd just received, didn't feel the fly when it landed and started sopping up her blood with its brush-like proboscis. Topo pulled her up by the arm and shook her. The fly, disturbed, flew over to the corpse on the floor and made its way into one of the many wounds. The corpse shuddered.

Topo reached into his pocket with his free hand and

pulled out a handful of crumpled and bloody bills. Sharon's one good eye widened in surprise.

"That's my uncle's money, Topo," she said. "You said he didn't have no money on him!"

Topo increased his grip on her arm and she winced.

"Two hundred dollars? Two hundred dollars? That ain't no money bitch," Topo snarled in reply as he waved the money in front of Sharon's battered face. "You made it sound like he had him some real money. What you think we can do with only two bills?"

Topo walked over to the apartment door, kicking upturned furniture and debris from his path, and dragged Sharon along behind him. He kicked the knife she'd dropped earlier and it skittered to a stop against the dead man's leg. When Topo got to the door, he turned and stuffed the money into one of Sharon's grimy hands.

"Go to Fatty Dee's place over on Myrtle Avenue," he said. "Bring back a couple of jumbos, and about ten nickel hits." Sharon nodded excitedly, gripping the money tighter in her fist.

"You better hurry too," Topo continued. "Don't stop to talk to nobody and you better not smoke none on your own."

Sharon shook her head and tried to smile. "I..." she began.

Topo spun her around and shoved her face into the apartment's old wooden door. Paint chips splintered and fell off, falling into her hair and settling on the floor. She tasted some in her mouth but she was too afraid to spit them out.

"Don't think I'm playing with you, Sharon," Topo growled. "You better run there and run back, and don't smoke none over there by yourself or I'll kick your ass from Fatty Dee's all the way back here. You understand?"

Sharon nodded as much as she could in her present position and felt relieved when Topo finally let her go.

"Go ahead then," he said.

Sharon nodded her head again and Topo opened the door and pushed her out into the dimly lit hallway. A large rat, unafraid, watched her as she ran out into the searingly hot dusk. The rat, smelling blood, slinked toward the apartment. It moved forward in quick spasms of movement, its tiny muscular legs a blur. Topo watched the disgusting creature until it was almost to the apartment door and then slammed the door shut. The rat, disappointed, bared its long incisors and turned away. There will always be blood another day.

Topo turned and surveyed the wrecked apartment. 'I got to put Sharon out on the street so she can make me some money,' he thought. 'This little bit of money I got here is gonna go quick, but she's still young and cute enough to make me more. That little bitch'll be working the street until she's too ugly or too dead. Then I'll just hook me up another young bitch that'll do anything for some crack. There's a lot of them. Their mamas too.'

Topo walked over to the corpse on the floor, it was covered with a moving, living mat of flies. As Topo watched, the rhythmic movement of the flies made the body seem as if it were breathing. He kicked the body savagely, causing the flies to rise in an angrily buzzing cloud. One fly landed on his lip.

"Damn!"

Topo brushed the fly off and swatted at it as it flew away. It landed on the body again and made its way inside.

Topo watched all of this with building revulsion. He

eyed a nearby closet and decided that now would be as good a time as any to move the body. He opened the closet door, tossed most of its contents out into the room behind him, and then turned and bent in order to drag the body in by its legs. Topo stopped. Something was different. The body didn't look the same somehow. Topo felt the hair on the back of his neck stand on end as superstitious fear walked its cold, bony fingers up his spine. Slowly, he straightened up and took a step back. Warily, he circled the body, looking for any impossible sign of life. The only life he could make out were the flies and their newly emerging offspring. Maggots. They were everywhere that he saw exposed flesh, resembling thousands of tiny grains of rice.

Topo shrugged off his fear. 'The guy probably just had a spasm or something,' Topo thought. "I heard about stuff like that happening in funeral homes.' After stalling for a few more minutes, Topo resumed his position at the dead man's feet and pulled him toward the closet, leaving behind a trail of blood, slime and wriggling larvae. Sharon's knife, wedged under the corpse, was dragged in with the body.

Hours later, Sharon snuck back into the apartment mostly empty-handed. She crept through the doorway, wanting to enter unnoticed. At the same time, she knew how futile this was since there was no place to hide in the tiny apartment, and Topo would be expecting her. Sharon tip-toed inside anyway in the hope of delaying the punishment that Topo was sure to subject her to for being late.

When she'd gotten to Fatty Dee's crack house and saw all those other people taking all those delicious hits from their pipes, she just had to do some. She didn't think that she'd get so caught up in smoking that most of the money would be gone. Topo, she knew, would be enraged and would beat her mercilessly. Hopefully, however, if she wasn't hurt too bad, things would go right back to normal and the two of them would stay like they were. Together forever. Young. In love. And high.

Cautiously, she peered into the minuscule kitchen, her eyes wide with fear and apprehension. Topo wasn't there. She stepped over her uncle's body and looked in his bedroom as well as in the dingy bathroom, they were empty as well. Puzzled, she stepped back into the middle of the living room which, with its fold-out couch, also served as her bedroom. She looked around at the apartment's devastation and at the items scattered all over the floor that her uncle had so lovingly and dutifully collected and cared for. Her uncle had told her on numerous occasions that he was a powerful Voodoo priest. The tiny statues that now lay broken and scattered about the floor were representatives of Orishas or Voodoo Gods. The other things that had also fallen from the small table that had served as a shrine were offerings or stuff used in rituals. When Sharon was small she was fascinated by the statues, the rituals, and the stories her uncle told her by the quivering light of the candles. But as Sharon grew older, she became bored with all of his mumbo-jumbo; she often wondered that if he was such a great voodoo priest, why did they live in such a tiny, crappy apartment in such a crappy neighborhood? Why didn't they drive around in an expensive car? Why couldn't he buy her the latest clothes? Sharon shook her head, why couldn't he stop them from killing him?

She stood there wondering where Topo was and what she should do next when she became aware of a strange sound.

The sound was faint, but not unfamiliar. She looked around, trying to figure out where it was coming from. Finally, she was able to pinpoint it. It was coming from the closet.

'Topo is hiding in there,' she thought. She stepped over her uncle's body, barely giving it a glance, and slowly put her hand on the doorknob. She placed an ear against the door and then pulled her face away quickly. The sound coming from the closet's interior made the door vibrate. It was a weird buzzing noise, and it was louder now too.

"Topo?" Sharon called through the door. "Topo, what are you doing in there? Sounds like you're messing with the electricity. Can I open the door?" Sharon turned the knob and pulled the door open, an apology and an explanation already on her lips.

The closet's black interior exploded in her face as thousands of flies, buzzing agitatedly, swarmed all over her. They became entangled in her hair and in her clothes. They flew into her nose, her ears, and her mouth. She flailed her arms about wildly, backing away from the closet, and tripped over one of her dead uncle's outstretched legs. She landed on the floor with a heavy thud, barking her elbow on the hard linoleum, and had the wind knocked out of her. She lay on her back for a few seconds trying to regain her breath and composure as flies slowly crawled all over her.

As she finally raised herself up on her elbows, her eyes strayed to the open closet...and she screamed. There was Topo. His eyes and mouth were opened wide with terror. Fresh blood stained the front of his tattered shirt, running from a dozen or more knife wounds in his torso. Maggots bristled from his hands, chest, neck, face, even his tongue. Slowly, they waved in her direction, as if beckoning to her. As Sharon watched, one of Topo's eyeballs rotated crazily in its socket and sank from view. It was replaced almost immediately by a wriggling mass of fly larvae that boiled from the eye socket and splattered onto his sneakers. Sharon screamed again.

Unfortunately, the screams of the terrified or dying were common in this dark, forlorn building. Its residents, long the hostages of crack, crime, and indifference, were used to death. Anyone that heard Sharon's cry merely shivered at its timbre and turned up the volume on the television set.

Topo's body swayed and Sharon, terrified that it would fall on her, dug in her heels and scooted backward. Without warning, a swollen hand grabbed her ankle and held her fast. Despite the oppressive heat, Sharon felt gooseflesh rise over her entire body as her spine turn to ice. She stared at the hand uncomprehendingly, until suddenly her uncle, the Voodoo priest, raised his head to hers. The skin of his face and hands rippled with the living multitude that swarmed underneath. Sharon watched as maggots pulsed from a wound in her uncle's heart. They rushed through his arteries and veins, replacing the blood that she helped to spill. He smiled and more of the maggots dripped from the corner of his mouth.

Just then, Topo's body toppled forward and landed on top of her, spraying her with blood and larvae. Sharon screamed, again and again, ...until, at last, all that could be heard was the lazy drone of the summer flies.

Mowgli Encounters a Bear
Carey Azzara

One lazy summer day, Marci and Shauna are lounging in their backyard. On this particular afternoon, they are home alone taking care of the two dogs, Mowgli and Anya, their two birds, and two new kittens, Percy and Duke. Although it is summer, it's a pleasant day, not too hot, typical of New Hampshire weather in late August. The girls are having a quiet chat and sipping cold drinks. Like most siblings, Marci and Shauna have moments that are, well, let's just say tense, and sometimes downright argumentative. However, when the chips are down, they can always depend on each other to be fiercely protective.

Percy and Duke are on Shauna's lap, and Anya, a 135-pound Great Dane, is sitting at Marci's feet. Mowgli, who is a 120-pound German shepherd, is sunning himself in the yard, and the birds are resting quietly (for a change) in the house. Everything is peaceful, a rare but welcome moment for this busy household.

Although Anya is a big dog, she frightens easily. Often, after initially barking fiercely, she slinks away and hides behind one of the girls when a stranger approaches. Mowgli, on the other hand, is both protective and friendly. He will happily meet and greet anyone, with few exceptions. All dogs seem not to like certain people, and the girls always pay close attention to Mowgli's "sixth sense" about people. The dogs take care of the girls and the girls take care of them. It's a wonderful set of relationships and makes the girls' mom feel secure when she must occasionally leave them home alone.

As the afternoon wanes and evening approaches, a gentle breeze cools their faces. The sun is still warm when it peeks out from behind the clouds where it has been hiding on an off the whole day. The girls laugh at Mowgli, who flops over on his side and then rolls onto his back. He now has his legs spread-eagled and his tongue is hanging out one side of his mouth. He yawns and then flips over to his other side. It's a lazy day indeed.

Marci and Shauna are just about ready to go inside when Anya jumps unexpectedly to her feet. She obviously hears or smells something. Mowgli does, too. His ears are up and he is on full alert. No one moves. Then the cats both screech and leap off Shauna's lap, rushing as fast as their little kitten legs can take them toward the back door. The sisters send bewildered looks at one another and their faces become anxious.

Marci whispers, "What's going on? Do you see anything?"

Shauna shakes her head no. "What could it be? Is there something out there?"

Then there is a rustling in the bushes at the tree line. Mowgli is on his feet and the girls get up, too. Anya has her tail between her legs and is slowly making her way behind the girls.

To everyone's amazement, a massive bear with coarse bristly fur emerges from the woods and lets out a spine-chilling growl. Then it begins to march toward them.

Of course, the question of what type of bear they are facing is not the uppermost thought on either of the girls' minds. However, knowing what kind of bear you are confronting is important. Black bears are good climbers, and their claw marks are deep enough to permanently scar the bark of an aspen tree. If you startle a black bear it will typically run away and then often up a tree.

By contrast, a startled brown (grizzly) bear may charge and occasionally attack, making grizzlies over twenty times more dangerous than black bears. Sometimes it isn't easy to tell them apart. The joke is if you don't know, simply climb a tree. If the bear climbs up after you and eats you, it's a black bear. If the bear shakes the tree until you fall out and then eats you, it's a brown bear. The fact is you should never climb a tree to escape from a bear. Your best course of action is to throw food in one direction and run as fast as you can in the opposite direction...but clearly, I digress.

As the bear begins to approach them, the girls let out horror movie screams. Everyone except Mowgli heads for the back door, where the cats are nervously waiting to escape into the house. The commotion startles the birds and they start cawing away, making the situation even tenser.

Mowgli confronts the bear with loud barking. The bear reacts by standing on her hind legs, which makes her look even more dangerous. Her mouth is open and she is growling back at Mowgli while slashing her front paws in the air. Mowgli stands his ground. His bark turns into a deep and persistent growl. His jowls are drawn back, exposing his long white teeth. It's clear he is serious and has no intention of running away. Although Mowgli is not backing down and the bear seems to take note of the threat, she's not backing down either.

Marci opens the back door. She and her sister are frantic. They shout at Mowgli, "C'mon boy, c'mon in, Mowgli! Come in the house!" Although the girls holler repeatedly, Mowgli is not backing away. He is fearlessly defending his two girls and nothing is going to make him stand down. Anya, on the other hand, is hiding behind Shauna with her tail between her legs.

When it is clear that the bear is not backing away, Marci begins to step out the door. She isn't sure what she's going to do, but she can't let her shepherd get hurt. Just then, Anya finds her grit and squeezes between the girls, nearly knocking Marci to the ground. She runs out barking madly and positions herself to protect Mowgli's left flank. Her barking quickly turns into loud, frightening, and aggressive growling. Her lips, like Mowgli's, are drawn back to show her teeth, and she takes up a pouncing stance. Her love for the girls and Mowgli gives her courage that he and the girls, up to now, have not been aware she possesses.

Together, the big dogs pose a formidable and dangerous opposition. Now that Anya is joining in the fight, she and Mowgli stand a better chance of warding off the bear. However, the bear is still growling and shaking her head angrily. The standoff continues...and then the bear seems to reconsider her options. Suddenly, the girls spot a small black nose peering from behind a tree. It looks like a bear cub, but no—there are *two* bear cubs!

The cubs playfully scamper from left to right behind their mother. When they safely arrive on the opposite side of the clearing, the mother bear returns to a four-footed stance. She slowly turns and proudly walks away. She is still growling a little and shaking her head defiantly. She looks back to make sure she isn't being chased and then trots toward the woods with her cubs in tow.

The dogs know they have won. They stand guard but they don't take any offensive action. Each dog lets out a few barks to warn the bear that they are still there watching her. When the mother bear is close to the edge of the woods, she calls to her cubs and walks them deeper into the forest area. It is obvious now that her actions are about protecting her cubs and she has no intention of harming the girls, the dogs, or the cats.

Once the bear family is out of sight, Anya and Mowgli run to the back door where they are greeted with hugs and a torrent of pats on the head. The girls are laughing and tears are rolling down their cheeks. Mowgli jumps on Shauna and knocks her down. He licks her face and she laughs so hard her stomach begins to ache. Marci has her arms around Anya's neck, and when she lets go, Anya gently licks her face. The two sisters come together and hug each other tightly. They cry a little and then laugh aloud as Mowgli and Anya each give the other a couple of licks, too.

Marci says, "Hey, sis, this is a story we can tell our grandchildren!"

Shauna agrees and adds, "Yeah, but let's hope we don't have too many more stories like this to tell."

When the girls' mom comes home, they tell her every detail. After a few hugs and rewards for the courageous dogs, she makes some phone calls to the authorities, who immediately put out warnings around the area. Within a few days, they catch the bears and ship them to a wilderness area further north in the state.

That night Mowgli and Anya are treated to a special meal and receive more than a few affectionate hugs, ear scratches, and belly rubs.

Vegas Demon
A True Story by June Lundgren

One would think that all dark energy comes from negative entities such as demons, minions, and ghosts. But this is not true; 90% of the negative energy in the world is created by man. What does that say about mankind?

You don't have to see the dark ones to know that they are close by. You can feel it, the air suddenly gets heavy, you experience nausea, the room suddenly feels freezing cold, you may smell rotting meat or sulfur and you feel a sense of uneasiness in the pit of your stomach.

I was in Las Vegas, giving a lecture in preparation for the completion of my first book. People were calling and coming to my host's home for healings and readings. I had just stopped to take a lunch break when suddenly I sensed a presence of evil close by. I looked over at my host and asked, "When is my next appointment scheduled?"

She checked her schedule book and said "The next person isn't scheduled until one o'clock so we can have some lunch. Why do you want to know, is there a problem?"

I looked at her and shook my head. "Someone's coming, and they have a demon attached to them."

"How do you know someone's coming?" she asked.

"Because I can feel them coming, right here," I said, holding a fist over my stomach area.

I felt an internal coldness and a sense of foreboding that always warns me when evil is present. She looked at me nervously, and then the doorbell rang.

"Don't worry about the demon it can't get past the line of protection surrounding the house. That's why I had you place a line of blessed salt around the house, so nothing negative could enter prior or during my visit." The doorbell rang again and she looked at me nervously then went to answer it. A young woman stood in the doorway.

"I've been trying to get through on the phone for the past two days. I wanted to schedule an appointment for a healing. The line was always busy. No matter what time I called, I could never seem to get through. I decided to take a chance and stop by the house to see if I could schedule a healing." The woman said, looking over at me.

I looked at my host, "Lunch can wait, I need to take care of this right away." I said, giving her a meaningful look. "Let's go somewhere private so we can talk." I took her into another room.

Shutting the door, I asked, "So how long have you had the demon attached to you?"

She looked at me in shock. "Is that what's wrong with me? All my life I've felt like I had a black cloud hanging over my head. I've had nothing but bad luck for as long as I can remember. I lost my parents when I was twelve; my stepbrother has been stealing money from my trust fund and I've always been in a lot of physical pain."

Again, I sensed the dark presence; turning my head I could see the demon outside the property and it was furious. I opened myself up to contact the angelic plane.

"God please send me some help in the form of an

Archangel to remove the demon."

I heard a soft voice say "Child I will send Ezekiel and Michael to deal with the demon. Tell the woman that the demon had been trying to prevent her from contacting you. It knew that if she did come, its presence would be revealed and it would be banished."

I felt an overpowering warmth spread through my body and knew that the Archangels were next to me.

The next moment I felt them leave. Looking out the window I could see Michael was on one side of the demon and Ezekiel on the other side. They seemed to be wrestling with it. The next thing I knew all three of them disappeared. I smiled to myself and said "thank you," out loud. The woman looked at me in inquiry.

"I asked God to send an Archangel to take care of the demon. He sent Michael and Ezekiel. They were here for a moment and then I saw one on each side of the demon and it was struggling to get away. Then all three of them disappeared. You won't have to worry about the demon anymore." I smiled reassuringly at her. "Are you sure it won't be back?" she asked nervously.

"When God has a demon removed, it never comes back."

"God said to let you know that it was the demon who was trying to prevent you from coming here. Our phone line was not busy all the time, it was the demon trying to prevent itself from being found out. You'll find that your streak of bad luck and that dark cloud hanging over your head will no longer prevent you from living your life.

"I can hardly believe it, I feel so much lighter as if a great weight has been lifted from me. Thank you, thank you so much for your help in removing it." She said, starting to cry.

"Don't thank me, thank God, He's the one who sent the Archangels to remove the demon. I think your brother is going to find that the shoes on the other foot. Now it's you who will be set free, free to live your life in the light."

I did a reading for her to let her know that the future was indeed filled with light, and she wouldn't have to worry about the dark one anymore.

It is possible for a person to have a demon or a negative entity attached to them and be unaware of it. It does not happen often but when it does your life is pure hell. Most people pass it off as bad luck or they may think they're cursed when in actuality it is so much worse than what they think.

Night Songs
Anthony V. Pugliese

Something wicked lurked in the swamp's mist. Something about the insects' haunting trills, the way their tremulous warbles penetrated the sodden air.

Elijah 'Shaky' Nash fidgeted in the stolen motorboat as he batted away finger-sized mosquitoes and paddled cautiously between the eerie, gnarled cypress casting vein-like shadows against the brackish Mississippi.

A bright white moon melted against the darkening sky. In the distance, an owl shrieked like some ghostly messenger forewarning the approach of death.

The swamp withheld a lethal secret soon to be revealed and as he tried to catch up with his reflection in the murky river, Shaky listened to his partner Cain swear while he kicked the clogged outboard motor. Cain noticed his destination 200-ft ahead.

"There it is, boy!" Cain's eyes were wide, all his large tombstone-shaped teeth showing as he grimaced in joy and stood up on the boat. "Look, I can't believe it! This old place is still standin' after all these years!"

When they reached the 8-ft pier, Cain reached out to a twisted cypress tree and tied the boat around its knotted trunk. "Let's get movin', boy," he said, "We don't want to be out there when it's dark."

Shaky didn't argue. Cain Levi Roche was a former truck driver and a vicious hulk of a man. 50ish, 6' 2" with a 275-pound frame with a leathery, haggard complexion, his death sentence had been commuted in 1979. He was later sentenced to life for rape and murder. The son of a Croatian mother and a French/Choctaw Indian father in Shreveport, Louisiana, he had inherited his father's large ominous features.

He scratched at the thick, knife scar stretching from his left eye to the edge of his thick, box jaw. He hopped off the boat and proceeded to walk down the pier barely visible below the stalks of honey-colored wheatgrass and thick stabbing weeds.

Shaky thought about the blood trail left along the way following their fortunate escape from Angola prison two days ago.

As far as the law had ascertained, Cain had killed only one person on the outside. He had killed several men in prison but Shaky was convinced he had murdered far more in his past nationwide travels.

"C'mon, boy," Cain prodded, waving him along.

They both headed toward the abandoned house ahead, Shaky in fear of Cain's predatory ways.

Cain protected him from the other prisoners when he had first arrived 5 years ago, He had taken a liking to him. Shaky helped create makeshift weapons. He became involved in cigarette and gambling action, became Cain's eyes and ears, conferring with the local snitch to find out who was plotting to kill him. And he did these things whether he wanted or not. But had it not been for Cain, he may have been raped, beaten or worse. Maximum security prison was no place for a young man like him. All along, he knew there would come a day when this symbiotic relationship revealed its true price. Today would be that day.

Two days ago. Road detail. Sixteen prisoners in all, including him and Cain. Shackled together at the ankles like a feral charm bracelet, each one worked in the brain-boiling humidity under the watchful eyes of work boss, Cletus Gant.

Nothing for miles except road, dust, telephone poles and the faint swishing of swing blades cutting wheatgrass.

Cain signaled him with a nod. He had planned it for weeks, made all the arrangements. He expected Shaky to do his part.

Gant never conveyed any emotion or indifference behind his wary eyes. He stared out from the mirrored shades beneath his Stetson and stood as still as the telephone poles flanking the road. Rifle cocked with a .38 holstered around his torso, he was primed and ready for trouble. Too many guards around, Shaky thought. Sweat poured down his face as Cain mouthed in ire. *"What're you waitin' fer?"*

Guards paced like cats and spat at the ground, wiping their brows and cursing the southern heat. Their keys jangled on their belt loops and their boots trod the dry soil beneath as they fiddled with their weapons as if they would vanish if not touched every few seconds or so. Dead silence.

Shaky started his performance. He yelled out in pain, hit the ground and grabbing his gut as he had been instructed to do. He writhed, moaned, and kicked.

Gant rushed over, teeth gritted, one hand clenched into a fist as his right wrapped about the waist of his rifle. "Whatsa' matta', boy?" he growled. "You'd betta' git yer ass off that ground, son, or so help me, the tip of this rifle will be buried up yo' ass so fa', you'll be feelin' it in yo' throat!"

Shaky cried out, "can't—boss. Stomach—much pain. Oh,

GOD, it hurts so much!"

"Yeah? Well, my foot in yo' ass is gonna'—

The swing blade descended upon Gant's head, his Stetson flying off into the weeds, blood everywhere. Deader than road kill.

Gant's keys and rifle had been in Cain's hands before Shaky could even blink.

Cain had given him the .38. He pulled a matchbox from Gant's pocket, lit a match and tossed it into the tall grass.

Pandemonium ensued like a Chinese New Year festival gone awry. Rifle fire all around with Cain in his element, shooting and killing like an outlaw from the Old West, Cain smiling the entire time as he fought his way through the gauntlet.

The other prisoners fled. Some guards began the chase while others stayed behind to extinguish the raging fire in the fields.

Shaky had been ordered to use the .38 as Cain made his way toward the prisoner transport bus. He demanded he shoot to kill, but Shaky just shot into the air. He didn't need murder charges added onto his sentence if their escape failed.

They drove down what seemed to be a deserted, never-ending road. Miles and miles to nowhere, passing towns and parishes. Cain later ditched the bus in a drain gully. The two walked until exhausted, hungry and thirsty.

Everyone would be looking for them, and for an instant, Shaky wanted to be found. He worried about the future. And about the psychopathic asshole, he was with.

Cain killed a man who owned a fishing cabin, grabbing him from behind and snapping his neck like a carrot stick before stealing his Alumacraft motorboat and some supplies. He filled several canteens, found food, and gas for the boat. They embarked on what Cain called, a journey back to his roots.

They headed north, down the Okefenokee Swamp. Cain mentioned a 'safe-house' he had on the banks of the Mississippi River. Cops would never find them there. Nothing but swampland. Shaky was glad to be out of prison, but he wished he had never agreed to this journey into hell. He blotted the sweat from his forehead with the sleeve of his bright blue jumper, evaluating the dreary, humid landscape as he stared at the dilapidated, 2-story, clapboard house smothered beneath dense vines and Spanish moss.

The paint-chipped door had broken glass louvers and the partially collapsed roof was missing shingles.

Insects everywhere. Crickets, grasshoppers, and cicadas, dotting the area like paint-ball stigmata. Some leaping, others flying, pelting against the old house with violent fury. Their trills and warbles ended when Shaky and Cain crept by. So silent now, only desperate footfalls on the dock. He needed food, sleep, and shelter.

The insects started singing again. Shaky thought about how insect songs used to be soothing. He had grown up listening to their night songs. Now they would always remind him of Cain, prison, murder, and the dead house ahead.

The insects' compositions increased in volume. He felt the humming vibrations in his inner ear, the sun's flaming crown disappearing behind the horizon. "There's something very wrong with this place, Cain," he noted in his syrupy drawl as he lifted his hands to his ears in an attempt to filter out the din.

"Relax, Bubba," Cain said. "Ain't nothin' ta fear."

Shaky turned and watched the boat bobble next to the cypress barely standing above the water on stilted, tangled roots. He thought about running to it and leaving Cain behind for good.

"Let's get inside," Cain demanded, grabbing Shaky's shoulder. "It's gettin' dark, boy. I don't wanna' be out ch'ere anymore."

As they walked ahead, Cain halted in mid-gait, one massive hand in the air. "Hold up fer a minute," he said.

"What's wrong?"

"Shush up. I thought I heard somethin'."

"What? How can you hear anything above these bugs?"

"Be quiet and give me the thirty-eight."

Cain brandished the gun, lifted its barrel. He walked toward the front door. "Follow behind me," he said, "and keep yo' mouth shut, you hear?" He crept to the door and nudged it open with his large right shoulder; its decayed hinges squealed eerily. Inside, something shuffled around in the darkness. Night fell quickly, the swamps' greens and browns transforming to blacks and grays.

"Prob'ly just an animal, Cain," Shaky said, his voice trembling.

"Maybe a raccoon."

"Racoon my ass. There's someone in here. I can smell 'em."

Shaky heard the subtle click of the gun's hammer being pulled back.

"Go find the kerosene lanterns," Cain said. "There's some around somewhere."

"In the dark?"

"Just do it, dummy."

Shaky felt around and banged his knees into an old

coffee table. He found tree lamps with wire handles and rusted metal housings sitting rusted on the surface. He handed one to Cain.

Cain pulled out his matches and lit the lamp's blackened wick. He lifted it to face level. His face took on a demonic glow. He panned the room with the cold predatory eyes of a Copperhead, grinning from ear to ear, unblinking, his face like an evil Cheshire cat with large square teeth. "I know someone's in here! C'mon and show yourself, or things're gonna' get complicated when I start shootin' in the dark! Ya' neva' know what I might hit, huh?"

A dark presence raised its arms into the air from behind the threadbare sofa and stood erect. A girl bathed in lamplight. She was attractive. And in the wrong place at the wrong time.

Tan with rounded features, the girl wore a sleeveless t-shirt with blue-denim cut-off shorts. Her rounded neck-length, flax-colored hair gleamed in the dim light and her wide, round coal black eyes assessed her surroundings. She showed no fear. She never even struggled with the cloth strips binding her to the paint peeled, ladder-back chair. Shaky thought this unsettling.

Cain slithered up to her, leaning inches from her face. He pressed the gun against her left temple, his lifeless, unblinking eyes
fixed on hers. "You gotta' name, missy?"

"I'm Melody. Melody Latone"

Cain growled under his breath. "French-Creole, eh?"

"Half."

"Mind tellin' me, what in the name of Christ on a stick yer doin' all the way out ch'ere?

"I'm a student at the University. I came out here to

study insects, my course of study is entomology, which is the study of—"

"—I know what it means!" Cain said. "I ain't ig'nernt just 'cause I ain't in college, bitch! So, where's yer boat? We didn't see any other boat up yonda' as we paddled in."

"It was caught in some mangrove roots and sank into the bog. I'm stuck here with no cell phone or laptop now. They were on the boat and I have no idea how I'm getting back."

Cain sighed his eyes like slits. "Well, Girly-Q, you are way in over yer pretty little head, I'd say."

Shaky had bad vibes about the woman. He walked up to Cain and whispered in his ear, *"She might be a cop."*

Cain regarded him with a gritted frown. "I don't recall askin' you a goddamned thing, you get me? If she were a cop, where's she keepin' a gun and badge? Ain't no cop got the sense to come out here, boy. Tell you what...keep yo' pie-hole shut. Go sit by the winda' and keep watch or somethin'."

Shaky dragged a straight back chair to the window facing the black river. Light sparkles danced on its rippling surface like stars. The second most beautiful thing he saw in this hell-hole all day, he thought. He parted the moldy, tattered drapes, trying to sift through the dirt and cobwebs that coated the cracked panes. He felt something cold against the nape of his neck. Cain's gun. "Are you going to kill me, Cain?"

Cain snickered, "awww, just keepin' you on yer toes, son." He spun the revolver's chamber once and placed it against Shaky's head. "I don't think I want you talkin' to that girl, got it? I've got a funny feelin' you can't be trusted. You hear?"

"Sure, Cain," Shaky said, ignoring Cain's sadism.

"Lots of insects out tonight, huh?"

"It's mid-August, dummy. Always are a lot out this time of year."

"My mama used to say if you see a cricket, put it in your hand and make a wish."

"Yeah, I know you believe in all that hocus-pocus, hoodoo, boy. But I don't."

Shaky believed in many things. He recalled the stories his Irish great-grandma had told him when he was a boy. Witches, fairies, and the Will o' the wisp. She said these ethereal beings lived in the swamps and had power. She said *haints* and demons walked the earth, always watching.

"Odd," he started, "whenever I heard insects sing, I'd never actually *seen* them. Little bastards are everywhere. They're really loud, too. Louder than I've ever heard."

"Bayou hokum, boy. They just seem louder 'cause it's quieter than a priest's tomb."

"What about the girl, Cain?" He looked at Melody. "She isn't even scared. Not one drop of sweat on her face. Hell, I've been sweating all damn day!"

Cain stroked the gun barrel across Melody's lips, his eyes glazing as he combed his unkempt salt & pepper hair with his free hand. "You wanna' go back to, Angola? Is that what you want, huh?"

Shaky shook his head.

"Good. Now you listen to me: When my daddy wasn't drinkin' himself blind and kickin' me and my mama around the house, he'd put my ass to work in his sugarcane and rice fields. He said when the humidity is high, insects get plentiful. In other countries, grasshoppers would go apeshit and eat eveythin' in their path in dry weather. Nature, that's all. Ain't nothin' voodoo about it, you *hear*?"

"Yeah, I understand, Cain, but—"

Cain grabbed him by his loose shirt with one hand, lifting him to nose level. "Boy, I don't wanna' be here either, but we ain't got no choice. I'd rather be down in N'or'lans!" Cain punched him in the gut and threw him back into the chair. The warped floorboards beneath cracked and split from the impact.

Shaky thought his ribs had wrapped themselves around his lungs. He scrunched his eyes in agony, trying to regain his composure. Cain stared him down, his eyes wicked and hateful.

Something about the swamp made him different. He never talked back to Cain before. He found confidence. Deep within himself, within the most primal area in his mind.

Cain belonged behind bars like a rogue gorilla. Somewhere along the way, Cain's life took a twisted turn and his mind (if he had one) had become as polluted as city air, as convoluted as an elderberry tree, and as rotten as a week-old melon.

Shaky feared not only for himself but now, he also feared for Melody. She didn't seem to fear for herself so he'd do it for her.

He looked at her. Young, gorgeous and sweet. The perfect victim for Cain, a present from the Devil himself. She'll be dead before sun-up, he thought.

Cain watched her all night. He knew HE was being watched. His face became gaunt, veins popped from his thick neck as he walked over to Shaky. "I guess you know what um plannin' to do to with 'er, am I right, boy?"

"Yeah, I know, Cain," Shaky said, calm as possible. He tried to be strong. Cain sensed weakness.

Cain's eyes squinted into slits. "Got somethin' on yer mind?"

"Please don't kill her," Shaky said. "Just be more blood on our hands. Killing's what got you in prison in the first place. That stripper in Norfolk, Virginia? You raped and killed her, left her on the road naked."

Shaky's head almost spun completely around when Cain struck him with a fast, hard, right cross to the left.

"Don't you ever bring that up again," Cain said. "Keep the preachin' to yer rich, drunken, self-righteous daddy! And don't let me catch you tryin' to help that girl, eitha'. 'Cause if the 'gators and quicksand don't get ya'...I will."

Insects catapulted against the house, punctuating Cain's final word. Whirrs and whistles sliced through the dark like tiny buzz saws.

Shaky remembered their songs, how they used to lull him to sleep at night, take his mind off the slamming iron doors, the screeching prisoners being raped, and the dominant voices booming LIGHTS OUT!

He gazed at his shadowy reflection in the window, trying to distinguish his form from within the cracked glass. His short, dirty-blonde hair laid pasted to his forehead and temples and he appeared older than his 26 years.

He wished he had never entered the bar in Metairie. Wished he had never let his friends talk him the tragic joyride three years ago.

Sky like blue velvet. Residual clouds in the night sky stars shining like sparkles in a snow-globe. He met two older boys after running away from home to get daddy's attention. Dad only cared about his church and his congregation. He threw money at him to keep him happy. And there was no love. Only beatings after a few drinks.

The boys had been high on ecstasy, mushrooms, and Southern Comfort. Shaky stayed in the car. He didn't know they were robbing the convenience store. They had run outside with a bag of money, the angry proprietor holding a rifle as he followed behind.

"Drive!" one boy had told him, a gun to his head. "Drive or die, yard-bird!"

The owner had been shot, killed by the blonde kid with the big mouth. The other boy with the tousled hair grabbed the wheel and made Shaky crush the man beneath the tires, the owner's wife running outside screaming, her baby crying in her arms.

The blonde had shot her dead as they drove off. Shaky watched her fall onto the pavement, the baby still clasped in her arms. The blonde turned, stared out the windshield and snickered. No remorse showing in his dead pea-green eyes.

Shaky's mother took her life with a lethal dose of laudanum after he was convicted and sentenced to twenty years in prison. His father disinherited him, cursed him in the name of *Gawd* and warned him never to return to the plantation again.

He had lost everything, been shunned by his family, friends, and the rich elite. No more college money, no more stipend, and no more life. His education, as useful as a toilet seat being thrown to a drowning man. An escaped convict, a fugitive hiding in the rectum of the world with an eerie beautiful woman and a maniac with a taste for blood. Welcome to your new life, he thought.

Cain sat sprawled out on the floor, hypnotically spinning the gun's chamber and enjoying it like a child playing with a toy truck.

"Hey, gal," Shaky tried to say in a whisper. "Aren't you afraid?"

"No," she said, shaking her head. "Should I be?"

"Damn right you should be. Cain plans to kill you. You *do* know that, don't you?"

"Don't worry," Melody smiled. "This will all be over soon." "I don't wanna' hear talkin'," Cain said, rising from the floor. "And didn't I tell you not to talk to her, boy?"

"Leave him alone," Melody said. "If you listen, you may learn something. Although, I doubt you have any gray matter in that gourd you call a head. You should listen to the outside and heed what it's trying to tell you. Pay attention to the toad, the grasshopper, even the ant. For they know everything."

She was a witch, Shaky thought. Her words, like an incantation. No: more like a revelation. His grandma always said sweet, young women with confidence and strength were either witches or inhuman. As if a woman couldn't be strong without being supernatural, he would laugh. In this case, she may have been correct. No angelic young girl would talk to a man like Cain in that manner.

Cain's massive jaw dropped. "You gotta' lotta' guts talkin' to me like that, sweetmeat."

"I know what you are," Melody said with superiority and restrained rage. "I know...and soon...*you* will know who *I* am." "You need a little knockin' around," Cain said, fists clenched.

"Beware, Cain," Melody said in a calm sing-song tone, "Beware the night singers and the guardians of the earth. They sing for
YOU!"

Insects bounced and thumped against the flimsy structure. The roof and floorboards shuddered. Shaky jumped up, hopping from one foot to the other.

Cain cocked his fist. "You talk a lotta' crap, girly—

41

I'm gonna' ram my—"

In the distance, a low humming sound like a low flying plane intensified. Rumbling shook the house to its foundation.

Everyone dropped to the floor.

Insects edged through the windows, squeezed through the louvers in the door. They exploded down from the buckled staircase on the second floor in a spiral formation entering every room, making it impossible to see through their shapes and flying forms.

Crickets, grasshoppers, cicadas, and katydids perched on various places. Their bodies dimmed all the lanterns. They shit, pissed, made the diluted air foul with an eye-burning stench. They drilled relentless tunes and flew in helix formations in mid-air like minuscule twisters.

Other insects squirmed and crawled on everything in the rooms, including each other.

They covered the walls, the cracked ceilings, and the overhead bulb sockets that were ready to snap and fall from their frayed cloth cords.

Shaky wrapped his arms up over his eyes, his jumper flapping like a flag as he fought his way through the living blizzard.

Songs, unbearable static grating against his eardrums. Insects hammered his exposed forearms and torso like blunt darts. He looked over at Melody, the chair covered with a tremendous insect pile, Melody buried beneath the squirming fray.

The insects' shrill decibels gradually decreased into complete and utter silence as he made it to the door. Insect shadows moved like black ghosts against walls, ceilings, and floors.   Melody's chair hit the floor. The insects flew off, Melody gone as if eaten away.

"Dammit," Cain said, brushing bugs from his hair. "We've got to find her!"

Shaky felt unfettered rage. It didn't matter anymore. He didn't care what Cain did to him. They were all going to die anyway. "No, Cain," he said. "She's dead. And even if she wasn't, she's got nowhere to go. We've got as much a chance surviving here as a possum trying to cross a highway. We're beaten, Cain. Are you that stupid you can't see that?"

Cain lifted the gun from the floor, wiping off bugs. "Beaten my ass, boy! I'm gonna' find that sweet little gash and put a bullet between her eyes!"

Shaky blocked his path as Cain headed toward the door. He balled his fists and held his head high. "No Cain. If she really is out there, leave her be."

Cain's eyes narrowed. "I'll kill you! You little pile of shit!"

Shaky felt a sudden jolt, a boost of strength welling up within him like a geyser ready to erupt. Melody, alive. He felt it. A witch. One who had given him potency, energy, mightiness, adrenalin.

Or could he be reverting back to the man was before prison?

He kicked Cain in the groin as hard as he could muster.

Cain groaned, grabbing his privates as Shaky snatched one of the lanterns from the table.

Cain lifted himself, rubbing his crotch, the gun in his other hand. He tried to maintain an accurate aim as he prepared to shoot.

Shaky swung the lamp and knocked the gun from Cain's hand.

Cain roared and leaped like a hungry Mountain Lion.

Shaky swung the lamp again, making contact with

Cain's huge head, sending him crashing to his knees. But Cain didn't fall. He slid across the bug-covered floor with a bloody gash, his eyes rolled back in his head like a zombie from a movie Shaky once saw at a drive-in long ago.

Shaky swung again. Cain swayed for a moment, lashing out at Shaky with immense, desperate hands. Shaky swung the lamp two more times, one left side, one right. Cain tilted forward, crashing to the floor like a felled tree. White-hot flames still burned within the lamp as Shaky grabbed the gun from the floor and tossed it out the window.

He snatched the other two lamps. He threw one against the floor and the other against the right-side wall. Fluorescent blue flames transformed into orange and spread throughout the room.

He placed the remaining lantern between his teeth and dragged Cain's limp bulk out the door. He dropped his ex-partner on the grass at a reasonably safe distance and tip-toed down the stone walkway trying to avoid bugs, frogs, toads, lizards and the other swamp life. All the creatures retreated once the flames engulfed the infested hideout.

Shaky made his way through the wriggling masses. The full moon rested against the sky like a scoop of vanilla ice cream in tar.

Up ahead, the boat swayed in the oil black water. The fiery house's reflection shimmering and bowing on its silvery surface, cotton thick fog roping around the swamp like a smoky serpent. Visibility impossible but he reached the boat. Toads, frogs, lizards, and salamanders writhed inside, their fleshy shapes gnarling into a wet, slimy mass.

"God, now I *am* afraid"

"DO NOT FEAR ME!" said an echoing feminine

voice ahead.

Shaky raised the lamp. "That *you*, girl?"

Ten-feet away, a silhouetted figure moved within the graying mist.

"Melody?"

The woman waved her arm and the fog dissipated as she stepped into the light. She glowed with a white light and she levitated inches above the ground. "I AM NOT YOUR ENEMY," Melody said in two voices. She wore a dark robe with wide flapping sleeves, her face like a black hole inside the wide cowl covering her head. "DO NOT BE AFRAID." Fireflies flew around her and pulsed with intermittent amber light like tiny planets as her cloak undulated in the ashen breeze. She looked sainted, not evil.

"You're beautiful," Shaky said, lifting the lantern higher. "You a witch? Or are you the Will o' the Wisp?"

Something snaked around his neck as he spoke and dragged him backward. Cain, empowered by fury and madness. He placed the gun to Shaky's head. "Now I've got both of you! This all ends HERE!"

"CORRECT," Melody said in polysyllabic language, a symphonic tone added. "IT *WILL* END HERE!"

Windows imploded in the house as the roof plummeted into its blazing frame; its thunderous peal reverberated throughout the swamp, the entire structure collapsing like a giant deck of cards, burning like a monstrous bonfire.

Melody lifted her arms like a fluid ballet dancer. Four hairy insect legs jutted out from within her thick sleeves, their jointed segments moving up, down, back and forth like robotic ropes in fluent, smooth movements. She slipped off her robe, allowing it to dribble down to the ground.

Cain's jaw dropped as he released his grip on Shaky. "So," Cain started, "you really *are* responsible for this plague!"

The creature's bulbous insect head responded with a singular nod, elongated, segmented antennae curling and coiling, melon-sized eyes staring. Shaky saw duplicates of his reflection in their multiple honeycombed-shaped lenses.

Her mouth, partially human, scaly plates around her lips, chitinous body covered with an indigo-colored exoskeleton. The fire's flaming image could be seen on her lustrous, boney plated form.

"I'm goin' ta kill this monstrosity," Cain said, firing the gun.

The monster exploded with loud, mocking laughter.

Cain groaned and roared in frustration and he fired again.

The creature emitted an ear-shattering shrill, causing him to fly back into the squirming insect carpet below. Cain slowly lifted himself. He sat upon the ground, knees in the air as he shook his head. His eyes showed confusion, defeat, and fear.

Shaky grinned and nodded. He had never seen Cain scared and vulnerable. Shaky turned and faced the monster advancing toward him. The swamp creatures cleared her path like windblown leaves. "What happened to you?" Shaky asked. "Why do you look like a beast?"

The creature's face morphed back into Melody, eyes as big as baseballs, black and shiny. They glistened in the limited light. "This pig," she started, "this horrid excuse for a human being brought me to this swamp long ago. He beat me, raped me and tortured me repeatedly before throwing my bloodied corpse into the sludge of this bog.

"As I hovered above my grave, I had encountered an ethereal life force, an elemental spirit of light and sound—the *Will o' the wisp, the hinkypunk, the hobby lantern*—whatever name you prefer.

"It sung to me, beckoned me to join with it. It told me my soul would be lost forever if I did not. I welcomed its embrace. I conjoined with it, with the swamp, and its night creatures. It had been wandering here for centuries, and it was alone. We were as one thereafter."

Papery, rainbow-colored wings melded into one another, unfurling from her back. She lifted herself from the ground and hovered over to Cain who had been corralled by insects and other swamp life.

"I HAD BEEN WAITING FOR YOUR RETURN," Melody boomed in ear-splitting, amplified, vocals "YOUR TIME IS SHORT. AND YOUR SOUL IS MINE."

Shaky heard sirens in the distance. Voices, bloodhounds, and fan-boats. He saw tenuous light shafts skimming the black river in the distance.

"GO," Melody said.

Shaky hesitated. "But I don't want to go back to jail."

"YOU WILL NOT. THE SWAMP WILL PROTECT YOU. NOW GO."

Shaky nodded. He jumped off the dock and into the river. He hid behind a cypress. Something jumped in his shirt pocket. He reached in and pulled out a tiny black cricket. It chirped as he placed it in his hand. He made a wish, tossing the cricket on the dock.

Something large splashed around behind him. A gator. It bellowed, its maw opened, ready to strike. He turned, the gator blinked once, its jaws forming a smile.

47

It snatched him and pulled him under the black water, the surface becoming smaller and farther away. The gator tore him like sackcloth, rolling over and over again.

Shaky's hands vanished. So, did his body. He saw *everything,* past, present, and future.

He saw Melody, Cain, and the police. He was finally at peace.   Melody rocketed up into the air and burst into colorful light specks like a giant firecracker. The specks scattered into four different directions, vanishing into the darkness as the Sun started its ascension from under the vermillion horizon.

Shaky stretched his cellophane wings, flying high into the air.

The night creatures stirred once more. The insects droned to a cacophonous fever pitch as they covered Cain. His screams were quelled by their piercing shrills.

Mysterious Mind
Amy S. Pacini

My head is a block of madness
Blinded by a vortex of insanity
Emotions run amuck
In a cerebral forest of fury.
Lost somewhere in mechanical darkness
Running from one hemisphere to the other
I try to untangle a congealed cluster Of haphazard
musings and notions.
Searching for a way to mold this gray matter Into a
systematic vehicle of meaningful expression.
It isn't until my mind enters a nocturnal trance
When the episodes of the day begin to dance
Creating a multifarious collage of faces
Mingling together in familiar places
Sometimes,   random   images   appear   An
amalgamation   of   reality   and   illusion   Barely
recognizable to the conscious soul.
On a subliminal level,
They are concretely tangible
Existing beyond a metaphorical grasp Awakening
the spiritual psyche And reinventing the intellect.
It is only in my dreams
That I am completely undiminished
Where I discover a chain of anecdotes Which define
meaningful expression No matter how logical or
enigmatic.
In the daylight hours,

My canvas is blank again
But when the night darkens,
My mind prepares itself to paint a colorful landscape
Exploding with distinctive images And authentic characters.

The Last of the Siamese Tigers
Danny Campbell
1

Krung walked home from the padi field, where he had been lurking all day. Through the pregnant stalks of burnt gold rice, to the narrow little trail at the forest's edge, and then into the jungle. The forest was cool and dark under the canopy of giant trees, throwing a blanket of relief over the brow of the twelve-year-old boy. He adjusted his eyes to the gloom, and the homespun cotton bag he carried on his shoulder while stepping past the leeches racing towards his feet. He came to the edge of a fast-flowing shallow river, which had cut a swirling path along the limestone valley floor. On a warm grey stone on the opposite side of the riverbank, a black and yellow water monitor lizard lay basking in a spotlight of sunshine. The gargoyle-faced creature fixed Krung with a blank, reptilian look, before skittering off in search of solace. Krung waded across, his feet automatically seeking large stones in the water, to prevent his ankles being dragged asunder in the current. On the other side, he followed the trail as it veered upwards, eventually coming to a clearing where the earth was a rusty red underfoot. There, rising from the steep slope of a hill, was the village of Soblan where he lived.

* * *

A heavy sun bounced off of the leaf thatched roof of

the house he shared with his mother, father, and little sister Kob. Beneath the roof, a bamboo floor and walls were held in place by four upright wooden posts. Underneath the one-room structure, pigs were penned in a wooden corral. They turned the red mud black, with urine and feces, which trailed down the slope in a rivulet mudslide. Krung's mother, Meowh, was at home, doing the never-ending jobs which all mothers know need to be done. Although she was thirty years old, the deep lines on her pretty, and quick-to smile face, showed a lifetime of hard work. Kob sat nearby peeling pale green, cucumber-like, *nam tao*, and putting them into a pot of water. His mother looked up from her work, cutting the loose threads on homemade clothes when he came in, and asked him: "Where have you been, Krung?"

"Out hunting."

A smile formed on his mother's lips as she watched his efforts to sound grown up. A *Pwa-Ka- Nyaw* child grows up soon enough.

"Well then, what have you caught?"

Krung put his hand into his cotton bag and pulled out a large rat, which was stiff with rigor mortis.

"One of the rats that eat our rice mother."

"Well done. That will be part of our supper tonight. Now, you go off and have your wash. Your father has gone to Mae Lam Kham to arrange to sell the rice surplus."

` She took the rat from him and placed it in a sack which hung from one of the many pegs upon the bamboo wall. Krung turned and left the hut, jumping the last steps on his way down.

* * *

Men and boys were making their way from Soblan down to the river. The water there was fast and clean, and its coolness washed away the grime and heat of the day. The men were grateful for it. Krung saw Pati-Mussu, his father's best friend, knee deep in the river, his *pakhoma*, tied in a knot at his waist, and gathered up in a bunch between his upper thighs. As he bent over the water, lathering soap in his hands, his slight pot belly hung over the knot of the sarong. He turned his head when Krung's shadow passed in front of him.

"Oh, *sawasdi* Krung, I did not see you," he said absentmindedly.

"*Sawasdi Khrap Khun* Pati-Mussu."

The boy smiled at him. He was a man he had known all of his life, and his down to earth ways had always made Krung laugh.

"Yes, yes. Go and make your blessings to the *baan phi.*"

Pati-Mussu smiled back and pointed with his thumb towards the small bamboo shrine built by the riverside. Krung walked over to the model house. The miniature structure mirrored the village homes and was covered in flower garlands, some fresh, and others in decay. A few balls of sticky rice rolled by many fingertips had been placed there to slowly turn grey, or be dismantled by ants. Krung raised his hands three times in a *wai*, high on his forehead, to ask the water spirits to keep the river flowing. He then retrieved his own sun-faded pakhoma from a tree branch, where it had been left to dry since his last wash at midday. Some of the other village boys were fighting with each other, tussling to see who could throw who over in the water. But Krung affected maturity, and ignored their smiling and waving invitation to join in the fun.

"Krung, did you know that Phor Luang is coming to our village tonight?"

"No, I did not, I am pleased to hear it. He tells such good stories."

"Yes. The old man with the long tongue."

Krung chuckled at the absurd image. He was very pleased that Phor Luang was coming, for they would have an entertaining evening. He rinsed off the soap in the cold water, ducking himself under to get it out of his hair. Then hurried out as fast as he could, waving goodbye to Pati-Mussu on his way.

2

Night time rolled across the village like a black cloud. The villagers, safe in their homes, cooked rice over open fires. Krung's mother stirred the rice in her cauldron, which was suspended from a bamboo tripod over a hearth of sand. The red embers of the fire crackled busily and cast a glow onto the cooking utensils. The tripod was tied together at the top with string made from the robust fiber of jungle plants, and though it looked fragile, it easily held the weight of the metal pot and its watery contents. She removed the bubbling scum from the surface with the edge of a wooden spoon and flicked it onto the hot ashes of the fire, where it vanished in a puff of steam. Kob sat playing with a frayed, old rag doll, alternately chatting to it, to Krung, and to her mother, joining them all in her made-up world.

* * *

As they cooked, Pati-Teyeh came home. He wore a woolen cap and a homespun poncho. Across his shoulder was the ubiquitous Pwa-Ka-Nyaw bag, which had in it everything a man might need in the course of a day: a knife, string, a small bowl made from a large bamboo pipe for eating rice. He had a kind face, with twinkling eyes, but like Meowh, the crow's feet and hollow cheeks of his face suggested that more work than play was the sum of his existence. A thin, drooping mustache and beard dripped from his nose and chin.

"Good evening," he said to his wife, who smiled at him in reply. "I have some dried fish in my bag, and I have arranged to sell the rice. The price was not bad."

"Good. Here, give me the fish. Look, Krung has been catching rats today. I am making a curry."

Pati-Teyeh turned to look at Krung. His eyes, full of paternal pride, saw the skinny boy in his black t-shirt and ragged jeans, the smooth—as yet unworried—pale ochre skin, the heavy mop of thick black hair.

"You are becoming a man my son. To be a hunter is to be Pwa-Ka-Nyaw, one of the people."

Krung allowed his own pride to rise in his breast at these words, for they made him feel taller. When the food was ready, they sat cross-legged on the bamboo floor and began eating. The rat curry, dried fish, and rice, was washed down with a green and bitter tea.

* * *

When the families of Soblan had finished their rice and chili paste, they gathered together in a circle around a large fire in the center of the village. They talked among themselves, catching up with gossip and news, and watched embers floating upwards like tiny Chinese lanterns. Men sat, or squatted with men, and women with women, the children mimicking their elders. Except, of course, the smallest, who were slung in blankets about their mother's bosoms. A tall man stood up from the group of men and moved away from them. He was distinguished by his spectacles, fisherman's hat, and Mackintosh, which contrasted oddly with the red, black, and white homespun blousons worn by most of the other tribe members. He moved closer to the fire so that its flames were reflected in his eye-glasses, and a curious smile spread across his lips. He raised his eyebrows so that his whole face formed a cynical and very knowing appearance. Everyone turned to look at him. He raised his hands, palms upwards as if he was lifting an imaginary bundle of feathers. He was ready to begin:

"It is good to see you, my friends."

Hush greeted him, along with the wide eyes of innocent children, and the appreciative glances of those who knew what was to come.

"I shall tell you a story tonight. About *Suah*, who lives in the mother forest."

Krung's ears pricked up at the sound of the word Suah—tiger.

"Do not be fooled. You do not see him every other day, as you do *Ngu* the cobra, but he is there. It is true that he is not as many in number these days. For us, that is just as well, for men and tigers cannot live together. When I was a boy, just like *you!*"

He widened his eyes and pointed his thumb at the children, raising his voice with the last word, making the more nervous among them jump. Keeping a mildly intimidating gaze fixed upon them, he continued:

"Just like you, I used to hunt in the forest, and guard the padi against rats. Once, when I was near the stream of the sweet *nam wan*, I stopped to take a drink. Then, I heard the purring of a giant cat, and the bamboo creaking under heavy paws. I can tell you I was very afraid. I knew what those sounds meant; I was facing a very great danger. What could I do? Those growls came closer, and the tiger was stalking me. He moved in circles, always to the left. What a nasty noise he was making! I could almost feel his breath on the air, and see the glint of his teeth, and his maddened yellow eye! I called upon the *Khwam*, "do not desert me, put fire in my legs and my arms, put weapons in my hands". I faced his direction, never giving him my back. I tried to make myself big!"

Lowering his voice to a whisper, so that the sound of burning embers almost drowned his voice, Phor Luang said:

"As the forest grew quiet, and my breathing slowed

to nothing, there came, a ROAR…"

There were gasps of surprise, and terrified children buried their faces in their mother's clothes, while the older ones, including Krung, tried to hide their scared imaginations and put on the serious brow of grown men.

"Yes, my friends, I could barely breathe, and a cold sweat covered my body. Surely this was my end. But, my friends, Suah had spoiled his own plans. When the men of Soblan heard his victory cry, they came running with their own war whoops, and the spears of their own anger. I was saved. But remember. He is out there."

Phor Luang pointed with his thumb into the impenetrable darkness of night, his face, a resolute warning. The crowd began to disperse, the children in awe of the old man and his tales.

* * *

Some of the men stayed on, talking with Phor Luang, about matters more immediate than the distant threat of man-eating tigers. Concerns about the forestry commission, and the illegal loggers who, year by year, seemed closer and closer to the hamlets of Mae Lam Kham. The five villages were connected by kith and kin and were carefully independent of the outside world. Most needs could be met by themselves, or sometimes pigs and rice could be sold in the markets of Chiang Mai to buy tools if needs be. Their voices were low, soothed with rice moonshine and coarse tobacco. Eventually, the last of them succumbed to tiredness and made their way back to the huts with the help of flaming torches. Phor Luang thanked Pati-Mussu for a blanket on the crowded bamboo floor of his home, and, removing his spectacles carefully, settled down among the other dozing bodies, closed his eyes and fell asleep.

3

If we were to move now, away from Soblan, and go to the gently undulating jungle beneath the Thanon Thong mountains, we would come to the domain of a creature which fires the human imagination. Phor Luang calls him Suah, and he has been busily searching in vain for others of his kind. As Phor Luang had observed, once there were many tigers in the jungle, especially when he was a boy, but those days are gone. Now Suah is alone. Although he is a solitary hunter, like other mammals, he enjoys the scent of others. When his male needs rise he dreams of taking a wife. But now the scents are stale, and there no tiger encounters to be had. So, he wanders around looking for animals to kill; gaur or sambar deer if he is lucky. Suah is as beautiful as he is ferocious, with wide feline jaws, and a white imperial beard. The black stripes which slash across his orange fur, form a moire camouflage, as he stalks behind pipes of bamboo. He has always been admired and feared by the Pwa-Ka-Nyaw, so, like a prince of the forest, tales about him have been woven into the fabric of their culture. Suah—the Siamese tiger— (call him what you will) roams a diminishing environment. His instincts told him, that wherever he went, and whatever he wanted, were his by right. But he was sensing that all was *not* right. Indeed, things seemed desperately wrong. The reality of inhospitable borders grew all around him, and, little by little, made smaller his once limitless forest world.

* * *

The towering shadows of the trees sang with the sound of cicadas. The murky jungle night is occasionally illuminated, with the surprising green glow of fireflies. Suah is not blinded by the night. His night vision serves him well enough. The sambar deer need to be on their guard. Fearing the dark, and the smell of the tiger, who is anxious to eat. Both are taunted by *Nok-khun-tong*, the-gold-man bird, who caws annoyingly, "Suuuaaahhh, Suuuaaahh", more for his own entertainment than as an altruistic warning. On the periphery of their sight, the deer see the bamboo crisscross in an unmistakable way. With a sudden kick of their hooves, they are gone, bounding into the forest. Suah has missed his strike. Life is becoming harder for the last of the Siamese tigers. With hunger in his belly and frustration in his heart, the beast wanders in search of sustenance. He moves in a circle covering miles of terrain, stopping to drink from a stream or spray the trunk of a tree with his scent. To let the world, know that *he* had been there. That this is *his* land. Tired and hungry, he climbs into the catacomb of a limestone cliff wall and sleeps, dreaming of wild pigs and deer.

4

As for Krung, he dreamed of tigers. He was confident in his hunting ability, aiming a catapult directly between the eyes of an enraged tiger, which was threatening his family. The big cat shrank to the size of the rat he had killed earlier in the day. Krung was about to become a great hero in the village of Soblan, and beyond. Krung the tiger killer, the bravest man in the north of Siam. But suddenly, in the way that dreams have a life of their own, the tiger grew to huge proportions, and Krung's confidence then vanished, as he ran for his life. The tiger cornered him in the crevice of a rocky jungle outcrop, and its slobber dripped onto Krung's arms as he shielded his face. The tiger roared a savage cheer of victory. Krung started awake. A film of cool perspiration covered his body, his face wan, his throat dry. He was grateful for the sudden light which pushed its way through the gaps in the bamboo walls, and the shadow of his mother, as she fussed around the tight living space they shared.

"Are you alright my son?" she asked, noticing his pale face and wet brow, "do you have a fever?"

"No mother, I am ok, I just had a bad dream about a tiger. That is all."

He clambered from underneath his blanket and reached for his pakhoma. His mother nodded knowingly and said to him:

"Don't you worry about tigers. There are no tigers. Not anymore. Phor Luang, he likes to tell stories and give you children a good fright. You are better off worrying about Ngu when you are walking in the padi, and you had better beware of soldiers, and strangers with guns. Tigers, hum. After you have washed go and help your father."

Krung nodded his assent to her every word, knowing that way lay the fastest route to peace. With her words ringing in his ears, he ran to the river to wash.

* * *

At the river, he saw his father kneeling in front of the baan-phi. He waited quietly, while his father chanted. Eyes closed, lips moving, Pati-Teyeh was lost in an intense devotion at the foot of the spirit house. Waiting and praying came easily to the forest people. Sometimes, there was nothing else to do. Famous Buddhist monks had extolled the virtue of waiting, contemplating, searching for answers to unanswerable questions, throughout the Kingdom of Siam. As if waiting was a spiritual end in itself. Had not Prince Siddartha wandered for years as a mendicant, before awakening as the Buddha? Pati-Teyeh was not chanting a Buddhist prayer, however. It was one of animism. He was asking the spirits which flowed with the river, from the heart of the sacred forest, to keep it flowing freely. He had luck and fortune, was *hikko*, a shaman, and he knew that his fortune was due to an avid attention to the lay of the land, and an appeasement of the spirits which dwelt in all things. Rocks, trees, water—all had phi—ghosts within them. Even human beings were possessed with these spirits, and their health and luck were dependent on the thirty-seven *klar*. These little magic beings, which the Thai called *khwam*, were want to make trouble with a living body if they were ignored. This was known by the forest community, and further abroad. Those who ignore spirits do so at their peril. Mountains crumble, and the world shakes, trees fall down, water dries away to nothing, animals vanish as if they had never existed, save for their preserved and ancient bones. Humans can become ill and die before their ripe old age if the klar chose to abandon them. Krung knew this. He was lucky to have a wise father, a man who knew how to talk to the invisible world. Pati-Teyeh finished his chant. He opened his eyes and saw Krung gazing at him. The boy had a touch of awe in his eyes at the magic his father could work.

He smiled and said:

"Come, my son. Let us go to the padi field."

* * *

They moved easily along a trail, a smooth boreen formed by footstep after footstep. The ground was red and dry where the sun shined upon it, and moist, where it lay hidden beneath broad leaves. Pati-Teyeh stopped suddenly in his tracks, noticing something at the side of the path. He squatted, and pulled a machete out of his bag, and dug carefully around the base of a small palm-like plant. Krung watched, as he exposed a parsnip shaped root, and then brushed the mud from it. He held it up for Krung to see.

"This is good *jin noh* my son, it will help you when your stomach is bad."

He placed it into his bag and carried on walking. Through the gnarled trees dressed with lianas, and the coarse and angry bushel spikes, and the tight clumps of enormous bamboo. The path veered upwards, and they climbed a hill. Toes dug into the ground, backs bent forwards, up they went, in an almost crawling momentum. At the top of the hill, the forest was no longer tropical. Instead, the jungle gave way to coniferous trees and a carpet of pine needles. The sparse flora allowed a view of the surrounding hills and valleys. They seemed endless, and among them, gibbons and birds called their hearts out.

* * *

Over the ridge, they followed another path down. The landscape changed again and became fields of golden brown rice which moved slowly, waddling like pregnant women when a dry breeze blew in from nowhere. Pati-Teyeh watched them under the tropical sun. The fields were square in shape and looked as if they had been painted there by Vincent van Gogh, and they made the rice farmer happy. This is the difference between starving and eating, and, sometimes, doing very well indeed.

"This will be a good harvest," said Pati-Teyeh, nodding to himself.

"We will be very busy then father."

Pati-Teyeh said nothing, as he was lost in private thoughts. He bent down and took one of the rice stalks in his hand. He carefully unwrapped the cylindrically folded blade, exposing the nestled grains of rice within. "*Khao*. A good year," he said, and then saw a rat running for cover from the field. He looked over at Krung. "You stay here. See if you can kill *Noo*, before he eats all of our rice." Then, with a smile, he raised his hand and turned to leave.

* * *

Krung sat under the shade of an overhanging branch at the edge of the padi field. He watched his father walking away through the padi fields, until it seemed as if he were a shadow on a yellow blanket. After Pati-Teyeh disappeared into the green, luxuriant forest, Krung took his slingshot out of his bag. He sat there patiently, lost in his own world of possibilities. He daydreamed about the life he led, and the things that could be, until Noo became bold. The rat stuck his face from out of a tangle of vegetation, and looked around suspiciously. Krung's first shot exploded in the earth very close to Noo, who quickly vanished in the bush, only to reappear soon after with his nose twitching frenetically in the air. They played this life and death game; Krung, hands deftly loading the slingshot, taking aim. Noo, now you see me, now you don't. The rat overcoming his reticence, the boy improving his aim, but there was to be no winner today, only a stalemate. Eventually, Krung became bored, and gave up the adventure.

* * *

Walking back home, Krung stood at the highest point of ground, among the pine tops. He looked out across the trees, and imagined a different life; one in the city of Chiang Mai, or even further south, in the city of *Krung Thep*, for which he was named. But it seemed unlikely that he would ever live such places. He imagined that it was fabulous there in the great cities, where everything was possible, and everyone was incredibly rich. A place where people ate *khao mun gai*, or *phat ka pow kai dao* every day. He had eaten these dishes once in Chiang Mai, when travelling there with his father and Pati-Mussu, in the latter's old pick-up truck. They had sold a large rice surplus, and Pati-Teyeh had money to spend on tools, and other things to make life easier. Krung had never seen so many people in the same place, milling around purposefully. Why were they in such a hurry? The night market seethed and shouted and waved its hundreds and hundreds of hands, holding cloth, food, jewelry, spices, everything. If Chiang Mai was like this, what must Krung Thep be like? The thought excited him. Pati-Teyeh and Pati-Mussu drank rice whiskey and became very animated in their conversation. Krung ate mouthfuls of the soft white rice, and spicy strips of chicken, and the fried pork with holy basil, until his belly swelled as if it would burst. Then he remembered how the townsfolk had looked at them. Unkindly, and on occasion, with hostility. Was it their darker skin, or the traditional clothes that they wore? Were they dirty, did they smell? Krung felt the disdain, and saw that the older men felt it too. Nonetheless, he still dreamed of seeing the great city again.

* * *

The fields that Krung had left behind, now became a playground for the hungry rats. they kept to their runs, and tried to avoid traps, snares and Ngu the cobra, who was generally feared throughout the forest. Twilight brought a new visitor to this crossing place, where the man-made world met the untamed one. There was no mistaking the heavy paws, sinewy gait, and throaty, growling breath of Suah. If there had been deer in the vicinity, they would have long since fled. The rats were not unduly worried. The great beast, hungry though he was, would hardly deign to make a meal from so un-alluring an animal. Suah looked at the rice field with a withering contempt. He was dangerously carefree, and his tiger's ego, felt that the whole forest sensed his unhappiness. He looked at the open sky turning pink with the falling sun, and growled an angry, horrible, growl of discontent. Then, he padded off into the coming night.

5

When Krung arrived back in the village, he paused outside Pati-Mussu's home and called out:

"*Sawasdi Khrap* Pati-Mussu!" but instead of his father's friend, a young girl, only slightly older than he was, came out. She had a delicate face with bright almond eyes and full lips, and when she smiled at Krung, it was with genuine pleasure.

"My father is with your father and they are at the *long-lien*," she said, "I think they are talking about Ka-noon's marriage to Oy."

She said the word marriage breathily, over-emphasizing it in a clumsy way. It made Krung squirm with embarrassment, for in truth, he had begun to notice Gulab, as the girl was named, in ways which made him uncomfortable. She gave him a coy grin, and pressed the folds of her white dress down, self-consciously, yet also delighted at the effect she was clearly having on him. The two had been playmates for as long as they could remember. In a small village, the choices made in marriage are ones of proximity and familiarity. Krung waved his hand and mumbled something incoherently, and ran off to find the men. Gulab returned to the household chores which she believed most likely, she would one day do for Krung as his wife.

* * *

The long-lien was the largest structure in the village. It had corrugated iron walls and a concrete floor. The roof, however, was made with the same dry banana leaf thatch, which the other houses in the village used. The men had built this schoolhouse ten years ago when a young man had come to live among them. Komol was a young university graduate and idealist. He was supported by wealthy philanthropists in Krung Thep. A society of devout Buddhists who believed in karma and that the making of merit meant action and not just good thoughts. They had recruited young and idealistic teachers, just like Komol to their cause; to bring education to the poor throughout Siam and eventually, Democracy to the nation. Komol spoke flawless PwaKa-Nyaw and was also a teacher, and he was driven by a sense of social justice. He was determined to carry out his duty to teach the children of the forest. He was determined to bring reading and writing to the forest community. It was the first time an outsider had shown a purely altruistic interest in them and the villagers wasted no time in welcoming him.

* * *

For a while, Soblan had a school and its children began to learn to read. Komol played another vital role in the life of the village. He acted as interlocutor for the village headmen, especially Phor Luang, who had a rudimentary education himself, in their dealings with the forestry commission and the other outsiders they occasionally had cause to deal with. When illegal logging of the forest had begun, Komol organized legal help and raised the matter with liberal journalists, who then published stories. The shaming of the crooks destroying the forests of Chiang Mai was to be Komol's downfall. He was gunned down by hired assassins. With his loss, the future prospect of education in the villages of Mae Lam Kham was gone. No further teachers came to Soblan and the monolithic long-lien was a pathetic monument to what might have been.

* * *

Krung found the men there, drinking tea and

talking. He noticed Pati-Mussu casting a melancholy look around the longlien, which he and the others had helped to construct. They often looked glum when they gathered in the building, as they had just received some shocking news. The mood improved though when they began talking about the forthcoming marriage. This was something to look forward to, something good for the perpetuity of the village, something bringing new life into what was a decreasing Pwa-Ka-Nyaw world. Pati-Teyeh acknowledged his son with a nod, and Krung raised his hands in a wai towards the group, who then beckoned him over to join them.

"Did you catch a rat Krung?"

"No father."

"*Mai pen rai*," said his father, meaning that it was not a grave matter. Krung sat on the floor just outside of the main circle formed by the men. Seeing Phor Luang among them, he caught the old man's eye and asked him:

"Khun Phor Luang, are we going to go to Chiang Mai?"

"Perhaps," came the reply. But Pati-Mussu saw the light of expectation in the boy's eyes and saw in him another young boy excited by the possibility of a different life. He had seen his own son follow the course of his curiosity and go to live and work in Krung Thep. He had tried to advise against the move, but his son was determined. It was an increasing development among the Pwa-Ka-Nyaw. Their sons and daughters left the tribal homes and the countryside ways behind them. That movement was a bigger threat to their existence at this time than ever before. When Pati-Mussu had visited his son in the metropolis to try and persuade him to return, he knew

70

the advice he had given was sound. His son, driving tourists and businessmen around the city in a *tuk-tuk*, was making a hard living. His skin was permanently stained with the grime of the streets, he drank heavily, and his brow was scarred with worry lines of insecurity. Pati-Mussu realized, even before asking, that his son would be too proud to admit that life was worse here and would refuse to come back with him. But it was his duty to try. He looked at Krung and said:

"You know Krung, however attractive the city appears it is only a temporary place. I know of cities of old that have returned to dust or have been swallowed whole by the jungle. In eight hundred years to come, perhaps Krung Thep will be forest again, as it was once before. Try to remember that."

* * *

The conversation drifted along on the current of their moods, questions, and decisions. The things they usually kept quietly in their hearts, until the black night sky told them that it had had enough of their philosophizing. It was time to go to bed. They rose and wrapped pakhoma's around themselves, to ward off the cold night air, and lit torches made from the wood of pine trees which burned slowly and guided them home in the dark. It was silent, save for the various grunting's of domesticated pigs and the occasional cluck of wildfowl.

6

Suah followed the smell of the humans, along the pine ridge path, towards the hill-side hamlet of Soblan. On his way up, he came eye to eye with Ngu. They looked at each other warily, neither cat nor serpent wishing to take on the other. Hungry as he was, Suah knew he had no business with the king cobra, for a bite from him, could kill even *Chang*, the elephant. Suah showed due deference and stood patiently, as Ngu slithered lazily away, keeping one eye on the cat. The snake vanished into the undergrowth, as a worm into its hole. Suah followed the path up to the highest knoll, to where the pines framed a window view, exactly where Krung had stood earlier that day. From the naked jungle side of the hill-top, came the sound of laughing monkeys as they played in the trees. On the other, Suah saw houses and the dying embers of a fire. Behind the drifting odor of the wood smoke and ash, he could smell the scent of pigs and dogs and fowl. He also smelled the smell of something else. An alien scent that with foresight, he ought to fear, but a tiger knows no better. He made his way towards it, stalking the village as stealthily as he could.

* * *

Tigers do not tip-toe, but that is what Suah seemed to be doing, as he crept into the village. The animals, pigs corralled beneath their owner's homes—so that the Pwa-Ka-Nyaw could protect their wealth, restless cocks in cages, and clucking hens, asleep with open eyes, were suddenly aware of an unusual presence amongst themselves. The animals began to babble, a lazy pig snorted, a chicken squawked, a sleepy dog raised an ear from where he lay with his nose pressed close to the dying fire. At the edge of the forest, Suah inspected the man-made dwellings. This was no world he was used to. He appeared silver in the moonlight, and his black stripes moved across his back in a confusing, lateral sway. This *chiaroscuro* blended him and the forest cover, making him almost invisible. His breath slowed to the point where it became silent. He could not, however, disguise his smell. If it had been a guar or sambar deer that he stalked, he knew at some point this would give him away. The trick was to get as close as possible until it was too late. But here, these animals, the pigs, chickens, and humans, were kept in boxes like birthday gifts waiting to be opened.

* * *

The animals knew now, unlike the humans, that something was dreadfully wrong. Like the ripples from a stone thrown into a pond, a sense of animal hysteria began to spread throughout the hamlet. Then the grunting of the pigs became a frightened squeal and the chickens began a cacophonic refrain. The dogs ran away into the forest. Pati-Teyeh stirred, aware that the animals were panicking. Then, without further warning, came an enormous crash of breaking wood, followed by an animal noise of terror. The pig's pitiful squeal resembled a human scream. As Pati-Teyeh lurched for the door to see what had happened, he saw his terrified family huddled together in a corner of the room. He picked up his machete, fearing that whatever had caused the disturbance, would need more than the chop of a knife to stop it. Squinting into the dark, he could vaguely see a large, shadowy shape disappearing into the black jungle. Soon, the entire village was awake and torches were being lit. They were curious to learn just what malevolent spirit had disrupted the harmony of their homes.

* * *

Pati-Mussu was the first to ask his friend:

"Are you alright?"

Although it was clear from the expression on Pati-Teyeh's face that he was not. He feigned bravery and said:

"I am alright. But if that was what I think it was, we are in some trouble."

Together they surveyed the damage to the pig pen. It was a bloody mess. Both men knew that the only animals powerful enough to carry the pig away in that way were the Siamese tiger, or maybe a leopard. Both were unlikely to attack a village. The realization that one or the other hand, was something that they did not in their worst dreams countenance. The tiger, it was believed, had long since vanished from the forests of Chiang Mai. The Asian leopard, though its trails and spoor were still found on nearby trails, was a far smaller creature. Pati-Teyeh was sure it did not have the strength to break the pen apart as easily as it had been. Everyone thought that Phor Luang's stories were just that; stories told by an old man to excite the imagination of the young. The moral survival tales which lent weight to their culture and colored their existence with belief, legends and law, drifted through time. From the original to the apocryphal. Sometimes the stories seemed like a long lost and distant joke. But here there was nothing funny. An old tale had become something real. For an unprepared village people, an unafraid tiger was more reality than they had bargained to deal with.

* * *

Pati-Teyeh and Pati-Mussu with Krung helping them, fixed up the pen as best they could, all the while being stared at fearfully by the visibly shaking pigs inside.

"We will have to do something about this," said Pati-Mussu, looking around at the superstitious faces watching them as they worked.

"I know."

But he did not really know what to do. This was an unforeseen occurrence. He had offered prayers to the forest and the wilderness. This is how they had answered. It did not bode well for a village headman, to be the victim of spiteful ghosts and their horrible manifestations.

"I will go and talk to Phor Luang about this," Pati-Teyeh said to his friend. Pati-Mussu looked at him, as did Krung, and what they saw was a worried man. A friend and a father undeserving of this bad luck.

* * *

After the attack, the inhabitants of Soblan suffered from fitful sleep and bad dreams. Meanwhile, as they struggled with that sleep, far away, Suah devoured the pig. Safe in a den under a limestone boulder, deep in a valley of the jungle. Having been so long without a kill, he busied himself with gluttonous abandon; bones, muscle, flesh, were crushed and chewed between his powerful jaws with little discrimination. When he was sated and his stomach could take no more, he lay against the dry earth of the slight cave, among the crawling plants and insects and fell soundly asleep. His snoring came as a deep growl and could be heard reverberating like the unwelcome hum of a swarm of hornets. Other animals of the jungle knew to allow him a wide berth as he slept unless they chanced to wake a sleeping tiger. Even the *mak nai*, those ruthless jackals, adept hunters themselves, would not dare to steal Suah's kill. Undisturbed, his swollen belly heaved up and down with the effort of digestion. And as he slept, the surrounding natural evolution, creatures and things which live and die hidden from the prying eyes of mankind, sang one of its most extraordinary inventions an awkward lullaby.

7

The following morning, panic infused the village of Soblan. People found reasons to walk past Pati-Teyeh's house to see the damage. Pati-Mussu came to see his friend at first light and warded off the nosey types with tough looks born of the loyalty he felt toward his good friend.

"Sawasdi."

Pati-Mussu just smiled as he heard the greeting and saw Pati-Teyeh walking down the steps of his house.

"So, to Mae Lam Kham and Phor Luang," they said almost in unison. "And to hunt Suah we come!"

The two men laughed at their own bravado. Krung followed them after a few steps, bag slung across his shoulder in anticipation.

"No Krung. You must stay. There are tasks your mother will need help with," said Pati-Teyeh sternly to his son. Krung's face flattened, showing his disappointment. But instead of erupting in protest, he meekly obeyed and went back inside.

* * *

As they left the village behind, they entered the dark world of the forest. Along the way they observed and relaxed at the sight of familiar things; a baan phi, a banyan tree, a boulder which looked like the head of an elephant. These sights were as familiar to them as a favorite shop, the traffic lights and a zebra crossing are to the city dweller. Phor Luang's village, Baan Mae Lam Kham, was slightly larger than their home of Soblan. Phor Luang's home was modest, indeed, it was indiscernible from the other baan's in the village. It was only upon entering the house and seeing the secondary school diploma hanging on the wall, that one knew he had had something of an education. The men and women who came to him during the day to ask for advice also set him apart from more ordinary men. Phor Luang was hikko and was, therefore, an important man. In this, he was not unique. Most headmen were hikko, as was Pati-Teyeh himself. But Phor Luang came from an ancient and distinguished line of hereditary soothsayers. One which had arrived with the original band of Pwa-Ka-Nyaw that had replaced the *Lua* tribes, who had lived and tilled the land before them. Their migrations further afield had left the fertile, watershed mountains open to the new arrivals, many, many years ago.

* * *

Phor Luang stopped talking to the man in front of him when he saw Pati-Teyeh and Pati-Mussu loitering outside. The man was having problems with his wife, who nagged him, and on occasion had fought with him physically. The isolation of the forest existence and the need for strong communal bonds did not allow for *in camera* misfortunes. Communities such as theirs lacked the flexibility of better off people, who lived far away from the village world of fixed predicaments. He turned back to him and said: "Nuttarot, I am sorry, but if you are not happy, you must separate."

Nuttarot looked at Phor Luang's face with hurt and sensitive eyes, as if he was seeing the truth for the first time. He sighed, gathered his composure and straightened his back as in preparation to bear a heavy load and said:

"But I do not want to Phor Luang."

With that recognition and admission, that he and only he held the key to his own happiness, he thanked Phor Luang and said goodbye.

* * *

Phor Luang greeted his next guests warmly and bade them sit cross-legged in conference, on the bamboo floor of his home.

"Nuttarot will not be happy until he lives alone. He will be no use to women after his experiences. For some men, it is better to never have a wife, as it is better for some women never to have a husband," Phor Luang said, vocalizing his thoughts more than attempting to draw further analysis of the situation, "but in Soblan you have a more pressing and dangerous matter to attend to."

Phor Luang scrutinized his guests. His glare widened until he looked quite mad with intensity, waiting to hear from their lips what he had already heard of and knew what to do about.

"Suah, Khun Phor Luang. Suah has come to my village and destroyed our harmony," Pati-Teyeh said, looking evenly at Phor Luang. "This is very serious because Suah, if he dares to attack men, has decided that they are nothing to be frightened of." "And then no one is safe," Pati-Mussu added.

Phor Luang looked at them with the kind of look a grandfather gives when he hears another old story told as if it was new.

"Yes, of course, very far from safe. In very great danger. You must hunt and kill this tiger. It is the only way."

Then he added, unable to stop himself, an "I told you so" boast.

"My story seems very prescient now. Eh."

He had the grace to show a little shame when he saw the anguished look on Pati-Teyeh's face and then said:

"None of you have hunted the tiger. Here is how

you will do it. In India, where this sort of thing is more common, they wear masks on the backs of their heads. Suah does not like to attack from the front, he is a sly old cat. If he thinks you have eyes in the back of your head, it may stall him. You can whittle some from bamboo. Then, you need traps, and bait, and your rifles. Hey! Take Nuttarot with you, he could really do with some time away from that wife of his. Most of all you will need good luck."

* * *

With a plan forming in their minds, Pati-Teyeh and Pati-Mussu went to pay a visit to Nuttarot. They found him, with a long, miserable face, sitting on the steps to his home. From within the gloom of the little hut, they could hear his wife, Phueng, intoning as if in prayer:

"Oh, why did I marry you, when I think of what could have been, I must have been a fool."

She stopped when she heard the talking outside and came to see what was going on. Her face was unlined for one whose life was lived in such obvious turmoil. When she saw the visitors, her expression assumed a delighted aspect and her luminous, large, brown eyes danced with a thinly veiled mania.

"What is this visit in honor of?" she said, cowing them with her glare.

"Phor Luang has asked us to take your husband with us. We have to hunt a tiger."

Phueng immediately began to fuss around her husband, admonishing him with expressions of concern. When he was finally able to collect the things, he needed and escape with the men, Phueng was left alone with her thoughts. They buzzed busily around in her brain and emerged in occasional verbal outbursts to herself, invoking and castigating a god of her own self-pity.

Swallowed by the Beast

8

Elsewhere, Suah roused from his slumber. He had slept and dreamed well. He awoke to a ready meal. What remained of the pig was covered in ants. Nearby, in holes and cracks in stones, rodents slept equally content, their bellies full of purloined meat. Suah finished off what flesh and gristle were left, licking the bones until they were clean and then stretched in satisfaction, like the proverbial cat who had got the cream. If he could have had any idea of the repercussions which would arise from his foray into the village, it would have made no difference. He was old and hemmed in by edges of a once vast world. It was only a matter of time before he returned to where the hunting was easy. Wooden fences would not stop from taking what was rightfully his. Suah walked, a big catwalk, to nowhere in particular, in the ever-decreasing circles of his territory. Smelling the stale scent of previous patrols. Marching, as was his habit, for mile after mile.

9

The hunters arrived in the valley of Doi Inthanon after walking for many hours. On the backs of their heads, they wore the masks carved from bamboo, exactly as Phor Luang had advised. Pati-Teyeh led, and only he was spared the disconcerting sight, of goggle-eyed faces walking perfectly backward across the terrain. The mountain when they were close, was a purple, sleeping giant, rising lethargically upwards above the dancing heads of aspiring hills, which for all of their rolling beauty, seemed to kowtow in wonder at their brother king-peak. Pati-Teyeh, Pati-Mussu, and Nuttarot busied themselves with clearing enough space to be comfortable among the inhospitable thickness of the jungle scrub. They had chosen the spot well, for there were no ant nests, or angry, buzzing pockets of the nemesis of man; the mosquito. Nuttarot had a small piglet in a sack which grunted and squealed unhappily. He released it and tied it to a stake, where it cowered from the men. This morning it had been wallowing contentedly with its siblings, as happy as a pig in...only to be seized and stuffed into a bag and carried uncomfortably for a very long time. The men laughed at its reaction and jokingly attempted to pacify it with sweet words and rolled fingerfuls of sticky rice. The piglet, however, was unimpressed with their false friendship and its clever little eyes revealed profound distrust.

* * *

The men had left their tobacco and moonshine behind. Instead, they had brought bitter and moist leaves rolled around rock salt. They chewed the *miang*—fermented wild tea leaves, slowly. Their energy and senses were heightened as a result. Pati-

Teyeh began to conduct a ritual with a candle stump, some pieces of homespun string and the ubiquitous ball of rice. Pati-Mussu and Nuttarot closed their eyes and knelt, listening to the earnest prayer. Pati-Teyeh spoke to the trees, believing that they really heard him and could help them.

"'O mother forest, please protect us here during this night."

It was a low song, sang to gods of wood and stone and the multifarious creatures that dwell among them. His voice penetrated the still forest air as if it carried the essence of magic, which for him and the others, it did. He was communing with an invisible world and the safety of family, friends, and community depended on the forest listening. Had Pati-Teyeh and the others known much about the ideas of science, it would have made little difference to the world they lived in. That world was far away from modernity, it was a refuge of wilderness.

* * *

They dug pits and placed bamboo pipes sharpened to a point in them, afterward covering the deadly holes with leaves. They cleaned their rifles and waited. They felt as ready as they could be for something utterly unknown. The conversation, as the night drew quickly in, turned to the more ordinary experiences of their lives.

"Nuttarot, why do you stay with that woman of yours. She is unhappy, and only makes you unhappy?" Nuttarot was quiet for a while, his face struggling to conceal a twitch of resentment.

"How can I leave her?"

The plaintive words shut the other men up. They saw that his mindset, that he found the idea of separation difficult and perhaps even impossible to contemplate, was hard for him to budge. Besides, they also knew that breaking the chains of a bleak and tainted love, was the business of the protagonists. Nuttarot wanted sympathy, but no more. He was not prepared to change his mind.

* * *

It was black now. Save for the silver rays of the Moon piercing the thick canopy sparingly. None of them felt sleepy, their nerves heightened by chewing the bitter miang leaves. They observed the changing tempo of the forest. In the dark, the sounds which emanated from its seemingly anguished bosom calmed and it was the time of night hunters. The shrieking, gibbering inhabitants, which seemed to taunt, laugh, fart and splutter, simply for making noises sake during the day, were quieter now. The language, the cries of love between primates and birds and even the long whistle song of cicadas making the most of a brief adulthood, diminished enough for creatures with wide, moon filled eyes, to stalk bugs and larvae fooled by a cover of darkness.

"It has been some time since we did this," said Pati-Mussu, addressing Pati-Teyeh.

"I think we should do it more often, tiger or no tiger," came the soft reply.

"No, I don't think so. I miss my bed already. A belly of rice washed down with *lao khao*, followed by a good sleep, that's the life for me."

"Some hikko you would make, heh, too busy worshipping a rice wine god."

They allowed themselves a quiet chuckle at this thought before Nuttarot started nervously:

"What's that?" he said in response to an ugly fox's bark which rattled the trees.

"Don't worry," said Pati-Teyeh. "That is the sound

of the maknai. They have better noses than most, and will keep away from our smell."

He looked at the younger man in the dark thoughtfully, distracted momentarily from the purpose of their hunting and considered why it was that a man like Nuttarot found life so difficult. A man like Pati-Mussu, even though he had endured greater adversity than the kind Nuttarot was enduring, seemed, like the tiger, to stalk life bravely, and without complaint. The night passed long and with thoughts like these. The three men, believing in ghosts, thought that they saw them often. * * *

The next morning the gibbons called them awake.

"Whoop, whoop, whup, whup, whup, whoooop!"

As a primate language, the sounds veered from an excited gabble, to a long, slow, melancholy *whoop*, as if the singer possessed a profound sadness. As humans sometimes want, they could not or would not be comfortable in their own skin, until they had got the matter off their chest. The hunters stirred and moved around stiffly, listening to the calling as they focused bleary eyes. Pati-Teyeh listened to the voices of the gibbons and thought to himself, "O to see what you see, and travel as quickly as you do from tree top to tree top." He then looked at the palms of his hands and saw the same outline that he had always seen, except that now, those strange clutching claws at the limit of his desires seemed older and less eager to grasp. Pati-Mussu, looking at his friend scour the tree line for the apes, read his thoughts and said:

"Hey, if we could move like those apes our search would soon be over."

Pati-Teyeh looked at his friend and wondered and wondered. How does a man stop a tiger? How does he change his destiny? Why has this beast come to trouble us?

"Come on," he said, "we had better find another place for tonight."

They packed their camp away, and left the forest floor, save for some disturbed plants and earth, as if they had never been there.

10

The virgin forest was unrevealing, clothing the tiger with its impenetrable cloak of paradise. For the men, stripping away fold after fold and only finding more, the effect was tiring and frustrating. Even patient people can reach the point where that virtue is exhausted. As it was now, for Pati-Teyeh, Pati-Mussu, and Nuttarot, their faces blank with fatigue and disappointment. Only the whittled, phantasmic faces on the backs of their heads showed any animation. It was for Pati-Teyeh, as the aggrieved victim of the tiger's assault, and as headman, to decide to call off the impossible hunt.

"We can no longer do this. We must accept that we have failed. It is nearly time for the harvest, and we have duties that cannot be ignored."

The others did not argue. They were tired of being in the forest. Tired of hunting for a ghost. The little pig they had carried all this way in a wide loop through this isolated terrain, at the limit almost, of their understanding of the forest, would be carried back. It would be offered a brief reprieve before its assured slaughter in honor of the harvest and, this year, a marriage feast.

* * *

As the men trudged back limp with failure, the picture in their minds was uniform. The harvest - the waiting golden rice ready to give birth after just enough time lazing under a blazing sun. A life cycle ended and begun anew, as some of the millions of offspring grain would be kept and planted at the most opportune moment, just before the rainy season. Harvest was the last leg of a grueling marathon of rice cultivation. A last effort and grain silos would be filled. The Pwa-Ka-Nyaw would not go hungry. Pati-Teyeh looked behind him as they neared the forest's edge and for a moment, he felt a wave of anxiety about what it contained.

* * *

They arrived at Mae Lam Kham first, and Nuttarot's head hung liken a condemned man's when he saw his wife waiting on the steps of his baan with an accusatory look in her eyes. He smiled weakly and said goodbye, with a look of panic which he did his best to conceal, yet was there, obvious to his friends. Pati-Teyeh and Pati-Mussu were welcomed back to Soblan by their families.

"You need to go to the river!" said Meow, smiling at the grubby, tired and battered appearance of her husband. Krung and Kob embraced him and Pati-Teyeh felt as much love for them as he ever had. Pati-Mussu's sons and his only daughter Gulab - his own wife having died during childbirth - made the same kind of fuss over him, which he jokingly brushed off with:

"You are not thinking, "why didn't he stay out there a little longer," and they hugged and laughed with relief.

* * *

The jolliness was quickly replaced by the need to get ready for the harvest. The village seemed hot and exposed to the hunters after the gloomy light of the forest. Beads of sweat appeared on Pati-Teyeh's head as he removed his woolen cap. There were storerooms and silos to be swept clean and sacks and sheets to get ready. Scythes to sharpen with stone. Work to be done. He looked around at the bustle of the villagers and at the smiling faces of his family and friends. He felt proud to be a part of them and honored to lead them as his ancestors had. But that thought was accompanied with the unshakeable knowledge that real danger surrounded them. Suah would lurk in their dreams like a recurring nightmare. Something must be done.

11

Phor Luang returned to Soblan that night, to tell his stories and assuage the anxiety of the villagers. The mood was serious this time, as once again the glow of a large fire illuminated the listener's faces. There was a shared sense, that Phor Luang's words before had been eerie prophecy. What tricks would his tongue play now? Phor Luang knew this and confronted their thoughts head on.

"Dear friends, I know what you are sitting there thinking. When does a myth become reality and the reality myth? Eh? Am I right? Don't try and answer. The answers to questions like that have occupied greater minds than ours since the beginning of time. These stories are built into our existence, they are the part of our survival. It is this way for all human beings."

He studied the faces gathered around him, looking each and everyone in the eye as if challenging the foolish among them to argue with him. He then continued:

"'We are the Pwa-Ka-Nyaw, we have lived in these valleys and hills for eight hundred years. The ghosts of our ancestor's dwell here among the trees and mountains, as surely as all things must change their shape; mountains to rocks and stones, water from sky to river and lake, saplings to giants and then to earth again. These things just are. They follow a cycle, changing their shape without interruption. What has happened to the tiger? I tell you that his cycle has been interrupted. If the noble Suah could think and feel as we do, he would be ashamed of what he has become. The greatest hunter of all has become a sneak thief. Why has this happened? In the past, it would be that the tiger was old or injured and could not hunt in the usual way. Or people had made their homes in parts of the forest which were his natural domain.

People and tigers cannot live side by side and so tigers have been hunted for reasons of safety and, it is true, for sport. The animal we are presented with is at the edge of his kingdom. For all, we know he is the last of the Siamese tigers. I would not be surprised. Now we are affected because there is less of the forest today. There shall be still less tomorrow."

* * *

Krung went to his bed with Phor Luang's monologue embedded in his mind. The men and women of the forest led hard and unremitting lives. There were only the hills and the trees and the padi fields for an occupation. The wise old hikko bound them to the past and the future with his stories. It was not for everyone, this ability to commune with the spirit mysteries of existence, to understand nature on its own terms. Krung began to feel the power of this knowledge in his heart. He began to realize that perhaps this was his own calling. But that was for *tomorrow*, a word heavy with promise, for now, meant the harvest and more hard work. After that, a marriage, to coincide with the time of plenty. This was to be a big celebration and a time to forget the problems of life. Phor Luang's words about rocks and rivers, trees and tigers, turned to pictures in Krung's mind in an attempt to understand his place in the world. He was glad to have his father back. He felt safer and proud that he was the son of a strong and wise man. The ghost of the lonely tiger haunted his thoughts, tearing a twelve-year-old mind between empathy, a need to prove his worth and an unabated horror at the savage potential of the beast.

* * *

For his own part in this story, Suah had returned to the hills surrounding the hamlet of Soblan. After another of his epic marches, he was now irrevocably drawn to the glow of the fire torches, which the villagers carried around like fireflies and, of course, the chance of an easy meal.

Something else drew him there. He had found no others like him, not mate nor cub, nor even adversary. He was, as far as he could tell, utterly alone. Quietly gazing at the silhouettes of humans in the distance, he watched their companionship and heard the conversation and laughter. He watched and insofar as it is possible for tigers to feel sadness, he gave way to a feeling of abject melancholy. Then he turned and meandered into the thick forest scrub, his horizontal stripes appearing as so many bamboo pipes bending in the wind.

12

The mid-morning sun was merciless as the Pwa-Ka-Nyaw went about the business of the harvest. The golden-brown carpet of the padi fields were covered with people moving across it like ants on the forest floor. This was last back-breaking effort. Afterwards, there would be some respite, until the rains came, and it would begin all over again. Man following nature's rhythms in the way that he always had, dependent on her whims, sometimes regardless of how hard he worked. As Pati-Teyeh swung his scythe in a wide arc, twisting at his waist, he understood the relationship profoundly. Sweat ran steadily down his face and neck, his back and thighs, a wide, conical hat protecting his head from the sun. When the pain in his back and arms became too much and his breath heaved so much that his lungs hurt, he squatted and rested, close to the earth, surveying the scene around him. The blue sky and the omnipresent sun painted a vivid portrait of a tropical December. The Pwa-Ka-Nyaw men swung their scythes and as row after row of rice plants fell, the women gathered them in bundles in their arms. They carried the bundles to the red earth at the edge of the fields where they threshed the stalks against a nylon weave tarpaulin so that the grains were freed and danced spinning and jumping to the music of rice being beaten. Then, children's hands swept the jiggling grains into little piles and more hands scooped the piles into sacks made from the same nylon weave. Finally, the sacks were carried on the backs and heads of teenagers, Krung among them, to the waiting silos and storerooms of the village of Soblan.

* * *

Thus, the harvest continued for two weeks, during which the relentless work caused memories of the tiger to fade and almost, but not quite, be forgotten. Early in the morning, again the women, whose duties started before the men woke up, husked the rice with a *dhenki*, a long see-saw contraption with an outsized pestle and mortar at one end. Leaning on two armrests, a village girl pressed down one end with her foot so the beam with its pestle end fell into the wooden mortar bowl, crushing the grain and freeing the rice from its husks. 'Thump, thump, thump' all morning long. The coarse mountain rice, eaten with a chili and fermented crayfish paste, supplemented with wild weeds from the jungle, kept everyone healthy. Meat and a wider array of vegetables were far from plentiful, though mangoes and bananas were grown in a little hill-top fruit garden nearby. For the PwaKa-Nyaw, rice meant life itself.

* * *

The harvest was a good and bountiful one. Once the exhausting work was over, what energy was left would be used to have fun. Pati-Teyeh and Pati-Mussu visited a secret still hidden among the hills, near a stream with sweet tasting water which was used with the new rice to brew lao khao. The two friends were gleeful as they poured the murky liquid into five-gallon containers. They allowed themselves a few sips for quality control purposes, and their warm cheeks, twinkling eyes and sudden high spirits told them that the concoction was a success.

"That's good," said Pati-Teyeh.

"Oh yes," his friend agreed.

They had to rein in their enthusiasm so that they did not sit in a heap, waxing lyrical about the beauty of life while intoxicated. They carried the containers back, struggling with their weight, to the long-lien, where preparations for the wedding were being held. As they passed through the village, they were met with the admiring glances and toothy, or sometimes toothless smiles, of men young and old.

* * *

Lurking near enough to Soblan to smell the human activity; the fires, cooking, alcohol fumes, drifting and pungent, Suah knew instinctively he was failing to survive. He had stolen what was left of a deer carcass from the mak-nai, but he was still hungry. The bustle of the harvest around the village had made him wary of approaching it. His patience, however, was beginning to tire. He had once prowled as an absolute master. Now he slunk lazily on the outskirts of this other world, like an itinerant monk begging for alms from townsfolk. A sallow skin revealed the shape of his ribs, where once he was fat with muscle. This effect, along with his stripes, made him look like a skeletal, tiger apparition. A wandering manifestation of the forest's sickly soul.

* * *

Wherever man meets the wilderness, it does not remain so. Such is man's nature. The more land he needs, the more he takes and the forests disappear and the animals with them. The PwaKa-Nyaw were not guilty of this. They had lived in the forest for hundreds of years, as had before them the Lua, whose stone monoliths were still found in the jungle, lost in a historical celebration of a deity. Before them, who knows? Another nameless tribe in the story of man and the forest. The forest to the south and east was of Soblan was becoming farmland for plantations. To the north-west, the jungle hills rose into the foothills of the Himalayas. A place for pilgrims in search of

Buddhist shrines, or climbing madmen trying to get to the top of mountains.

13

Ka-Noon wanted to be a teacher. He remembered Komol's teachings as a boy and he had ever since been curious about the possibilities of knowledge. But now he was getting married to Oy and such dreams as he had, would most likely remain dreams. He was happy, however, because he truly loved Oy. That, as anyone knows, matters more than all other considerations. He was preparing to leave his family home, to go and live with his wife's, as was the Pwa-Ka-Nyaw custom. In such a small village, marriage matches were common, and it was often inevitable that the children of adult friends and, sometimes, even family members, would drift through their childhoods and then their adolescence, to become betrothed in natural progression. Krung and Gulab looked like following this very path, but they were not at the point where they would disappear to sit together, talking quietly and earnestly, gazing at the mirror of the river, until chores could be neglected no longer.

* * *

The wedding day, when it arrived, began with a cool morning, with clouds of mist rising from the dark green treetops below the village of Soblan. Four boys, taking advantage of the holiday atmosphere, played *takraw* on a small court placed at the edge of the village on the hill. One of them had wrapped a grimy rag around his favored foot so that when he kicked the hollow, rattan ball, it spared him the sting and welts of damaged skin. Using their legs, shoulders, and heads, the opposing teams tossed the ball around like a volleyball, the rattan making a thwacking sound whenever it was struck, the game only interrupted when sent out of play by a clumsy swipe. Meanwhile, at the long-lien, the smell of pork cooking in a curry, stirred and fussed over by perhaps, all of the women of Soblan at the same time, aroused even the laziest of men from a late slumber.

* * *

Above the tempting, unfamiliar smell of stew, came the sweet sound of voices singing. Carrying high, above the rooftops and the tall trees, the noise captivated with a firm grasp, the ears and emotions of the listeners. The source of the sound was soon revealed, as a procession began its route around the dusty tracks of the village. It was led by two young girls dressed in white cotton, ankle length dresses, fringed with pink tassels, the colors signifying their unmarried status. On their heads, they were red cloth wrapped in turban style, and in their hands, were baskets full of lotus and other flower petals, which they strew along the ground as they went like good and dutiful bridesmaids. After the girls came musicians, in the form of two men carrying pig leather drums. A bone-thin man puffed hard into a *khaen*, which sounded like a cross between bagpipes and an accordion. The family and the friends of the betrothed made up the rest of the line, holding out sticks with split ends, for those not in the procession to place lucky charms and sometimes but not often, small denomination *Baht* notes onto. The revelers snaked their way through the village, finally coming to a halt at the long-lien, which had been decorated with banana leaf origami, and bowls and cups made from thick bamboo trunks, intricately etched with good luck symbols, waiting in rows for the feasting to begin.

* * *

When the assembled guests sat down, the rice moonshine was passed around. It was drunk only by the men, who soon began to get overexcited. The women wore indulgent expressions on their faces and ignored them. Instead, they made a huge show of congratulating and complimenting Oy, who was wearing a black dress fringed with red for the first time as a married woman. She held the white dress of her childhood in her lap. They told her how beautiful she looked, as indeed she did, with a face like a Pwa-Ka-Nyaw Botticelli Venus. There she was, the center of attention, until then, in a dramatic flourish, Ka-Noon strode in brandishing two long-handled swords. The room full of eyes turned to the man as he stood still, initially ignoring the increasing tempo of the drummers. When he had summoned his nerve, he began to dance.

* * *

The sword dance was as old as the Pwa-Ka-Nyaw. Its meaning was in showing how the young groom could defend his bride and his village with skill. He placed the blades on the floor and everyone strained their necks to get a good look. The drummers beat out their rhythm, willing and encouraging the dancer to succumb. Ka-Noon's eyes fixed on the swords as if he was lost in a shamanic trance, oblivious to everything, except the drums and the swords. He pranced around in front of, and around them as if psyching himself up before even touching them. He slapped his elbows, and clapped his hands behind his knees, limbering himself awkwardly. After two more steps, he raised a wai and bent down to pick the swords up. Then, he spun them, one in each hand, until they resembled the rotor blades of a helicopter at the ends of his arms. Still, the drums crashed and the khaen blew, and the people cheered when he bent backward with the blades still spinning away madly. He twitched and halted, as if the spinning of the swords commanded the movements of his body and not vice versa. Then, with sweat pouring from his body, he bowed low in front of his wife and held out the swords to her with outstretched arms. She took them from him and in return, gave him her childhood dress. With that symbolic exchange, the solemn part of the ceremony was over, and the feasting and drinking began.

14

How they drank lao khao and sang poems through the night. They carried on into the early hours when the wakening insects and birds began to make themselves heard. A memorable night, one to be told in the future. From his vantage point, high on a hill, watching the revelers make a mockery of his loneliness, Suah knew that he had no future. In an almost self-conscious way, the tiger decided that he would enter Soblan again. He waited for the music and the song to die away, so he could claim what was rightfully his. As the villagers slept, he made his way into the village, licking the few scraps of food that were left unfinished by the chickens and dogs. When they smelled his scent, the dogs ran away again, and the chickens clucked their harrowed warning, but still, the people of Soblan slept. Suah's creaking bones, and a madness of old age made him vicious and nasty. The pangs of hunger in his belly drove him way beyond a residual fear of the humans. He stood on his hind legs and placed his flat, furry paws in the entrance to one of the stilted baans, sniffing blindly. Clinging on with his bent knitting needle claws, his chest pressed against the ladder steps, he poked his head in. The living and breathing forms of some kind of prey awaited him.

* * *

Suah hopped inside the hut with one swift movement. Gulab woke up with a fright, hearing the terrible growl coming from nowhere. Suah ended her life with one powerful swipe of his claw. The poor child's last expression was a wide-eyed, open mouthed one of shock. Pati-Mussu grabbed his rifle and fired blindly at the growling horror in his living chamber.

Suah, clipped by a bullet, burst from the hut and vanished under cover of darkness. Pati-Mussu looked at his daughter as she lay on the bamboo floor, her blanket flung to one side. A scarlet sash of blood stained her white dress, and he picked her up in his arms with tears burning in his eyes. He opened his jaws in a silent scream which caused his soul to crack apart. Pati-Teyeh, followed by Krung were the first to arrive. Pati-Teyeh felt as though his legs would fail him, while Krung turned his face away and could not bear to look at his neighbor and playmate.

* * *

Word soon spread among the village, in a murmuring rumble of fear and outrage, which rallied the discordant with fury. They milled to and fro with torches held aloft, and rushed to Pati-Mussu with sympathy, as cries and wails of sadness built a wall around him and his sons. They surrounded the girl's body, covering her with their grief, touching her head, and Pati-Mussu turned to Pati-Teyeh and said:

"I have had many sons, but she was my only daughter."

15

Gulab received a Pwa-Ka-Nyaw cremation. In the forest, high on a knoll, where the trees had been cut down to create a fire break, Pati-Mussu watched the lifeless body of his child, dressed now in a married woman's clothes, burn away to nothing but ashes. He was inconsolable. He knew that from now on he would never be happy in this life, and would have to wait for the next. He hoped that Gulab had already been reborn as her mother had, she who had died giving birth. He hoped that they were happy in whatever new life form they had found. Yes, life in the forest was hard. Pati-Mussu spent long hours staring at the flames, and then the ashes as they became cold. Finally, he scooped up handfuls of ash where his daughter's body had been and put them into the cotton shoulder bag she had carried around with her. The grey ash spilled from his hands, and floated in the atmosphere, dissolving when it touched his skin or rested lightly on a waxy leaf.

* * *

Pati-Mussu carried the bag across his shoulder, deep into the forest, looking for a particular tree. After a while, he found it. It stood there bleached white by the sun, dead but still standing.

At its base were small offerings of the kind left at baan phi's, and just the rotted remains of a cotton bag like the one he was carrying. Upon one of the branches, a thin, dried strip hung like a broken piece of a long dead liana. It was his daughter's umbilical cord.

He had placed it there himself, a duty his wife would have performed, had she survived the trauma of her daughter's birth. With twice the pain in his heart, he carried out this traditional task in the shade of Gulab's tree. For a moment, the forest seemed to stop moving. He knew it was only his own senses, heightened and raw in his grief, for nothing is ever truly still in this place, it just changes its shape, from one form to another.

16

Nothing would be left to chance again. There was a large gathering of men with arms at Soblan. They included members of the Royal Thai Forestry Department, who, in their pressed khaki uniforms, badges, and sunglasses, looked the part, and were experts on paper, but whose reputation for corruption in the past had sullied their relationship with the forest people. They had brought a television crew along with them, and the aloofness mixed with condescension they displayed, urging old people to 'get out of the way' made the Pwa-Ka-Nyaw trust them still less. Phor Luang removed his spectacles and rubbed his tired eyes. He was very emotional. Gulab's death, as it had the rest of the tribe, had deeply upset him. And now, as Chief Hikko of the tribes of Mae Lam Kham, he was being usurped and belittled by a bunch of arrogant outsiders. He also felt some guilt. As chief, perhaps he could have done more to hunt the tiger. But these days, he was an old man, like Suah himself, and not sure if he had as much fight left in him as the tiger certainly would. He looked at Krung— no one had told him he was too young to hunt the tiger—determined and eager with his slingshot sticking out of the waistband of his shorts. None of them had seen this before, except of course himself, and he was no longer sure if the stories he told were as real as he remembered them. He prayed that the mother forest would help them, the villagers acquiescing with bowed heads. Some silently angry that 'mother' should treat them this way. Some of the outsiders continued talking through the animist prayer and broke the power of its spell.

* * *

Vestiges of self-preservation were awakened in the declining tiger, as he smelled and heard men beating and calling in the forest. A prescience of sorts occupied his instincts and compelled him to flee the areas around Soblan. But to where? Where would his tired legs take him that was free of the men who now pursued him. He had no care of who or what he killed, child or man or deer, it was all the same. The smells and sounds drew in around him, confusing the snakes and the monkeys, which scattered blindly in panic across each other's frightened paths, while bats and birds flew in screeching circles, unable to settle. Agitated, his great head swung from side to side, as he paced to and fro. Suah finally found a cave among the limestone boulders of the jungle. He crept inside and rested there in the dark, like a child hoping for invisibility by sitting in a corner with his hands over his face. His head on his fore-paws, he looked at the light falling through the cavern's opening. The strong rays of sunlight illuminated a dust cloud of fine, dry, earth, rising in the wake of his recent tracks. He looked as the cloud dissipated, and as a great weariness descended, he fell as soundly asleep as a man in a prison cell.

* * *

The hunters strode and stumbled through the forest. Their plans were exact. Groups of men left the villages and swept out in an arc. The effect, a circular dragnet, closing in tightly over a very large part of the forest. With men and boys organized in this way, and determined as they were, they hoped the tiger would have no chance to escape. But still they would need the magic ingredient of luck, or as they preferred, the benevolence of forest spirits. If Suah could slip the net, then the horror would go on and on. Each man felt the dryness of throat and rush of blood which imminent danger brings, yet they remained steadfast. Krung walked along with his father, and Pati-Mussu, whose face was the very picture of the damned. For himself, Krung missed his playmate and was beginning to understand he had been deprived of a part of his life which he could never have again. That the loss of friends and family were as limbs, wrenched from the body of one's being. He shared the anger, and the excitement, of the hunt for the first time.

* * *

In his cave, Suah woke up and heard the men passing by. The beating bushes, the cries, the vibrating movement, formed a palpable and looming mortality in his animal mind. The danger spurred him, and he tentatively emerged from the cave, blinking in the sunlight. At the same moment, Krung, who had fallen a little way behind the others, happened to walk into the small clearing in front of the cave. Boy looked at tiger, in a momentary void between action. In the ensuing half-second, Suah seemed to swell to giant proportions, like a genie from the lamp, he filled the air with swirling tiger colors. At the same time, and without any hesitation, Krung drew and fired his slingshot at the tiger, in spite of the roar which blew past him, almost drowning him in its breathy humidity. The stone struck Suah between his eyes, with enough force to make him blink. The action gave just enough time for Krung to disappear between a cracked in half boulder, shrinking into the rock like a shadow.

* * *

An enraged Siamese tiger is one of nature's creations which can be truly called spectacular. Suah leapt onto the boulder, pawing at the crack in the rock, like a giant kitten frustrated by a piece of string. He scratched downwards at the quarry he knew was concealed within. Krung was flat on his back staring up at slits of the sky, darkened with the blurry orange movement of the tiger. A nightmare had come to pass, and Krung was duly terrified. He was sure that at any moment, the tiger would scoop him out from under the stone, in the way he had often done when tormenting the bugs found on the forest floor. Suah continued to dig at the solid rock with his forepaws, but got nowhere. Then, he looked, a yellow eye looking through the gap, and roared with rage. His open jaws gaped, and drooling saliva dripped down into Krung's eye. The fetid breath, sticky liquid, and harrowing sounds were too much for Krung to bear, and he fainted.

* * *

When he came to, the tiger had gone. He heard the muffled sounds of talking nearby, and he shimmied out of his hiding place. He made his way, still giddy, to where the voices were coming from, and then realized they were his father's and Pati-Mussu's. They had doubled back to look for him once they realized they had lost him. Although the frightening episode with the tiger had seemed to last for ages, it had really taken place in a matter of minutes.

'What happened son?' said Pati-Teyeh, seeing the groggy, and still petrified look on Krung's face. When he heard the details, he looked at Pati-Mussu, and in silence, they acknowledged how close another innocent had come to Suah's savage frenzy.

"You have been very brave. Now stay close to us, and we shall catch this killer shadow."

The three of them returned to the peripheral net of men and passed along the cry. The tiger was close,

109

indeed, almost within their grasp.

17

Tension held the jungle air until it was broken by a piercing scream. Villagers rushed to see what had happened and found a forestry official, his skin and clothes cut into ribbons. It was another sorry sight. Not quite dead, he was perhaps as good as, for it was a long way from expert medical help. The Pwa-KaNyaw did what they could to staunch his bleeding, and covered the shivering man with a blanket and kind words. As if it were even possible, hearts crashed more loudly in men's breasts, as one of them shouted:

"'There, there, Suah is there!" and there he was, cornered against a concave slab of limestone. To the men, who now had him surrounded, he suddenly seemed like nothing so much as a frightened and weary old tomcat, hissing with defiance at the catcher come to take his freedom and his life.

The volley of shots hit his tired old body, and he fell over on to one side. By the time Krung, Pati-Teyeh, and Pati-Mussu arrived, his eyes were already glassed over, with a final yellow glare. His final moments had been a panic addled scramble and one last vicious assault. If the bullets had not got him, then his hurting lungs and failing heart would have, sooner or later. So, there he was, Suah, or, the last of the Siamese tigers to have lived and died in the last forests of Northern Siam. He was strung to a pole and carried back to Soblan. The triumph after the tribulation. Here was the new story to be told. Although they did not know it yet, it would be the last from living memory of a real event. Krung looked at the tiger as it was carried past him, and thought about how beautiful an animal it was, and how small it looked in death, against the power of it in life and imagination. Pati-Teyeh and

111

Pati-Mussu looked at the animal with ambivalence. It had done its damage, the kind which cannot be undone, and thus would be always thought about and reflected upon. In Pati-Mussu's case, it had left a scar upon the soul, which, he believed, had killed something of his heart, and he knew that it could not be re-born while he still lived.

18

On a clear blue day, Krung walked back to the village of Soblan, carrying his grubby little shoulder bag. He stopped to look across the hilltops of Chiang Mai. In the villages of Mae Lam Kham, he noticed the changes, as they arrived slowly to the lives of the Pwa-Ka-Nyaw: the lines of wooden poles stretching through the forest for miles, and bringing electricity to the households which could pay for it. The red dirt trail roads were wider than he remembered them. They now accommodated increasing numbers of tourists, who, in the dry season, came to photograph the quaint little houses on stilts, and the old, turbaned women with wizened faces, squatting in their doorways and smoking cob pipes. Krung was fascinated by these visitors, and the distant world they came from. He did his best to make friends, and learn from them.

* * *

The tourists however, were often shown around by low landers, who had no real respect for the hill tribes and their way of life. They saw them as a commodity, to be exploited like any other. Then, the tourists would drift away when the rains came, and washed away the hillside roads like so much mud. In the heady days after Suah's death, Soblan, and Mae Lam Kham had been awash with such types. Along with the occasional scientists, or NGO officers, whose motives, though often purer than the former visitors, were often just as self-serving, pursuing knowledge for personal gain or acclaim.

* * *

The forests grow smaller, as the plantations grow larger. Krung and his father, and Pati-Mussu, carry on their struggle for life. The Pwa-Ka-Nyaw continue to live in the forest. They tend their mango tree gardens, and the padi fields which sustain them. The outsiders, so greedy for all that there is in the world, continue to put pressure on them by seeking ever more arable land. Or searching for treasures which are hidden in the depths of an ancient forest. Thus, it sometimes seems inevitable, that the tiger, elephant and bear, will one day cease to exist. Except perhaps, in stories, told by the old to the young to excite their imagination.

Interview with Bigfoot
Lila Pinord

It was a Sunday, my day off when I came face to face with the creature everyone calls Bigfoot or Sasquatch. I never believed any of the stories I read or heard since they never provided any definitive proof of their existence: no hair, no scat, any dead bodies or bones, no burial grounds. What do they do with them after they die? Maybe they never die—now there's a thought that made me shiver in my hiking boots! I smiled.

As usual, I'd left my Jeep about a half mile back at the end of an old logging road, grabbed my rifle—in case I came across a cougar or a bear—and began my trek into the wilderness above Lake Ozette. It was early Fall, but there was already a cold bite to the air. Bright red and yellow leaves fell like confetti all around me as if applauding a passing parade.

I enjoy my weekend jaunts, my commune with Nature, whether it's snowing, raining, or sun shining. It all feels good to me.

On this day, I stopped to admire a wide clearing, covered with a mat of wildflowers of every color imaginable. Beautiful. I lifted my camera that hung from a strap around my neck—another item I was never without—to capture this moment for future use— maybe to publish it in the newspaper I work for as the Features editor.

"What in the hell?" I lowered my camera, squinted

my eyes and scanned the area across the expanse to the tall trees that edged the meadow.

A figure stood there, staring back at me. He was tall, lean, with scraggly patches of long dark hair covering parts of his pale body. His long arms hung below his knees. I use the masculine gender for sure, it was a male standing just at the tree line in its shadow. He took a step out into the bright sunshine. Another step. In my direction.

For some reason, I was not afraid. Okay, I was a *little* afraid. Slowly, cautiously, we approached each other. My knees shook a little. We stopped when we stood about five feet apart.

This is one ugly creature! I thought. Its dark eyes, which were far apart and elongated, widened as if he heard and understood my thought.

"H—hello?" I stuttered.

Hello, he returned without moving his lips or facial structure. It was as if I heard his response inside my brain.

"Wh—why have you come so close to me? I understood you guys like to remain elusive, mysterious?"

The being took a step forward while I took a faltering step backward, not sure of his intentions.

I wanted to see you up close. People of your race are so odd looking. We stood sizing each other up.

"Oh. What is your name? Or do we keep on calling you all Bigfoot or Sasquatch"

He gazed down at his long hairy feet. I guess he was comparing them to mine since he immediately glanced at my much smaller ones.

We have no names. What is yours? Again, the voice in my head.

"Matt. I'm a reporter and I've always wanted to

meet one of you. Do you have a family, or are you all loners" *I have a brother Uguâ?*

Aha! I thought. *I caught him in a lie. They DO have names.* I watched as his long, craggy face registered only a slight change in expression. I wondered if they knew how to smile.

"Can I call you Mr. Foot, since you have no name" I smiled. I think he smiled back though I can't be sure. "Why do you show yourself to me," I asked again. "I know you guys like to be elusive. And how long have you existed here in the wilderness"

Thousands of years, even before the First People you call the Native Americans.

"I've heard that they've known of your race all along, is this true"

We have an agreement. We don't bother them and they don't bother us. They don't try to hunt us down or capture us as all the rest of you do. They don't run to the authorities to report a 'sighting' of a 'Sasquatch' so others will come to the area and search for us.

"I'm a reporter. How do you know I won't tell of our encounter today?"

No one will believe you.

"You're right. Readers will assume I made the whole thing up–

–like folks and their alien encounters."

A thought occurred to me. "How is it you understand our language"

We know all languages. All over the world. "So, you really are everywhere!" *Yes.*

"Why are there never any traces of your existence"

We have been here for thousands of years like I said. We learned how to cover our tracks, so to speak.

117

"My aunt on the other side of the lake has an apple orchard. Last week, she found huge footprints embedded in the mud beneath the trees and most of the apples were gone. Was that you or members of your family"

We didn't have time to cover our tracks then. We heard someone coming, so we slipped away.

"Which reminds me, what is your diet, how do you subsist out here in the wilderness and up in the mountains"

We don't eat meat so don't worry; I'm not about to dine on you. I wished he would have smiled when he said that. *We do eat fish and fruit, leaves and roots. Sometimes, we take your salmon.*

"So that was you! I'd laid out about ten salmon along a riverbank and gone out for more. When I returned, the fish were gone! I assumed a bear—"

Was that a guilty expression on his face? I doubt it.

"I really hate to ask this next question, but do you sometimes steal children to keep your race going" I'd heard this tale ever since I was a kid.

Never. Our race will continue forever until—

"Until *what?* Who are you? *WHAT* are you" No answer from 'Ol Stoneface.

I must go now. His shaggy ears perked up like he heard something, or someone, calling to him. I thought I heard a high whistling note, a sound smaller than a gnats, but couldn't be sure.

"Wait!" I called. "I've seen photos of your kind—"

All fake. We look nothing like big fat hairy bears! No one has ever captured an image of us.

He turned and ambled off across the wide meadow. I couldn't resist. It's the reporter in me.

I lifted my camera and snapped a picture just as Bigfoot lifted a long hairy arm in a waving gesture and

I was almost sure I heard him say *Goodbye*. In a blink of an eye, he disappeared into the shadows of the forest.

When I got back to my jeep, I lifted up my camera to view the photo, thinking I'd outsmarted him. Ha! I've got *proof!* But only the beautiful wildflowers covering an empty meadow met my unbelieving eyes.

His words echoed in my mind—*no Bigfoot has ever been captured on film!*

Then, upon closer inspection, I could see Bigfoot tracks trailing off into the woods. "Ah ha! It might not be proof of Bigfoot but it's better than nothing." I decided to hike back to the location and get some good close-ups of the tracks. When I got there, however, I was in for a surprise. The big, hairy creature had also returned.

"Wait! No!" I cried as I watched him sweeping the ground with a large limb from an evergreen tree, destroying his old tracks as well as his fresh ones.

I grabbed my camera, set it on video mode, and had captured at least 30-seconds of this activity before I realized it was futile. He wouldn't show up in the video. "Damn!" I stopped filming, lowered the camera and stood there watching him backtracking his own footprints, sweeping away the evidence, one step at a time. If only my camera could have captured that grin on his face.

I continued to watch him until he disappeared into the shadowy realm of the deep woods from whence he'd come and I was left with nothing, not a shred of proof of my encounter.

I returned to the Jeep, frustrated and disappointed, but decided to have a look at the video clip anyway. My head jerked back when I saw what I'd captured. Maybe I didn't have proof of a Sasquatch or even the footprints. But what I did have was something that would at least give my story some credibility. Or so I thought.

My story appeared in the paper the next day accompanied by a still frame from the video and a link to the paper's online edition where the full video clip could be viewed. What the readers could see on the clip was dirt, rocks, and leaves being swept to-and-fro by a large limb from an evergreen tree apparently being wielded by invisible hands. It was quite an astonishing sight and, in just a matter of hours, the video had gone viral across the Internet.

My hopes of some credibility, however, were short-lived. Nearly everyone was claiming the video to be nothing more than a clever hoax. My credibility as a reporter, the credibility I'd spent years building, was ruined. There was only one consolation—if you could call it that. I knew the truth. And, like Fox Mulder always said, "The truth is out there". The thing is, if you find it, you might also find yourself wishing you hadn't.

Bump
Dave Suscheck, Jr.

The barking jerked me out of a sound sleep, disoriented and confused. Whose dog was barking? My dog? My dog should have been sleeping in her bed in the corner of my room. I leaned over to look. Gone. That's strange. As I made my way down the hallway towards the back door, I was struck by a sudden wave of nausea that doubled me over. Gripping the wall with one hand, and my stomach with the other, I crept around the corner to the kitchen. As I looked out the kitchen window into the backyard, I could see my dog at the edge of the porch light, looking up, barking into the darkness of the tree. I felt the unsettling draft of the open back door across my bare feet. I looked over and realized how my dog, Molly, had gotten out. Both my storm door and screen door leading into the backyard stood open, like a silent lazy sentinel. I put on a pair of shoes and stumbled out into the yard heading in the direction of my dog's incessant barking.

"Molly, stop. Molly, stop," I repeated.

She yielded for a fraction of a second, startled by my voice, throwing me a quick backward glance long enough to see that it was me before she resumed barking at the silent, dark, fir tree. I stood there staring into the blackness as she continued her barking. The night was so crushing that in its darkness it absorbed the light completely. I couldn't

121

see anything, hear anything, or smell anything, but there must have been something in that tree to get Molly riled up. She was normally a quiet, gentle dog. Often times she would spook me with her wraith-like movements, appearing in front or behind me while I'd go about my business. She would stare quietly, studying objects, people, and other animals. To get her to this voluminous tirade must be something either unknown or dangerous. I grabbed her by the collar and led her reluctantly back to the house where I secured and locked both backdoors.

"We will investigate it tomorrow," I said looking down at her large pleading eyes.

She followed me back to the bedroom, the tapping of her nails on the wood floor the only sign she was following me. The rest of that night I slept fretfully, tossed and turned at nothing in particular.

The next morning, I woke to the ceaseless chirping of cicadas. It was another muggy, oppressive morning. I rolled reluctantly out of bed, padded to the bathroom barefoot, my feet sticking to the clammy wood where I took a cold shower. My thoughts were dominated by the weirdness of the previous night. What spooked Molly out of her normally docile character? It just wasn't like her to be so obstinate and loud.

After dressing, I headed out into the backyard to inspect the tree. Unlike last night, the tree was completely visible in the suns' burning light. Sweat began to bead on my skin. Not seeing anything from the ground, I needed a new plan. I went into the garage to retrieve my ladder. Once the ladder was secured as I could make it in the swaying branches of the tree, I began my shaky ascent to the top. At first glance, I didn't notice anything in, on, or around the tree that was proof of anything having been up there the night before. Perhaps Molly saw some sort of spectral shadow, some trick of light she saw that her dog brain couldn't understand. Just as I was about to begin my perilous climb down, I spied a patch of bark missing from the branch just above eye level. Peering as close as I could get to the patch of disrupted bark, I noticed what looked like claw marks. The strangest thing about these marks was that it appeared to have six digits per claw. I clumsily fished my cell phone out of my pocket to snap a few pics of it, and then hastened my retreat to the safety of solid ground.

Back in my house I went into my study and fired up the computer. I did a simple Internet search for animal claw marks. It brought me thousands of images, but none with six claw marks. Completely perplexed I gave up my digital quest and went to work doing what I actually got paid to do. Write. I wrote technical manuals for electronic gizmos, making the directions for the manuals understandable for the masses. It's not glamorous, but it pays the bills.

As dusk began to settle, Molly became restless. She kept pawing at my chair where I was reading. She wanted to go outside. As she started out the back she froze midstride. The dusk had created a grayish haze that shrouded my entire backyard in a film that made it hard to define specific objects. What was most startling was the silence. Absolute silence. Molly backed up and went into the house without a sound. I felt a prickly sensation run up my arms and when I looked down, I could see all my arm hair standing on end like I was standing near a giant static ball. I scanned the yard one last time and not seeing anything out of the ordinary shut and bolted both doors leading to the backyard. As I made my way into the living room, I spotted Molly behind the couch, peering around the corner at me. She was scared, but scared of what? I hadn't seen or heard anything out there. This troubled me because she never got this way about anything. If she was scared, I wasn't going to go confront anything that may be out lurking around. I double-checked all my windows, doors, and other possible points of entry, going so far as to check my fireplace. Confirming that the house was indeed secure, I coaxed Molly out from behind the couch and down the hall to the bedroom. We both tried to sleep that night, but the thought of something hanging around outside beyond the illumination of the yard light gave me the creeps. I had to talk to someone with more experience than I had, and I knew just the person I had to talk too. It could wait until morning.

* * *

The following morning, I got up and dressed, packed Molly into my pickup, and headed out to see a friend of mine. This friend was an expert in wildlife, his name was Rick Locke, and not only was he a childhood friend; he was also a Game Warden. If he couldn't figure out what made those scratches in my tree and spooking my dog, then I would start worrying.

The drive out to his office was idyllic. The sun was shining, wildlife abundant, and the traffic sparse. I always enjoyed driving out on old dirt roads on nice summer days with just my dog. Being in the country drudged up memories of my youth. I used to hunt a lot growing up. I hadn't been out that far in a while. I pulled into the parking lot of the Game Commission station a little after noon and parked on the side of the building in the visitor lot. Molly and I made our way to the front of the building and entered the cool, air-conditioned building. Locke was sitting at his desk at the back of the bullpen with his feet propped up on the desk, eating a sandwich and reading a magazine. He looked up from his reading as I approached; his face broke into a grin.

"Hey Sam, how the hell are you?"

"I'm good Rick. How're you doing?"

"As good as to be expected. Not many hunters anymore, so my job is preoccupied with catching teens fishing without licenses and the occasional poacher. What brings you out here?"

"Well, I don't quite know. Something has been in my backyard, spooking my dog, and I haven't been able to see it. I took a picture of some marks it left on a tree in the hopes that you might be able to identify it?"

"Sure thing. Let me see what ya got."

I pulled out the pictures I took of the marks and slid them across his desk. Rick took the images and spent several minutes looking them over, occasionally making slight noises while he mulled over what he saw. Finally, he broke the silence.

"You're putting me on, right?" he stated bluntly.

"No," I said. "I'm dead serious. That's what I found in the tree."

"I think you might have some kids messing with you, Sam."

"Why do you say that?"

"There are no animals with six-digit claws. They just don't exist in nature."

"How do you explain my dog's reaction then?"

"I don't know. Maybe they sprayed bear urine or something and they confused her scent receptors? The only thing I ever heard having six claws was a polydactyl cat, and that was a genetic abnormality."

"Well," I asked. "What should I do?"

"If you want, I can loan you one of our tranquilizer guns? Sit in your backyard until you see it and tag it. Then we may be able to identify it. Just don't tell anybody I let you borrow the gun."

"OK, I'll try it. This crap is starting to ruin my sleep."

"Haha. You're a writer who works from home. You don't need normal sleep patterns," He said as he punched me on the arm.

With tranquilizer gun in hand, I headed back to my truck, Molly in tow. I carefully put the gun and the box of darts behind my seat. I headed back home, Molly curled up next to me the entire way. She was tired. Whatever was in my backyard had made sleeping nights hit or miss. We were both exhausted.

As I neared my house I had another strange thought.

Once home, I let Molly out the back so she could do her business and I went to my den closet where I kept my guns. On the top shelf of the closet was a heavy reinforced lock box. Hefting it off the shelf, I placed it on my desk. I rubbed down the top of the case, removing the dust that had built up on the outside. Then I cleaned off the digital keypad and punched in my code and was rewarded with a soft click as the latch popped. Opening the lid, I gazed in at its contents. It was a Colt .357 Trooper MK III. Years ago, I used this gun to boar hunt down south and deer hunt around town. It was a solid shooting gun that, for me, was always shot true. Nestled next to it in the foam was a box of .357 magnum hollow point rounds. If this didn't take down whatever was in the backyard, I was in trouble. I removed it from the safe and took it to my bedroom where I placed it under my pillow.

Come evening, I would take it with me into the darkness.

The rest of the afternoon I went about my normal routine. I wrote some manual pages, cleaned, ate, fed Molly, and went about preparing myself for the coming nightfall. I was sitting at my computer when I noticed the cessation of noise outside the window. I had lost track of the time. I looked at my watch and realized that it was well into dusk. I looked over my shoulder at the window that overlooked my backyard and could see the gray haze of night steadily enveloping my yard in darkness. The birds had stopped, the cicadas stopped, and all other normal sounds of the summer evening were still. Complete, eerie silence had settled over everything. I got up and went to the window, peering out into the gloom as best I could to make out any shape that wasn't familiar to my yard. I couldn't see anything, partially because of the gray dusk made seeing things clearly more difficult, but also because I didn't know what to look for.

While staring through the window, to the extreme left border of my yard, I saw for the briefest of moments, a gray shape, a shade darker than its surroundings flash between the slats of my fence. At first, I thought perhaps it was my imagination, something to do with my wanting to see something that I somehow imagined it. When I saw it move again, this time on my side of the fence, I knew there was something physically there. My pulse quickened at the prospect of confronting the beast that was creeping my yard. I grabbed the tranquilizer gun and raced down the hallway to my backdoor. I paused at the door, took a deep breath, and slowly opened it, being careful to not let Molly out. I hugged the house as I moved to the left, being careful to stay out of sight of where I last caught a glimpse of the creature. When I got to the fence, I crouched in the bushes and ever so slowly moved towards the last spot I had seen movement. When I got to the edge of the bushes, I knew I was close. I could hear rustling on the other side of the fir tree. I carefully cocked the tranquilizer in the ready to fire position, took the safety off, and prepared to send it to dreamland. I took a deep breath and released it to calm my nerves. I counted to five and jumped out from behind my foliage fortress.

* * *

I leaped from behind the bush while aiming down the barrel of the gun, ready to put a tranquilizer dart right between the beady eyes of the beast when, to my dismay, staring back at me was nothing but a fat, slovenly possum. It slowly lifted its head and glassy, blank eyes to meet my gaze. I entertained the thought of popping it between the eyes with my dart anyway but did not want to waste it on such a vindictive action. I released my finger, feeling the pressure ease from the trigger. I was discouraged, but not completely disheartened. I retreated back to the house in the hopes that my attempt at discovering what was in my backyard was not lost. I went back into the house and hid behind the curtains of my kitchen door, silent in my vigil, hoping that I might catch a real glimpse of what was out there.

The hours dragged on in an uneventful procession. For the rest of that night, nothing happened. A few times I caught myself dosing off, leaning slightly forward until my head tapped the glass of the door. I was becoming extremely tired as night morphed into dawn. I gave up around five that morning, retiring to my bed. Molly slept soundly through the night in the corner of the bedroom.

As soon as the sun crested the horizon, light forced its way behind my lidded eyes. I rolled over and pulled the pillow over my head as I tried to shut out the orange of the day. The anticlimactic night left me feeling drained. Molly's whining is what finally pulled me from sleep. Her head was resting on the edge of my bed. Our eyes locked and her tail began to wag, her back end following suit as her tail increased its speed. I looked at my watch. It was later in the day than I expected, Molly was asking me for food and other business. I let her out and while she was doing her thing, I made up her dinner, giving her more than usual to make up for her missed breakfast. While she ate, I showered. Just as the dying light crept away, I took one last look around the yard. Nothing looked off. I shrugged and headed back inside to make my own dinner and catch up on work I had been putting off. I was starting to fear the whole thing was imagined, that I was somehow becoming unhinged, losing my touch with reality.

I was deeply focused, writing directions for the assembly of a new consumer trinket that was supposed to make can openers obsolete. It was boring. As I finished up the final steps, I was startled out of my chair by a loud bang on the window of my office. My heart began to pound. I went over to the window and lifted the curtain. The double pane window was cracked and there was a pinkish hue smear on the window. Then I heard another thud from down the hallway. I turned and went towards the sound. I heard the sound again, something crashed into the kitchen window. I could feel my heartbeat pulsing in my ears, the blood pumping causing my vision to narrow. The terror I felt in that moment, listening to the sound being caused by the unknown, was more than I could take. A tremor started in my hands, adrenaline coursed through my veins, pushing my heart faster than it was already going. There was a final smash against the window, cracking it. Then silence. I stood there for some time, trembling on my feet and afraid to move, afraid to breathe. I don't know how long I stood there in the kitchen, trembling like the last lonely leaf on a windy autumn day.

I took one, tiny step forward. Then another. Inch by inch I moved towards the window. In the light of the kitchen, I could see some residue on the outside of the window, similar to the marks on my office window. To the right of the window was a switch that controlled the back-porch light and I flipped the switch. The backyard was washed in yellow light, and the briefest of shapes escaped the illumination as it fled to the darkness at the back of the yard. I couldn't believe it. My brain couldn't process what my eyes had seen. I suddenly realized I was alone in my kitchen. Molly, my constant companion was gone. Now my terror turned to dread. I called out her name.

"Molly?" Nothing.

I searched the entire first floor of my house, frantically checking each room. I started to panic. That's when I noticed the door to the basement was opened ever so slightly. I pulled open the door and looked down into the abyss and called out her name again.

"Molly?"

I heard the slightest of whimpers. I rushed down the steps, turning the light on as I went. My basement was a mess. Boxes were stacked helter-skelter everywhere creating a maze snaking throughout the basement. Deep in the back, by the water heater, two reflective orbs stared back at me. Molly was tucked into the back between the cinder block wall and the water heater. Her ears were pinned to the side of her head, staring out cautiously. I made my way through the boxes to where she had herself tucked away. We spent the rest of the night down in the basement, huddled next to each other between the wall and water heater. Occasionally, I could hear the sounds of something hitting my windows. Nothing like the ferocity of the assault on the kitchen window, but enough to keep me up all night staring towards the stairs the tranquilizer gun and pistol completely forgotten. What I would find in the morning would make my blood run cold in my veins.

* * *

I knew it was morning because I could hear the alarm going off in my room. I stood up, pops and cracks coming from my knees and back. Molly followed me up the stairs to the first floor as I went and turned off my alarm. I went outside to horror. Under each of the windows facing the backyard laid mutilated corpses of small animals. Mangled almost beyond recognition, but enough pieces to identify squirrels, birds, possums, raccoons, and if I was not mistaken, some stray cats. Everything in my stomach was reintroduced to the world, right there in the grass. As I was doubled over spewing my guts out, I noticed the complete lack of noise around me. No animal or insect noises. For a moment, I thought that perhaps I had gone deaf. Then I heard a plane flying high overhead. All of the animals that were battered against my windows were the wildlife that lived around my house. Nothing was left alive. I had to fight through my urge to run. I needed to rid my property of the scourge. I couldn't do it alone. I needed help.

131

There was one person I knew that could help me with my problem.

Rick Locke came over right away.

"Holy Hell. This is sick man. You sure it was some kind of animal that did this and not some sicko messing with you?"

"No! I swear to you. I saw something running away when I turned on the light."

He could hear the panic in my voice and see it in my eyes. He set traps at strategic points around my property. I had a large oak tree on the border of my yard that he proposed putting a tree stand in and sitting up there with the tranquilizer gun.

"I can sit up there and see the whole yard. I can put on my scent lock gear. It shouldn't see or smell me. I see it I shoot it. Sound good?"

"Yeah. Just be careful, man. Look at what it did to all these animals. It's dangerous."

"I'm not some defenseless bird or squirrel. I'll be fine. I know what I'm doing."

I stood at my kitchen window and watched the night as it crept over the yard. As the minutes ticked by, seeing Rick in the tree became harder to do. I knew I wouldn't be able to hear the tranquilizer gun go off, it would be too quiet. The night passed into day. I rubbed my eyes with the palms of my hands; they were itchy and dry from lack of sleep. I looked into the tree where Rick held his vigil. Empty. I rushed out the back door, Molly quick on my heels. I rushed to the tree that should have held my friend. There were savage gouge marks from the base of the tree up towards the spot where Rick's tree stand had been bolted, gore hung in the branches. The trunk of the tree was painted with his blood. There was nothing of Rick larger than a baseball. There wasn't anything recognizable in the tree. I stared at the spot in disbelief. Molly started sniffing the ground, moving in the direction of some picked up scent trail.

I shadowed Molly as she moved. Her head weaved back and forth following the scent trail. She stopped at a gaping hole in the corner of my fence. Beyond the fence were deeper woods and the dirt around the twisted metal of the fence was stained with blood, not all of it fresh. Beyond that fence lay the thing that tormented and hunted my yard, the *thing* that killed my friend, unnerved my dog, and terrified me. I was determined to rid myself of this demon. I would use daylight to my advantage. I went back in the house and grabbed my .357, and a flashlight just in case. I went back out into the yard and headed for the breach in my fence. Molly was sitting there, patiently waiting for my return. The hole in the fence was big enough for both of us to crawl through. We ventured out into the woods, Molly following the scent trail as I followed her. I could feel my palms sweat as I gripped the gun. Each step forward pumped evermore adrenaline into my already overtaxed system.

I don't know how far we trekked into the woods, but Molly's nose led us accurately. We came to a thickening of the woods where buried in dense brush was what appeared to be the mouth of a cave. Molly tracked up to the mouth and caught a scent that stood all her hair up on end. She stopped just inside the cave and gave a low growl. She moved into the darkness of the cave until she was lost to my sight. I heard an ear-piercing yelp and she took off back towards the house at a flat out run. I watched her go, unsure of what to do. I turned back to the cave's opening. From where I stood the interior of the cave was a black void. I ran back to the house to get a flashlight and made my way back to the cave. I crouched through the entrance way into the belly of the cavity, the gun in one hand and the flashlight in the other. The passage I found myself in wound in a slightly downward direction. I was met by a strong stench of decay, a musky odor that triggered the most primitive part of my brain; an ancient warning urged my body to run in the other direction.

I sensed I was reaching the end of the cave's tunnel because I could feel the walls closing in on me in the gloom beyond my light. I came to what I thought was the end but was, in fact, the end of the central tunnel, the cave itself moved off to the left. I followed the path as it opened up into the main chamber.

The growl came out of the darkness to my right.

I froze and turned off my flashlight. I refused to exhale for fear that it would draw the attention of what was with me in the dark. Then there was a shuffling sound, scuffling and scraping noises as the beast came towards me. I started to back the way I came, knowing I had made a terrible mistake entering the cave. I raised the flashlight and the gun in front of me as I moved backward. When I got to the sharp angled bend I stopped with my back against the security of the bedrock and prepared to run at the slightest perception of movement. The tunnel would lead me out to what I hoped was the safety of the sunlit woods. My finger tightened on the trigger. With my other hand, I poised my thumb over the flashlight's toggle switch, ready to turn it on and see what was in front of me. I knew it was there, just outside my personal zone because the smell of decay and death got stronger.

I flicked on the light.

Yellow fangs dripped with saliva, graying silver fur,

and dark black eyes consumed my view. I could not recognize the face of the creature that stared at me, its head appeared as if completely free from the body, which was shrouded by the darkness of the cave. My mind shut down from a complete takeover of fear, I could feel a warmth spreading between my legs as my bladder emptied. My right index finger began to spasm independently of my fear wrought mind, pulling the trigger repeatedly until the hammer of the gun hit spent chambers, the clicking of the used shells lost in the noise of the expended bullets. Six bouts of flame shot from the barrel, the head disappearing back into the abyss of the cave. I don't know if I hit the beast, but the shots from the gun gave me enough of an edge that I dropped my gun and light and ran. My legs felt light and shaky with the fear and adrenaline coursing through my veins. I barely felt my feet touching the ground as I drove towards the light at the end of the tunnel. I burst from the cave like a diver breaking the surface of the water. I didn't stop when I hit the woods. From the deep recesses of the cave came a blood-chilling roar. I pushed myself on, racing towards my house seeking safety.

I didn't bother going through the hole in the fence, I vaulted over the top, my foot clipped the top rail and I slammed face first onto my lawn, the wind knocked from me. I laid face down on the ground, floating on the fringes of consciousness, my lungs and limbs burning from the exertion. I was able to raise myself up on my hands and knees and began crawling towards my house, blood draining out of my broken nose. I was halfway to my house when an intense pressure crushed my right ankle, my legs ripped out from underneath me causing me to hit the ground again. I was being savagely dragged back towards the cave. All the fight drained out of my body. I was resigned to my fate, my death in a pitch-black cave being gnawed on by some oddity of nature. I tried to look behind me to see what was happening as I was being dragged to my death, but my eyes were too bleary with tears to see clearly. As I looked towards my house, I saw a brown and white blur rocketing towards me. Molly rushed me, teeth bared in a gruesome expression I had never seen on her gentle face before, and as she reached my spot on the ground she leaped over me and crashed into the beast that was firmly locked onto my ankle.

The pressure on my ankle released, a great cyclone of fur and teeth gnashed at each other as the two animals fought. Unnatural, terrifying sounds, growls and screeches, came from both animals as they warred. I started to drag myself away from the melee of the clashing titans, my mind scrambled from fear and a concussion. A thought started to form. I needed to help Molly. I needed to kill the beast before it hurt anybody or anything else.

My fear propelled me towards the house, the sounds of the fighting behind haunting me. I feared for my dog's life, I feared for my life. I crashed through the back door, hands shaking violently with adrenaline, as I went for something to kill the monster. I went for the gun cabinet in my office. I pulled out an old shotgun my Dad used for hunting. I searched through the drawers and cubbies looking for some powerful lead slugs that he used for bear hunting. Two slugs were crammed in the back of the bottom drawer. They looked old but in decent condition. As I made my way down the hallway, I fumbled with the shells, loading them into the chamber. Molly let out a sharp yelp. I hit the back door at a stumbling run, raising the gun as I went. The monster stood on its hind legs, Molly firmly grasped in its jaws. With a flick of its head, it tossed Molly's limp body into the woods. I stared at the beast's head through the forked sight of the gun. The Beast's jaundiced eyes locked with mine.

All descriptions pale compared to the reality of the thing I was looking at. My mind was immobilized with rational thought. It looked like a hairless bear, with six razor-sharp claws, and large Komodo like teeth. I steadied my hands and squeezed the trigger. The slug found its mark squarely between the animal's eyes, burying deep into its brain. It staggered on its hind legs while I racked my remaining shell into the barrel and fired into the beast's chest, finishing it off.

I approached, afraid that it would rise up at any moment and kill me. I stood over the creature and nudged it with the barrel of the gun, making sure I wasn't too easy a target for its sharp claws. It didn't move. The gun fell from my grasp hitting the ground with a dull thud.

It was over.

So much had been lost to something so terrifying, something that defies explanation. Its massive paws were motionless as dark blood oozed from the quarter-sized holes in its head and chest. I stared at the body, my eyes burning with exhaustion and anger. How this creature came to be was a great mystery that I did not care to explore.

It was the most imperceptible of sounds. It grew in intensity and my first thought was that it came from the corpse at my feet. The resonances of the sound were more familiar and slowly occurred to me that it was coming from beyond the fence from the woods. It sounded like Molly.

I ran as fast as my fatigued legs could take me towards the source of the noise.

Not far beyond the fence, deep in the bushes, there was a flash of white amid the greens and browns of the woodland floor were visible. Molly was struggling to get up, whimpering as she tried.

She had deep gashes on her side; blood poured freely from the many wounds. I ran to her and administered first aid as best I could. I picked her up gently and moved quickly to my truck, and rushed her to the animal hospital.

I called animal control and the state police from the hospital while the vet worked on suturing Molly's wounds. I told them what had occurred out at there over the last two days. They may have thought me nuts but agreed to dispatch units to my house. The State Police called me back to tell me what they had found. They had met animal control and ventured into the backyard together, weapons at the ready. They saw all the dead wildlife stacked under the back windows of the house. They didn't see any beast in the yard but said there were large drag marks leading through the broken fence, which they followed down into deeper woods. The drag marks led away from the cave I had found, perhaps to another hiding place in some untouched region of the forest. Something as big, if not bigger, dragged off the corpse of the creature I had killed. They found what was left of my friend, in pieces, scattered in the woods. They weren't going to press charges because animal control identified the marks of an animal on the pieces they could find and it corroborated my story enough to satisfy the police. That was a minor relief. I went back to my house to meet the police for a more formal interview and to give them my statement.

* * *

Molly survived her wounds. I resigned to move away from that house and packed up a U-Haul with my stuff. I sold the house to the county for their fire department to practice on. They scheduled to burn it down the following fall. At my request, they were going to make the area off limit to hikers and hunters. Game Commission Wardens took day trips out to the woods to see if they could see what I saw, what I believed to have killed in my backyard. Their excursions were unsuccessful. After a while, it became a whispered legend, an American folktale that people told each other around campfires, at hunting camps, in bars. I know the truth in what I witnessed. There is something out in those woods. It's only a matter of time before it ventures out to meet humanity again.

Ninette: The Lair
Linda Jenkinson

Look
the lair's
now alight!
The lantern glows each time a soul falls
through the darkness— far as the eye can't see.

The Emporium
L. H. Davis

Captain Rigs didn't wake me until after we had docked at Jackson's Dome. As soon as I opened my eyes, he yelled in my face and yanked me out of my A-cell. I recognized the gleaming coffin for what it was, although at the time I didn't realize I'd been locked inside it for five months. After spending that much time in transluminal flight, the syrupy fog of the A-cell induced coma was practically oozing from my eyes and ears. I tried to understand Captain Rigs' instructions, but I suspected later—by the way things turned out—that I got something screwed up. But then again, had I known at the time he had kidnapped me, I would have killed him myself.

"I'll ride down in the lift with you," Rigs said, "but I'm not babysitting your ass until Finch shows up."

"Finch?" I asked. The word lingered in my mouth, tasting of burnt iron and onions. I'd never flown in space before, so I didn't realize the taste and grogginess were normal side effects of traveling faster than the speed of light. At the time I assumed I had just blown my entire paycheck again down at Mary's Place but would be fine after a hot shower knocked the edge off my hangover. Of course, it did worry me that a big man calling himself "The Captain" had hoisted me out of bed. I'd been drunk before, more than once, but never *that* drunk.

"This is your ID card," Rigs said.

The captain, a very wide, middle-aged man, stood well over six feet. I was barely twenty-one and just under four-foot-ten, so when Rigs pushed that plastic card into my hand and shoved me backward through the hatch, I went. Stumbling across the opening, I found myself surrounded by the blackness of space—and little else. Sensing freefall, my stomach, and bladder were on the brink of disaster when my ass kissed the outer glass wall of the boarding elevator. Captain Rigs then followed me inside, which I took as a good sign. The tawny green metal of the ship's exterior loomed beyond the glass wall behind Rigs, but standing so near the hull made it difficult to get a feel for the size of the spacecraft.

The distant horizon formed by the ship's spherical hull, however, indicated the vessel was quite large.

I looked up at Rigs and asked, "Where the hell am I?"

The captain smiled but didn't seem to be in a hurry to answer my question. I turned to the glass wall behind me as the elevator began to drop, hoping to see a landmark and get my bearings. Discovering we were still a thousand feet above the surface, I put a death grip on the handrail and choked down the stomach bile gurgling in my throat.

"Welcome to Wadi," Rigs said with a chuckle.

Wadi? What happened to Abydos? I thought. The taste of bile, burnt iron, and onions made speaking, if not impossible, highly undesirable. I had heard stories about Wadi, mostly while drinking down at Mary's. I assumed most of the wild tales, if not all, were fabrications, mellowed and aged by good whiskey. But as I looked out over the huge geodesic dome below, Jackson's Dome, and the sprawling city within, it became obvious the stories were at least somewhat true.

Wadi wasn't a real planet, not by any reasonable definition, although it was large enough to be classified as one—had it officially existed, which it didn't. Having disappeared more than a thousand years earlier, Wadi had been written off as dead and gone, destroyed by some catastrophic natural event. The place didn't look dead to me now, but it didn't look entirely alive, either.

The exposed surface of Wadi seemed to be a solid sheet of black rock, or maybe iron. Its undulating surface, smooth and continuous to the horizon, appeared as might a huge dark lake that suddenly solidified, capturing a few gently rolling waves. An enclosed walkway ran perfectly straight from the dome below us to another in the distance, possibly twenty miles away. Wadi had no atmosphere to diffuse or even dull the light of a billion stars, which seemed to hover just beyond the horizon.

"Now, listen to me good," Rigs said, turning me by the shoulder. "When we reach ground level I want you to keep moving. Don't stop and don't answer questions for nobody. You got a right to be pissed off, nobody denies you that, but you're here on Wadi now. And there ain't no way to get back to Abydos. The sooner you accept that fact the sooner things will start working in your favor. If you start kicking and screaming, or some nonsense like that, I'll just go back up to the ship and leave your ass down there with security. I'll admit right now that I kidnapped you from Abydos, but that was my job. You're here and you're healthy, so mission accomplished. No harm done."

"No harm done?" I said, sounding completely dumbfounded. Sadly, however, I knew he was right.

When I was a little kid, my mother and I used to wake up in so many different doorways that half the time I never knew where we were, and I'm pretty sure she rarely did either. One of my earliest memories was of her waking me up in the dark to strap a pair of rusty braces around my legs. The metal rods never did pull the bow out of my knees, but the pitiful looking devices did help keep our bellies full of food. Mom would truss me up and then prop me against a wall out by the sidewalk in time for the morning rush. I would smile and wave, and maybe throw in a little cough. It took a real hard-ass to walk by without dropping a few coins in my cup. We'd milk a street for a day or so and then move over a few blocks, set up house in a blind alley, and start working the new faces. Living on the street wasn't all that bad, except when it rained, and I never spent an entire winter outdoors until after she died. Mom always seemed to meet a nice man, usually one in uniform, just about the time the weather turned cold. He'd rent a room, and they'd moan and groan for an hour or so, but then he'd leave and somehow, we always managed to hang on to the place until early spring. It's kind of funny; Mom would have probably liked Captain Rigs. All of her boyfriends wore hats with gold braid thingamabobs, just like his.

"No harm done?" I mumbled again, wiping my tongue on my sleeve. *Someone should go to jail...if only because of this nasty taste in my mouth.*

"Glad you agree," Rigs said. "Just remember, nobody on Wadi gives a damn about anything that happened on Abydos or any other planet ruled by the Universal Imperium. You'll be welcome on Wadi, and free to do whatever you want, as long as you can produce that ID card and don't get in other people's business. Without that card, you're automatically guilty of spying for the UI, and they'll throw your ass in jail until you can prove otherwise. Try doing that from a jail cell on a planet where nobody knows you."

"But—" was all I managed.

"But nothing," Rigs said. "When that door opens, walk straight ahead and down the tube. The airtight emergency doors are about fifty feet down, just outside the dome. Right before you reach the doors there's an alcove off to the right. A security guard will be sitting next to the ID station. He won't say nothing if you don't, but he does expect you to insert that card into his machine. Just look into the optical scanner and put both hands on the glass plate."

I stared at the card he had given me, surprised to see my picture. It wasn't a good one, but then again there was no such thing as a good picture of me. Rigs had gotten my name right, too: Thaddeus J. Styx. I felt like thanking him for not spelling out Jasper.

"What do you think?" Rigs asked as I examined the card.

"T. J. would have been better," I said.

"Sorry," Rigs said, "but at least it's official. As captain, I can issue ID cards for my passengers, but it's still no good until you run it through that machine down there. It puts your data out on the Wadi net, which makes you a real person. No data goes on or leaves the Wadi network unless it's on one of these cards. That's how they can keep the location of this place a secret. That means you might exist on Abydos, but you don't exist here until your card is blessed by that machine. Any questions?"

"Do I have any question? You've got to be shitting me."

"Besides the obvious," Rigs said, "I don't know why

Finch wanted me to bring you here. He caught me as we were leaving for Abydos and told me he would cancel my bar tab if I brought you back with me. We were already in the jump routine, so I didn't have time to ask questions. I don't even know how he got that message out to my ship; that's not supposed to even be possible from Wadi."

"He canceled your bar tab?" I said certain I had misunderstood. *How much could this guy drink?*

"Well, yeah," Rigs mumbled. "Finch is an old friend of mine, but I hadn't settled with him in...well, maybe ten years...maybe twelve. I'd rather owe it to him than cheat him out of it, so it sounded like a good deal to me."

"A real bargain," I said. The elevator began to slow, so I knew I had to hurry. "Who is Finch and what did you mean by 'Besides the obvious?'"

"You really don't know who Finch is?" Rigs said as the elevator stopped.

"Not a clue," I said.

"Then the obvious ain't so obvious is it," Rigs said as the elevator door opened. "Move," he said, turning me around. He gave me a light shove, although not nearly as hard as before. "You'll know Finch when you see him," Rigs said. "He's...like you."

I didn't know if that was a slap in the face or not. I highly doubted Finch was a short troll, as I had been described on more than one occasion. Although, the only other option was that he had also been trained as a mechatronic technician and would have a tool bag slung over his shoulder, similar to the one I was lugging.

I kept walking to put distance between us, but, as I closed in on the security guard, I stopped and turned around. I just wanted to glare back at Rigs and hopefully make him a little nervous. To my surprise, he glared first.

"Go on," Rigs said, motioning me on. Turning his attention to something beyond me, he pointed and said, "That's Finch's dog."

Turning, my jaw dropped. *A dog? I'm not so sure about that.* The thing bounced, pranced, and spun in circles so fast I couldn't tell whether it was cute or ugly. And when it stopped briefly to smile up at me, I still couldn't decide; the dog was a robot. It stood about knee high to most people but thigh high to me--when it stood still. I had been trained in mechatronic repair while in prison as part of my rehabilitation, but I had never seen anything this sophisticated. Long, salt-and-pepper fur covered its ears and the top of its head. The bare metal of its jointed neck glinted under the lights, but fur also covered the top of its back and the last half of its tail. The rest of him was pure mechanism: shiny metal, embedded wires, and clear tubing. Other than being a little thin on fur, it was an excellent likeness of the real animals I had seen in books, although more technically advanced than the robots I'd seen on Abydos. Its green eyes sparkled as it bounced up, eye to eye with me. I thought it was a little strange that it had a blue ball in its mouth. But what part of my day hadn't been strange? It gripped the ball firmly in a set of silvery, needle-sharp teeth; the kind that would make anyone think twice before going anywhere near that mouth. I looked over at Rigs. He shrugged.

Turning back to the dog, I got a strong urge to say, "Sit." No robot I had ever seen would respond to voice commands from a total stranger, but then this creature seemed more alive than mechanical. For some reason, I thought it might listen. "Sit," I said.

And it did. Dropping the ball at my feet, it wagged its tail and smiled up at me. It didn't pant, although I half expected to see a fleshy pink tongue drop out any second.

"What's your name?" I asked, picking up the ball. I would have been surprised if it had answered--but not shocked. It didn't, but it did sprint down the tunnel toward Rigs. Skidding to a halt at his feet, the little guy turned around to face me and barked.

"His name is Gofer," Rigs said. "He loves to play ball. But son, you need to do what I told you. Get on with it."

As Rigs motioned me on, Gofer whined and let out another playful bark, so I tossed the ball to him as I turned back toward the dome. I slung my tool bag over my shoulder to free up both hands as I stopped in front of the security guard. Hearing Gofer's metal toenails clicking frantically on the deck, I looked around. He was running toward me, fast; his legs were a blur.

Rigs bent down to pick up the ball, which had rolled to his feet. "Fool animal," he said as he stood. Rigs then disappeared in a flash of white light as the ball exploded. A red mist filled the tunnel.

Knocked flat on my back, I slid headfirst through the open pressure doors. As I passed, they slammed shut, slicing the legs off the security guard. The smoke and mist cleared quickly, sucked out by the vacuum of space through a crack in one of glass panes near the elevator. Bits and pieces of Rigs clung to the glass and littered the floor. People swarmed over the screaming guard, although no one seemed to notice me.

Still, on my back, I watched the commotion between my feet, until a voice said, "Get up. We need to go." Rolling my eyes up, I found Gofer's ugly face staring down at me. "What?" I asked. Turning my head to both sides, I searched for the owner of the voice.

"Get up," Gofer said. "Security will be here any minute."

I stared at the dog's sharp teeth as he spoke--but I forgot to listen. "What?" I repeated.

"If you don't get up right now, I'm going to bite that ugly nose off your face."

That I heard, so I got up.

"Follow me," he said as he turned. He broke into an easy trot and without looking back said, "I'm not warning you again." So, I followed.

Jackson's Dome appeared to be just like every large city I had seen on Abydos; the streets were dirty, the alleys were filled with junk, and the homeless seemed to own the doorways. I began to suspect the only difference was that the sky on Wadi would always be dark, and I doubted if it was ever going to rain. Gofer trotted for about a half a mile without saying a word, which was fine by me; I wasn't used to having conversations with animals. Reaching a large stairwell, I followed Gofer down one level and stepped out into an entirely different, yet similar, city. Gofer started down the street, but I stopped and leaned over the handrail to see if there were more levels below. I didn't have time to count them all before being scolded about keeping up.

"Why should I keep following you?" I asked.

"Because your ID is no good," Gofer said, "and you don't want to go to jail again."

"Okay, but besides that?"

"Because I'll chew off your ass if you don't."

"Understood," I said. "Any other reason...that I might find agreeable?"

"Food, drink, and a pretty woman," Gofer said.

"Just one of those would have been enough," I said, picking up my pace.

I think we walked most of the night, but, since Wadi lacked a sun, we might have walked all day. I do know we walked until my feet hurt and then about twice that far again. I kept asking questions, but Gofer only had one answer: "You'll have to ask Sibylla."

I knew we had reached the far end of Jackson's Dome when the level above us suddenly disappeared, exposing the iron and glass structure of the dome itself. The sky remained as black as ink, but the stars were not as bright as they had been near the ship. When I asked about it, Gofer explained we were now on the poor side of the city, so the glass had probably never been cleaned.

"What do you expect after two thousand years?" he asked.

"Is it really that old?"

"Really," he said. "You don't know about Wadi?"

"Not very much," I said, which was a mistake.

"Wadi," Gofer began, "is the remnant core of a tiny star, even smaller than a brown dwarf. It's composed of mixed metals, some precious but mostly iron. A mining company originally settled Wadi two thousand fifty-four years ago. They went after the surface deposits first, the easy ore. Jackson's Dome is built over the original quarry, which was a solidified lake of pure titanium. After they dug out the ore, the company capped the quarry with this glass and iron dome. The iron core of Wad makes it easy to seal and pressurize. This dome was the first one they built, but now there are ninety-two others. After they capped this place the workers moved in and built the city to raise their families. The next dig was over at Harper's

Dome, which is where we're going. The workers lived in Jackson's Dome while they harvested Harper's Quarry, and then they capped that hole, too, and moved on to the next. Wadi is covered with these things, which are all linked together by surface tunnels."

"I think I saw one of them as I left the ship." Since I had him talking, I asked, "Why'd you kill Captain Rigs?" "You threw the ball," Gofer said.

That pretty much shut me up for a while. I didn't feel like talking again until after we entered the glass and iron surface tunnel leading over to Harper's Dome. A grating attached to the sides of the ten-foot diameter pipe formed its four-foot wide walking surface. A sign over the entrance read: "Harper's Dome, 18 Miles, Caution: Tunnel NGZ."

The tunnel didn't curve right or left, but it did follow the natural contour of Wadi's rolling iron ground. For the most part, the semi-gloss black surface of Wadi remained as smooth and undisturbed as it had the day it solidified. Roughly every hundred feet we would pass one of the original construction sites, where the workers had used lasers to cut and weld sections of the tunnel. These areas were covered with burn marks, odd pieces of steel, and broken glass. At one of these sites, I noticed a selection of abandoned tools, which I figured might be collectible antiques if I could figure out how to recover them.

"What does 'NGZ' stand for?" I asked, hoping the simple question wouldn't get me into trouble.

"Natural Gravity Zone," Gofer said.

"Which means...what?"

"It means that in about another hundred feet we're going to be completely out of Jackson's Dome," Gofer said, sprinting ahead.

151

I turned to see if someone, or something, was attacking us from behind. We were still alone, but I ran after him anyway.

"Why are we running?" I asked.

Gofer didn't respond, but he did jump and began to glide.

As I tried to process this visual information, the grating beneath me dropped away—sort of. Feeling as if I was running downhill, beyond my ability to keep up, my feet got all screwed up. I went down—headfirst. I wasn't sure what happened, but I had plenty of time to think about it before I hit.

"And that's why you shouldn't run in these tunnels," Gofer said as he walked slowly back. "You hurt?" he asked.

I wasn't, but we had been walking for at least twenty hours and stretching out in the reduced gravity felt pretty good. "I had no intention of running," I said.

"I know," Gofer said, "but I couldn't help it. Dogs like to run." I glared at him.

"Woof," he said, not even pretending to bark.

"Just admit it," I said, rolling onto my stomach. "You did it on purpose so I'd bust my ass."

"I can't admit that," he said. "I'm a dog; we're sneaky."

"Dogs aren't sneaky," I said, getting slowly to my feet. "Cats are sneaky, but you don't act like a cat either, or a real dog." "Have you ever met a real dog?" Gofer asked.

"I've seen them in videos," I said. "They're helpful and loving."

"Videos? So those could have been actors."

"I suppose," I said, yanking my tool bag from the floor. I pulled so hard in the reduced gravity that the bag nearly took my head off as it flew toward the ceiling. Struggling to get the bag under control, I asked, "What happened to the gravity?"

"Each of the domes on Wadi has a gravity-convergence plant," Gofer said. "GC plants generate artificial gravity and, as a side effect, create steam, which they use to make electricity. The gravitational field is proportional to the size of the generator, and we just walked out of range. In a couple of miles, we'll reach the G field of Harper's Dome. Between domes, you're on your own. Wadi's natural gravity is about one-tenth of a G. Just move slowly until you figure out how to glide. And try not to bounce."

I crashed a few more times until I got the hang of gliding, which I liked a lot. Once up to speed, we covered the remaining distance to Harper's gravity field in just a few minutes. Feeling my full weight return, I moaned, "Why don't they just turn off gravity? It's easier to move around without it."

"Apparently the miners prefer to work in one G," Gofer said. "The reason they installed the GC plants in the first place was to improve productivity. Mining is still the only real industry on Wadi, but now it's all underground. They export the metal on the black market and import everything else. Electricity and thrust

were just lucky side effects of the GC plants." "What kind of thrust?" I asked.

"GC plants and CG drives, like they use in transluminal ships, work on the same basic principle. They both focus the weak gravitational pull of millions of distant bodies into a singularity. With a little modulation, it achieves resonance and releases its energy in a small localized gravitational field. Small being a relative term, of course."

"Of course," I said, but I still missed the connection. "And thrust?"

"GC drive engines," Gofer said, "are tuned for maximum thrust, tension actually. They basically pull the spaceship toward those distant gravitational fields, approaching the speed of gravity itself. That's why they can achieve speeds greater than light. You really should have finished school."

"I didn't want to limit my options," I said. "I went to prison instead."

"Wise decision, I'm sure," Gofer said. "Spacecraft take advantage of the gravitational field generated by the GC engine, but GC plants are tuned to optimize that gravitational field, so the natural thrust vector is not nearly as strong. It's basically ignored, wasted you might say. Except here on Wadi."

"And what makes Wadi so special?"

"The Universal Imperium doesn't believe Wadi exists...because they can't find it. And why can't they find it?" Gofer stopped walking as if waiting for my answer.

"It's a big dark universe," I said, thinking I nailed it.

"Wrong," Gofer said.

"I'm pretty sure it is a big dark universe," I said.

"Okay, it is," Gofer conceded, "but that's not why the UI can't find us. They can't find Wadi because it's not where it's supposed to be."

I nodded, and we started walking again.

"You don't have a clue do you," Gofer said.

"Nope," I replied.

"Fifteen hundred years ago," Gofer explained, "after the mining company abandoned Wadi, someone...who will remain anonymous...pointed out that if all ninety-three GC plants networked their thrust vectors, we could modulate and control the planet's orientation and velocity. Not long after that...Wadi disappeared. It wasn't where it was supposed to be, so it was assumed to have been destroyed." "Why?" I asked.

"The only other option," Gofer said, "was that it had become invisible. Which sounds more plausible to you?" "I'm not stupid," I said.

"Then prove it," Gofer said.

I looked down at him and thought about giving him a good swift kick in the teeth, but then I decided I'd much rather keep my ass--unchewed. "Why would anyone want to move Wadi from one place to another?" I asked to clarify my question.

"The group that runs this place, the Free Society, doesn't want the UI to find Wadi."

"Why?"

"Maybe it's because the Free Society is composed largely of smugglers, escaped prisoners, and political refugees. And another reason...might be...that the twenty thousand miners still working this place don't want to pay UI taxes. Money made on the black market is tax-free."

"Why am I here?" I asked, hoping to catch him off guard.

"Good try," he said, "but you'll have to ask Sibylla."

"Not Finch?"

"Feel free, but I suspect he knows less than you do."

As we left the tunnel and entered Harper's Dome, I asked, "How much farther?"

"About a hundred feet," Gofer said as he hung a hard left, almost tripping me. After recovering with a small hop and a short foot-slapping jog, I found myself facing a wall of dark polished wood, fifty feet wide and twenty high. Two large doors, each seven-foot-tall and four feet wide, were centered in the wall. Each door was inlaid with twelve panes of amber colored glass, six rows in two columns. A hand-width of dark wood formed the structure of the door around the glass. Thin runners of wood separated the glass panes from one other, while shiny brass hinges held the doors in place. Although massive door pulls were provided, each the size of my arm, no locks or knockers were apparent. The remaining wall, above and flanking the doorway, was made of the same highly polished wood. I couldn't see a single fastener or seam in the entire structure. Finding this odd, I looked more closely at the entire façade and realized there were no fasteners or seams anywhere, not even around the doors. The hairs on my neck stood up.

"Like it?" Gofer asked.

He caught me off guard, and I jumped, ducked, and sidestepped all at once.

"That was some move," Gofer said.

"Damn!" I said, turning to face him. "Don't do that."

He chuckled. "Do what?"

"That thing gives me the creeps," I said, nodding toward the entrance. "What is this place?"

"Big letters above the door," Gofer said. "I'll even give you a clue. The first word is 'The.'"

I knew there was nothing over the door, but I looked up anyway—and nearly crapped in my pants. Thirty seconds earlier there had been nothing in the polished wood panel above the entrance, but now "The Emporium" was deeply engraved in ten-inch-high letters.

"That...just...appeared," I said.

"Gotcha," Gofer said with a laugh. "It's a hologram. One of my jobs around here is to make sure the sign is turned on every night: RF remote. I just wink my ass and the sign comes on."

"Really?"

"What an idiot," Gofer said as he turned. "We need to go in the back. Follow me, but don't look at my asshole," he said as he trotted off.

I followed, but of course, I couldn't look at anything else. "What does a robot do with an asshole?" I asked.

"I usually take them in the back door," he said, "so my friends don't see me with them." "Jerk," I said.

"Troll," he replied.

We walked a good two hundred feet back into the alley before we reached the rear of The Emporium. Dark and littered with debris, it was not a place I would have ventured alone. I followed Gofer along the scratched and dented corrugated metal wall, but I didn't see a door until Gofer stopped walking. Then one materialized—out of thin air.

"Did you just wink again?" I asked.

"Sort of," he said as we stepped inside.

As the blackness swallowed us, I whispered, "I can't see anything."

"Just wait for your eyes to adjust," he said.

I reached out with both hands and moved slowly toward the sound of his voice. I heard distant footsteps, but they seemed to be fading. "Who is that?" I asked.

"Hush," Gofer said.

So, I did.

The weak light from the open door behind us cast a pale wash across the floor, so I focused on that to retain my balance. I took another step, bumping into Gofer. He growled but said nothing. "What are we doing?" I asked.

"Waiting," Gofer said softly. A few seconds later he added, "I think it's clear."

A motor whined as the door behind us closed and

latched, plunging us into total darkness. I swayed, overcome with vertigo, but then a soft red light filled the tiny, empty room. Another door stood before us. I searched for a latch until a motor whined and the door popped open on its own, just a crack. Gofer nosed it open farther and stuck his head inside. I learned in above him.

Cluttered shelves and tables filled the inner room. Most were stacked high well above my head, but with what I couldn't tell; the details were lost in the shadows, although I sensed the value. The far end of the room opened onto a corridor, also filled with overflowing shelves.

A treasure trove of antiques. My palms began to itch.

"Don't touch anything," Gofer said as if reading my mind.

"Stay here."

"Hell no," I replied.

Gofer glanced up at me and said, "Wuss. Okay, but stick close and don't step on me."

"Why are we sneaking around?" I asked.

"We're not sneaking," Gofer said as he stepped inside.

"It sure feels like we're sneaking."

Well, we're not," he said. "Things will just go a lot smoother if we keep a low profile until we find Sibylla. There's another bot in here, like me, but she's not as personable as I am...especially with visitors." Reaching the corridor, Gofer looked both ways before turning left, as did I.

On my left, shelves ran the full length of the corridor, the highest tiers lost in the darkness above. A milky white fog obscured the far end, but I could see enough to know the building was much larger than it appeared from the outside. On my right stood the ends caps of freestanding shelves, which ran perpendicular to the corridor on twenty-foot intervals.

Gofer glanced down the first aisle as we passed but continued straight ahead. The mist at the far end of that aisle glowed warm and yellow as might a lobby or showroom, although I still had no concept of what they sold in The Emporium. Small amber lights hovered in the darkness, ten feet over head. Each offered little more than a six-foot oasis of visibility every twenty feet. The vast room was a hodgepodge of shadows and washed out colors, highlighted here and there by glints of light reflecting on glass and shiny metal mixed among the menagerie of objects.

Reaching the second aisle, I asked, "What do they do he—" I stopped as a blast of frosty air slammed into the side of my face, nearly knocking me off my feet. The scream of the high-pressure air bored painfully into ears. I turned to see what hit me, even before I considered running, which was the luckiest thing I ever did. Had I run, I would have been torn to shreds.

Although slow to react, I finally realized we had been discovered by Gofer's counterpart. Gofer, however, had dramatically oversimplified their similarities. The creature in front of me stood on all fours—yes, "like" Gofer--but as I looked up, the beast batted aside one of those distant overhead light bulbs-with its ear. The animal turned its long slender face toward Gofer with what appeared to be a stare of reprimand. Then, looking back at me, the beast retracted its lips, exposing a mouth full of glistening spikes. The monster moved closer, sniffing, but then it sucked in a great volume of air as if savoring my scent. Backing into the shelves, I squeaked, "Gofer."

The beast's nostrils were larger than my fists. A

frosty residue within hardened as it exhaled but then turned to slush as it inhaled. In between, a thick moist residue dripped from each crusty hole. I found myself staring, entranced by the pulsating horror less than a foot from my face. When the creature leaned nearer, I pulled back, striking my head on something behind me. Nearer still, the utter coldness of the beast drew the warmth from my body. I closed my eyes to wait for death and smelled the rancid odor of mildew growing deep within the thing's ugly head. The wolf—how I envisioned the creature in my mind—inhaled, drawing the hair from my scalp deep within its snout. I whimper and shivered at the sound I made. The wolf then exhaled, which struck my face like an explosion of ice. The horrid smell took my breath and forced open my eyes. Staring again into the mouth of the wolf, with its double rows of needle-sharp teeth, I screamed but managed to make only the sound of a dry retch. My lungs were empty--as was my bladder. As its warmth spread down my thighs, I gasped.

"Candy! No!" a voice said.

The beast withdrew, slightly, but enough that my lungs began to fill, putting out the fire ragging within. I was grateful for the air, but it was so saturated with stench I could taste the beast.

"Styx," Gofer said, "this is Candy."

His voice seemed small, miles away. I continued to stare at the wolf's great mouth as my mind tried to organize Gofer's words into a meaningful sentence. "What?" I finally managed. I glanced at Gofer and then looked back at the wolf.

"Back off, Candy," Gofer whispered. "Sibylla's coming."

Candy snorted in protest, washing me with a cloud of vapor, but then she obeyed.

"What the hell is that?" I asked.

"That's just Candy," Gofer said.

"Just...Candy?" At the sound of her name coming from my lips, the beast lunged forward, causing me to strike my head solidly on something behind me. My knees buckled. I thought the blow might put me out-- although I might have simply been fainting. Either way, as I struggled to stay on my feet, Sibylla spoke to me for the very first time. Her voice floated like sweet smoke down the misty corridor, yet it demanded obedience.

"Sit," she said, which I did without question. As I dropped, I turned to face her, as I knew I should.

Sibylla emerged from the darkness into a cone of light at the far end of the misty corridor. Pure white and totally nude, she seemed to glide through the fog as might an angel, exuding confidence and order. She moved swiftly with her breasts swaying gently and her silky golden hair billowing behind her, filling the full width of the corridor. As she passed again into darkness, I glanced at the beast above me and then down at Gofer. Both were sitting, eagerly awaiting the woman's next command, as was I. When Sibylla emerged beneath the next light, she seemed more mature, and her hair flowed elegantly around her face and shoulders. And to my great disappointment, she now wore a full-length formal gown, which precisely matched the color of her hair. A golden chain with fine wire links swayed tauntingly in the valley between her full breasts.

Smiling down on me, almost glowing, Sibylla said, "You must be Styx."

I stared up into the bluish-green emeralds of her eyes as she reached down to me with her delicate hand. Her fingers were long and slender with perfect nails, buffed but not polished. I hesitated to take her hand, but only because I didn't want my ugly paw to contaminate the vision.

"Please, let me help you," she said.

When I took her hand, which was soft beyond description, I seemed to float onto my feet.

"I must apologize for my children," she said.

Although faint, Candy and Gofer both whimpered.

In spite of my clammy pants, I said, "No harm done." *No harm done?* I should have been pissed, but for some reason, I just wanted to say whatever would make her happy. So, I said, "I'm sure it was just a series of misunderstandings and unforeseeable events."

"That's kind of you," Sibylla said. "But it was *not* an accident. Gofer wanted to see how far he could lead you inside The Emporium before Candy caught you. Candy's job is to guard the doors. You would have never made it all the way inside without my protection. Gofer knows."

"I wouldn't have let Candy hurt him," Gofer said.

I looked down at Gofer and asked, "Does she listen to you?" "Most of the time," he said.

Most of the time? His answer made no sense. Robots have protocols and Candy was either programmed to obey Gofer in a slave-master relationship, or she wasn't.

"A few years ago," Sibylla said, "Finch managed to load a subroutine into Candy that sometimes conflicts with her normal programming."

"Who is this guy Finch?" I asked. "Rigs mentioned--" I stopped, remembering the explosion. "Why did Gofer kill Captain

Rigs?"

Sibylla stared down at me but said nothing.

"I'm sorry," I said, afraid I had offended her. "I didn't mean to dig into your personal business, but would you mind telling me why I was brought to Wadi?"

"Does it bother you that Rigs is dead?" Sibylla asked.

I thought it was an odd question, although expertly phrased to learn who I was before admitting any association to the crime. I was pretty sure it was still a crime to blow up someone, even on Wadi. "My ears are still ringing from the blast," I said, "but I suspect they'll clear up soon enough."

Sibylla smiled and said, "I'm very pleased you were not seriously injured." She reached up, placing a hand on Candy's shoulder. The creature leaned toward her as Sibylla dug her nails into the animal's sparse fur. "What do you think of my children?"

I looked again at Candy, this time through eyes not clouded by fear. She *was* similar to Gofer in design but larger--ten times larger. Candy was powered by pneumatics, compressed air, while Gofer was fitted with hydraulic cylinders, pressurized liquid. Candy's bigger frame offered more space for the larger, yet relatively lighter, pneumatic components. "They're both amazing creations," I said. "I've never seen such advanced robots."

Sibylla smiled as I spoke, and I felt the need to continue. Something about her made me want to bare my soul to her--along with any other part of me she might want to see.

I nodded at Candy and said, "I think she has a burned-out solenoid valve in her condensation reclamation circuit, but I think I can fix it. And I'm sure Gofer needs a good kick in the ass...but all in all I'm impressed."

"I appreciate your candor," Sibylla said. "If you were to stay on Wadi, what on Abydos would you miss the most?"

I pretended to think about the question but already knew the answer. "Mary's Place," I said. "It's a hell of a place to kick back after work."

Sibylla's eyes sparkled as she spoke. "Please, follow me. I must show you The Emporium."

Sibylla took my hand and led me up the aisle toward the warm glow of the front room. We passed through a lighted section where an incomprehensible variety of collectibles filled the shelves on both sides of us. Countless boxes overflowed with coins of every imaginable metal. Statues, vases, and paintings were randomly intermixed with electronics and weaponry: knives to M20 lasers. We passed through a fifty-foot section of the aisle lined with body armor, antique on the right and state-of-the-art on the left. A peculiar smell made me suspect that a few of the pieces might still be occupied by the original owners or at least the last user.

We stepped out of the passageway into a work area behind a counter. Looking both ways, I realized we were standing behind a bar, a liquor bar, at least two hundred feet long. The dark wooden countertop, ornately carved and highly polished, spanned the full width of the room, clearly segregating the work area on the near side from the public area on the far side. Drinking utensils lined the shelves beneath the counter, mostly mugs in a wide variety of shapes and sizes. Further down, inverted champagne glasses sparkled in their hangers above a selection of gleaming shot glasses. The end caps of the storage area—which I later learned were called the stacks— formed the back wall of the work area behind the counter. These end caps were fitted with colored lights and glass racks, which displayed the largest selection of liqueurs I had ever seen or imagined. Seeing the exquisite decor and sheer expanse of The Emporium made me realize that Mary's Place had been a dump. *But I've called worst places home.*

Sibylla lifted a hinged section of countertop, so we could walk out into the public area. Seven distinct cones of weak, yellow light filtered down through the mist from unseen fixtures high above. Each island of light contained a dark circular table surrounded by seven high-backed chairs. The line of tables zigzagged across the room at forty-foot intervals. The nearest, centered in the vast room, sat no more than thirty feet away, but a gently swirling fog obscured the legs of even this one. A fine engraving covered the table's wooden surface. Although highly polished, the wear and tear from extensive use remained apparent. The backs of the chairs, each unique and rambling, looked as if they had grown from the seats of their own accord.

While the vast expanse between the tables would afford some level of privacy to the individual groups of patrons, the layout seemed odd. *It's only a ruse...to give the impression of privacy.* Electronic devices in the tables themselves would even struggle to record a conversation whispered directly in the ear. Either way, the room wasn't right. Just like in the stacks, the available space was much too great for the external structure of the building. The Emporium, like the robots, harnessed technology not yet known to the general public.

Releasing Sibylla's hand, I moved to the table in front of us and reached out to caress the smooth contours of the ornate chair. The wood felt quite warm—and squirmed—as my fingers made contact. "What the hell was that?" I said, yanking my hand away.

The Emporium groaned.

"This is Thaddeus J. Styx," Sibylla said as if introducing me. "He is our friend."

I turned to Sibylla with a hundred questions, but the complacent smile on her face told me all I needed to know: "My children."

"Please, sit with me," Sibylla said, slipping into a chair. The light over headed changed from yellow to pink as she settled in. She motioned for me to take the chair beside her.

Warily, I probed it with my finger. Nothing moved. *It's just playing dead.* I sat, anyway.

"Ask what you will," Sibylla said, again taking my hand.

The pink lights accentuated her beauty. I wanted to be with her more than any woman I had ever met. "I don't want to offend you," I said. *She kidnapped me; why am I apologizing to her?* However, my gut instinct screamed that it was important to keep Sibylla happy. Maybe the three years I'd spent in prison conditioned me, but I knew Sibylla was calling the shots and even disappointing her could be fatal. *She brought me here for a reason, and I will* not *let her down.*

"Ask," she said.

"Why did you kill Captain Rigs?"

"I admire your frankness," she said, "so I will reply in kind. There were several reasons. For one, Rigs was conspiring with Finch to murder me and take control of The Emporium. There were other reasons, as well, but mainly...I didn't like Rigs; he was a pig. When a man chooses to put his hands on a lady and refuses to pay for the privilege, he will not live long on Wadi. The reason I didn't kill him sooner was because of his association with Finch. There were details to work out, and Rigs was the tool I needed to accomplish my goal."

"Rigs thought I knew this Finch guy," I said. "But I don't. Who is he?"

"Finch is officially the proprietor of The Emporium. I don't like to deal with finance and legalities. I made Finch the legal owner, so he could manage those aspects of the business. This allows me to focus exclusively...on customer relations. But Finch is getting old, and I'm afraid he's gone completely insane."

"Why not just fire him?" I asked. "Or have Candy run him off?"

"I need him," she said. "Finch is legally the owner. If he disappeared, ownership of The Emporium would revert to Harper's Dome. I'd lose everything. The Emporium is my home...and my family."

Sibylla seemed genuinely distraught, but I sensed there was more to the story than she was telling me. "What makes you think Finch is trying to kill you?"

"Look what he's done to me," she yelled. "He's draining my energy...my beauty. I'm supposed to be a twenty-five-year-old woman!"

I don't care how old you are, I almost said, but then I reconsidered the wisdom of making any comment about a woman's age. "Then come away with me," I said. "We'll leave. I'll take care of you." I wasn't sure how, but if she wanted to leave I was willing to die trying.

"I can't leave," she said, burying her face in her hands. "Finch and Rigs have violated Candy. She has been programmed to kill me if I attempt to leave The

Emporium."

"But I just saw her obeyed you," I said.

"Candy loves me," Sibylla explained, "but she'd still tear me to shreds if I try to go near one of the outer doors."

"Have you asked anyone for help?"

"Since this began, Finch and Rigs have only allowed their close friends to come into The Emporium. They're all in on it. Finch has convinced them that *I'm* the crazy one."

"How do I know...you're not?" I asked. The look on her face suddenly told me I might have just stepped over the line. I hoped it wasn't that fine line between life and death.

But she smiled. "I like you more by the minute," she said. "You don't, but if I was delusional why would I be telling you this?"

"Why *are* you telling me this?"

"Before I can...terminate Finch, I must find someone to take over his position as proprietor of The Emporium; someone...like you. Would you be interested?"

Hell yes! But I knew there had to be a catch. "Why me?" "Why not you?" she asked.

"Not good enough," I said. "There has to be a reason you brought me a couple of light years across the universe. Why me?"

"I'd like to say it's because of your qualifications," Sibylla said, "but you'd know I was lying."

"I *might* have bought it," I said. "I'm pretty gullible around beautiful women."

Her face lit up. "I noticed, but to be honest, I asked Rigs to bring me someone with robotic training to take care of my puppies. And, I need someone who will not be missed on Abydos...or want to go back."

I had been thrown in prison on trumped-up charges and never understood why, but I did get certified in robot repair. My prison's robotic school had a reputation of being one of the best mechatronic training centers on Abydos. "Rigs said Finch asked him to bring me here."

"Because Rigs believed he did," she said, "but the message came from me. Finch doesn't even know you're here. And we

need to do this before he finds out."

"Do what?"

"I created Finch," Sibylla said. "I gave him his identity. Now, I want to give it to you."

As long as his ID didn't come attached to his head, or his heart, or any other body part, it didn't sound too bad. "You want me to become Finch?"

"I do," Sibylla said. "If you assume his identity, you take control of The Emporium, as well as her financial accounts." "What makes you think I won't screw you, just like Finch?" "Will you?" Sibylla asked.

I was scamming people on the streets of Abydos long before I went to prison. I was good at it, but I sensed Sibylla was better-much better. Besides, running a place as nice as The Emporium-even if it meant being this pretty lady's whipping boy--sounded pretty damn good to me. "I won't screw you," I said, and then I surprised myself by adding, "unless you want me to." *Why the hell did I say that?*

Sibylla smiled. "Thank you, Thaddeus. I will remember that generous offer."

"Call me Styx," I said.

"Alright...Styx. Let's complete this before Finch returns." "Where'd he go?" I asked.

"It seems an old friend of his was tragically killed yesterday," Sibylla said. "Finch went over to Jackson's

Dome to find out what happened."

I laughed and said, "I heard about that." I pulled on my ears. They were still ringing. "I heard it had something to do with a nasty little dog and a blue ball."

"*You* threw the ball," Gofer said from somewhere below the table.

Having lost track of him, I just about jumped out of my chair.

"Stop saying that," I said. "It was your ball, and you know it." "But you threw it," he repeated.

"Gofer," Sibylla warned.

"Oh, all right," Gofer said dejectedly. His motors whined as he trotted out from under the table and down the length of the bar. Crossing under at the walk-through, he disappeared into the gloom of the stacks.

"Gofer was fond of Rigs," Sibylla said. "They would play ball for hours."

"That's too bad," I said.

"He'll get over it," she said. "Are you ready?"

"Is this going to hurt?"

"I just need to capture some of your biometrics," she said, "and manipulate them into the system. We can do everything right

behind the bar. You'll find that I'm an expert hacker."

I grinned. "Well...you sure got the body for it."

She seemed confused at first, but then she smiled. "*Hacker*, she said, "not hooker."

"What?" Slowly, it sunk in. "Sorry," I said, a little disappointed. Realizing she hadn't answered my question, I asked again, "Will it hurt?"

She stared at me for a moment as if at a loss for words, but then she smiled and said, "Not at all." She stood. "Let's go back to my workstation." As we walked, she said, "Like you, when Finch came to me he didn't exist on Wadi, so I created an identification for him by loading his biometrics into the system. That makes me the administrator of his data and gives me the privileges needed to update or change them."

I followed Sibylla behind the bar to a kiosk on an end cap of the stacks. She opened a pair of large doors, exposing a monitor, keyboard, and various devices, which I assumed would capture my biometrics--whatever those were. Seeing the variety of complex looking equipment, I laughed and asked, "Do this often?" "Every fifty years or so," she said.

I laughed again, but she didn't. "Why don't *you*...become Finch?" I asked. "I mean you could just enter your own data." The question appeared to strike a nerve.

"Do you want the job or not?" she asked. "If you have any doubts about it, please speak up. Right now, you can just walk right out of here, but I'll be honest, once I give you his ID it'll be a lot harder to leave. You *will*...be him."

Being him has got to be better than being me. The first clean bed I ever knew was in prison. I looked down the expanse of the elaborate bar, loaded with its grand selection of fine liqueurs, and then back at Sibylla. *Drop-dead gorgeous.* "Oh, I'm taking the job," I said, "but can I change my name back to Styx? Finch sounds a little too...wimpy."

"I can make that happen," Sibylla said, "but not today."

"No hurry," I said. I watched her work for a few minutes but just couldn't let it go. "So why *don't* you use your own biometrics?"

Sibylla put her hands on her hips as she turned to

face me. "Do

I look like a man to you?"

"Not even close," I said. "Got it. Thanks."

"Besides," Sibylla said, turning her back to the monitor, "I'm already in the system. As the administrator I can update Finch's biometrics...palm, voice, and retinal scans...but only with new data that's not in the system. To use existing biometrics, I'd have to delete all prior instances and all references of the owner from the entire network, which is impossible. But since you bypassed security when you entered Jackson's Dome, you don't exist in the Wadi network. All I need to do is update Finch's ID with your data. And then you will be him."

"Lucky, I didn't get through the—" I stopped, realizing this woman had arranged that, as well. She had timed the explosion to prevent me from entering my data into the system. *Just one more good excuse to waste Rigs.*

She pulled me next to her and said, "Put your palms on this glass and look in here. Read the words out loud as they scroll by. You do read?"

"I like pictures better," I joked, "but I did learn how to read, so I could figure out what the words were on my diploma: Master of Science in Mechatronic Engineering."

She took my face in her hands and said, "I love it when you talk dirty." But then she slammed my face into the eye thingamajig and said, "Read."

I deserved it; my proclaimed fancy degree was actually just a vocational certificate in robotic repair. But I think she already knew that even before the machine made me reread several of the words.

"Congratulations, Mr. Finch," Sibylla said as the screen acknowledged the changes. "How does it feel to be the proprietor of The Emporium?"

"It makes me feel thirsty," I said, turning toward the bar. Spotting the beer tap, I moaned. Its jewel encrusted handle--at twice my height--looked as if it might be a challenge. But then I noticed the steps and the catwalk, which ran the full length of the bar. "Nice," I said, dropping my tool bag next to the steps. Climbing onto the catwalk, I ran my hands over the polished surface of the bar. The wood cringed at my touch, as the table had done, but quickly settled down. "We're going to get along just fine," I whispered.

"No celebration, yet," Sibylla said. "Follow me."

"But," I said, turning to protest. The look on her face told me to save my breath, so I grabbed my bag.

Back in the public area, we walked the length of the bar to an alcove hidden in the gloomed at the far end. I stopped short of the recess as Sibylla disappeared into the darkness. Slowly, a dull red light blossomed, revealing a massive metal door fitted with gears and three huge cross-latching draw bolts. The mechanism covered the back wall of the alcove from floor to ceiling, the first one I'd seen since entering The Emporium. Sibylla stared at the door, absently fingering the gold necklace around her neck.

"This will be the ultimate test of your new identity," she said.

"Only Finch can open that vault." "What's in it?" I asked.

For a moment she said nothing, but then she solemnly said, "The heart and soul of The Emporium and thousands of years of history."

She spoke so softly I thought she might be on the verge of passing out. "Are you alright?" I asked.

Realizing she had nearly zoned out, she turned to me with a look of surprise and then batted her long eyelashes. She grinned as she chirped, "And my best jewelry."

"Why would he lock up your jewelry?"

"He knew I wouldn't leave without it," she said. "It's been in my family for hundreds of years. Please...open the door."

Starring at the iron monster, I said, "That's a lot of door for a vertically challenged person."

"If you are Finch, it will open *for* you," she said. "Just grip the handle and tell it to open." She pointed to a long-tapered glass rod mounted horizontally near my chest. The rod appeared to be an inch in diameter where it attached to the door, but it enlarged to twice that size at the free end. Engraved with fine scrollwork, the glass handle glowed with a golden internal light.

"What if it's not buying?" I asked.

Sibylla stared at me as if I had suddenly grown a second head.

So, I tried again by saying, "I mean, what if this thing is smart enough to realize that I'm not really Finch. Will it fry me or something?"

"Open the door," Sibylla said, no longer asking.

"Yes," I said, no longer afraid. The door would either open, or I would die trying to open it for her. *Both serve Sibylla, which is all that matters.* Gripping the handle, I said, "Open." A burning sensation in my palm flowed up my arm, but it faded before reaching my elbow. I blinked as a beam of light swept across my face, hovering briefly over each eye. Motors whined as the handle began to rotate.

Grabbing my shoulders, Sibylla pulls me back and said, "You did good...very good."

Wrapping her arms across my chest, she squeezed me back hard against her. I could barely breathe. But feeling her breasts bulging around my neck and resting on my shoulders, I wished for nothing—except to turn to face her. When the door swung open, however, her grip increased, painfully shifting my focus from cleavage to air. I struggled, but Sibylla's hair snaked around my neck. Fear cinched my gut— until her animated locks began caressing my face and probing my ears. Under other circumstances, I would have enjoyed the sensation, but I had to assume that only my lack of oxygen had brought her curls to life. Dying in *her* arms would have been a victory; however, as I stared into the vault, I noticed many good reasons to live. *Look at all that shit! This has got to be Finch's personal stash.*

A huge ornately carved bookcase, with an integral desk, covered the wall to my left. The upper shelves were filled with large books and fat ledgers, gilded with gold and silver leaf. *That desk alone will take me years to explore.* At the far end of the vault, where Sibylla had focused her attention, stood a jewel-studded vanity with three large mirrors and a delicately engraved and upholstered stool. Matching wardrobes, each large enough to hold me—and all my friends—stood on both sides of the vanity.

Releasing me, Sibylla walked directly to the right-hand wardrobe. I followed her inside. Ancient weapons hung from the wall on my right, although not the practical battle-ready weapons like I had seen in the stacks. Fabricated from precious metals and studded with jewels, these swords, lances, and daggers, were the toys of kings, certainly long dead.

"Nobody's made this kind of stuff in ten thousand years," I said, reaching for a sword with a blade as long as I was tall.

"I wouldn't touch that," Sibylla said. "Things are

175

rarely what they appear to be in The Emporium." She didn't have to warn me twice.

"Come," she said. "I need your help."

Turning, I stared into the now open wardrobe, where dozens of heavy necklaces hung from the crossbar on small silver hangers, curled at the ends to cradle the chain. All of the chains appeared to be identical, each formed of links made from the gold wire as thick as my little finger. Sibylla removed one of the chains from its hanger and sat at the vanity facing the three mirrors.

"I'm ashamed to even look at myself," she said, averting her eyes.

"But you're beautiful," I said.

"Yes, I am," she replied, "but you have yet to see me." She lifted the ends of the heavy chain to her throat, allowing the golden links to drape across her breasts. "It feels wonderful," she signed. "I'm stronger already." Rocking slowly, she began to moan.

I knew women appreciated jewelry, especially middle-aged women, but the amount of pleasure she appeared to be getting from that necklace seemed a little over-the-top. As I watched her face in the mirror, her eyes sparkled like diamonds. Then they began to twinkle and flicker. As I leaned in for a better look, her eyes flared with high voltage.

What the—? I stepped back but held my tongue, hoping to keep it a little longer.

"Please," she said, waggling the ends of the necklace behind her neck.

I took them but had to study both ends of the clasp before deciding how they should mate. Sibylla moaned loudly as I engaged the ends and twisted, snapping the clasp.

"Remove the old one," she gasped as if in pain.

"I'm sorry if I hurt you," I said. She shook her head in reply, so I reached for the fine thread of gold she had been wearing all along. "This necklace is almost worn through," I said, grasping the clasp. "I hope I don't break—" was as far as I got.

Blinded by a flash of hot, blue light, I staggered back, with the buzzing bees of electricity swarming my arms. Coming to on the floor, I stared up at the ceiling, feeling as if my hands were on fire. I held them up and discovered I was still gripping the necklace. Its clasp remained fastened, but the chain had parted. Noticing white smoke curling off my fingernails, I dropped both halves of the chain, which fell onto my chest. My shirt started to smolder before I finally managed to I roll over and get rid of the damn thing.

"What the hell was that?" I asked, getting to my feet. After shouldering my tool bag, I turned to Sibylla. "Are you okay?" She still sat at the vanity, but she didn't reply or move. And I was fairly certain she was not okay. Her hair had woven itself into some kind of golden shroud, or cocoon, which now tightly encased her entire body. "Sibylla?" I reached out, but I couldn't summon the nerve to touch her; my hands still hurt from the last time. Spinning toward the open door, I screamed, "Gofer." When he didn't instantly materialize, I ran out to find him.

Gofer and Candy sat near the bar looking as if they had just been scolded. A small man, an older version of me, stood facing them. "He's like you," Captain Rigs had said, so I knew the man had to be Finch.

"Thaddeus, what have you done?" he asked.

"Call me Styx," I said, "and I didn't do anything; Sibylla did it. Who are you?" I asked, hoping to bully him first, so he wouldn't bully me.

"I'm the one she calls Finch," he said. "Is she in there?"

"Sort of," I said. "She changed."

"Did you put a new necklace on her?"

"Well, I might have helped...a little."

"Damn," Finch said, stepping back behind the bar. Glasses rattle beneath the counter.

"Make mine a double," I said, climbing onto a stool.

Stepping up onto the catwalk, Finch placed a silver dagger on the counter.

He certainly does look like me. Suspecting my drink wasn't coming,

I asked again, "Who are you?"

"Are you really that dense? I'm your father."

"I don't have a father."

"Get over it," Finch said. "You're obviously my son. I sent your mother to Abydos as soon as I found out she was pregnant." "And you're obviously insane," I said.

"Possibly," Finch said, "but I sent your mother away so Sibylla couldn't kill her and take you as her own...as she did me and my father...and his before him. Sibylla is evil."

"You abandoned me and my mother to a life in the gutters. My mother died coughing up blood in a filthy back alley. And you have the nerve to call *Sibylla* evil?" I jumped from the stool and started back toward the vault. Finch caught up and turned me.

"You don't understand," he said, waving the dagger in my face.

The polished edge of the blade quickly grabbed my attention, but my mouth didn't seem to care. "You're right...asshole, I don't have to understand."

"Sibylla is evil," Finch said, "but I do love her."

"You sure have a funny way of showing it," I said,

"but then I suppose you loved my mother, too."

"No," Finch said, "I never did."

That rattled me. "Okay," I said, "I'm glad we got that cleared up." I pulled away and started again toward the vault.

"Your mother was a prostitute," Finch yelled after me.

I couldn't believe my ears. Turning turned back to him, I said, "Every time you open your mouth shit falls out. What the hell are you trying to tell me?"

"I sent your mother to Abydos to protect *you*," Finch said. "I never intended to have a child, but Sibylla drugged me and brought in that woman. I would never have known about you or your mother if she hadn't been so greedy. She was taking Sibylla's money but wanted more, so she came to me. I sent her away to save both of your lives."

"She's been dead since I was ten. How do you possibly think you saved her life?"

"That's ten years longer than she would have lived on Wadi," Finch said. "As soon as you were off your mother's tit, Sibylla would have killed her and taken you as her own child." "Ten years of sickness and hunger," I said.

"Ten years of life...and freedom," he said. "My father worked for Sibylla before me, as did his father before him. The males in our family have always worked for Sibylla, and the females have always died young or disappeared." "How old is Sibylla?" I asked.

"Nobody knows," Finch said. "She's a mechatronic device of some type...a robot. There are no records of where she came from or who made her. She's thousands of years beyond our best technology, even now."

"That explains a few things," I said, rubbing my

179

palms on my shirt. They were still buzzing. "What's the deal with those gold necklaces? That little one shocked the crap out of me."

"She makes electrical power by breaking down the metal. I think she uses some type of fusion process. Each one lasts her about twenty years. My father, your grandfather, figured out what she was doing and modified the vault, so she couldn't get inside for another chain. He added a DNA scanner and locked it with his own genetic code...our genetic code. I wouldn't open it for Sibylla, which is why she made sure you were born. It's the only reason she brought you here." Finch shook his head and turned toward the vault. "We almost had her this time."

"But she could buy gold on her own," I said.

"No, she can't," Finch said. "She's a robot, which means she can't buy or sell anything. She can't own property. Ownership of The Emporium has been passed down from father to son for countless generations. Sibylla controls The Emporium by controlling us. My father wanted it to end with him."

"Sibylla is a beautiful woman," I said. "Men will give her gold if she wants it."

"That's why my father brought The Emporium to Wadi, fifty years ago. Wadi is a mining outpost and has been thoroughly studied. There are no deposits of gold on Wadi. Almost every piece of gold on Wadi is locked up in that vault. My father bought most of it, and I bought the rest. What's not in that vault is in the hands of people who wouldn't even sell it to their own mothers, much less give it to Sibylla."

"If your father had everything locked up inside that vault fifty years ago, why isn't Sibylla dead?"

"Because I love her," Finch said. "I couldn't bear to watch her die. My father sent me to school on Abydos when I was eight. I was there for ten years and never came back...until I heard he was dying. Sibylla was killing him. She was running out of power, and he wouldn't let her into the vault. My father knew she was killing him, but he accepted that as the price he had to pay for his freedom...and for my mine. He was ready to die; it was Sibylla that sent me the message. She needed my DNA to get inside, and once I was here...well, then it was too late. She can manipulate young men quite easily. I think it's what she was originally designed to do. Nothing else makes sense."

"But why?" I asked.

"I don't know," Finch said, shaking his head. "Maybe she was built as a covert weapon. She could take out a lot of men in one night if she wanted to."

"So now she's a weapon of mass destruction," I said. "You've got to be kidding me."

"I know you can feel the power she has over you," Finch yelled. "You know what I'm talking about."

I did, but I said nothing. *I love the way she makes me feel.*

"I was your age when I came back," Finch said. "She was too strong for me then, and I let her into the vault...just like you did. But as we get older it's harder for her to control us. And when she is low on power it's even harder, which is why I must do this now." He glanced down at the dagger in his hand and then stepped around me toward the vault.

I grabbed his shoulder and turned him. The blade in his hand brushed the strap of my tool bag, which parted, spilling the contents onto the floor. I stared down at the blade. "What is that thing?"

"An ultrasonic blade," he said. "I don't know what material she's made of, but this will cut through anything."

"You can't just kill her!"

"I promised my father I would see her dead," Finch said. "I hoped she would just run out of power and die peacefully of old age. I do still love her. She aged a lot over the last year, maybe twenty or thirty years, so I know she was running down. But you let her in, so I have to kill her before she regenerates. When she's like that, in that cocoon, she's upgrading and maintaining her circuits. She won't feel anything."

He turned toward the vault, but once again I pulled him back. "If you don't like it here, old man, just leave."

"Our family has lived in The Emporium for generations," Finch said. "This is our home."

I shook my head and said, "My family died in a gutter on Abydos."

"I gave your mother everything she needed to survive and build a good life for you, but she squandered it all away. She was just an ignorant slut."

"You don't know anything about my mother."

"But I'm afraid I do," Finch said. "The good captain and I were friends. Whenever he went to Abydos he would find her. I always sent him with money."

I thought that son of a bitch looked familiar. "Then you knew we were living on the street like animals."

"Yes," Finch said, "but you were free, and you had a chance to make something of yourself."

"After she died...what chance did I have then?"

"A better chance," Finch said. "If she hadn't died, she would have continued to drag you down."

"Did Rigs kill her?"

"No," Finch said. "At least, I don't believe he did. All I told him to do was to make sure you found your way into a good prison. The penal system on Abydos is hard, but those that try come out with valuable skills.

We have many talented technicians on Wadi that were trained in the prisons of Abydos."

"Wadi? A planet of smugglers, criminals, and political refugees.

That's the grand future you see for me?"

"You can build a good life for yoursel—"

"And he will," Sibylla said from the doorway of the vault.

I instinctively turned to her soothing voice—a little afraid of what I might find. After listening to Finch, I had a vision in my head of Sibylla that frightened me. When my eyes found her, however, I knew the monster Finch had described was a figment of his imagination. The beautiful young woman standing before me could never harm anyone. The gold necklace danced between her bare breasts with a blinding brilliance as she glided across the room. Sibylla, now no older than me, had indeed changed. Her mere presence was overwhelming.

"Styx...my children...come to me," she said.

I moved toward her without question and took her hand as she reached out to me.

"Sibylla," Finch yelled. "You have what you need. Let the boy go in peace."

She looked at me. "Do you want to leave?"

"No," I said. "You promised I could stay."

"And you may," Sibylla said. "After all, you are the new proprietor of The Emporium. My children and I...are here to serve *you*."

"We can play ball if you want to," Gofer said.

I looked down into Gofer's gnarly face and laughed. "Hell no," I said. "But...maybe later, after I learn how things work around here."

"Then what *should* we do?" Gofer asked.

I looked at Sibylla. "What would *you* like to do?"

She slipped her arm around my waist, pulling me close.

Oh, hell yes!

"We've been stuck on this dump for fifty years," she said. "Why don't we go on the road for a while and see a little of the universe? We can stow The Emporium for transport and have a

MULE here by midnight." "What's a mule?" I asked.

"A Multi-Utility Landing and Extraction vessel," Sibylla said. "I know a couple of nice pilots that fly an independent operation. They drop in every now and then to...see me. They owe me a few favors." Sibylla then whispered in my ear, "Why don't we try Calypso Twelve for a few months? It's a water planet with two small suns." She nibbled my lobe and added, "I'd love to work on my tan."

Feeling her lips against my skin, I forgot the question. But after enough blood finally trickled back upstairs, I said, "Hell yeah. How do we call in the MULE?"

"Thaddeus," Finch yelled, "don't be ignorant. The Emporium must stay on Wadi. I've already explained that to you."

"Ignorant?" I repeated dryly. "Sorry, but I guess I take after my mother. And don't call me Thaddeus." I turned back to Sibylla and noticed that Candy had taken a seat in front of the vault door. "As far as I'm concerned," I said, "the vault door will remain open." "Thank you," Sibylla said, squeezing me gently.

I nodded toward Finch and asked her, "Are we done with that asshole, yet?"

Sibylla smiled and said, "Entirely."

As if on cue, Candy let out a deafening snort of compressed air and leaped over our heads. If Sibylla had not been holding me, I feel certain I would have collapsed. Landing on all fours a few feet in front of Finch, Candy unhinged her jaw. Moving in a blur, she engulfed Finch's body from head to toe before he could even look up. With the tips of his shiny black shoes protruding from her mouth, Candy leaped over the bar, disappearing into the dark mist between the stacks. The whine of Candy's large pneumatic pump soon drowned out Finch's muffled screams. Whatever she was doing to him certainly required a great deal of compressed air.

"Damn," Gofer said. "I hope Candy waits until she gets him outside. She never thinks about how somebody--me--has to clean up after her." Gofer stood and trotted off after Candy. Reaching the pass-through in the bar, he stopped and turned back. "By the way," he said, "welcome to the family, Captain Styx." Gofer let out a little bark and then sprinted off into the darkness.

"Captain?" I asked, turning to Sibylla.

"We might not have engines, but this is still a class-one spacecraft," Sibylla said. "Do you want to see the laser cannon?"

"Hell yeah," I said. "If I'm the captain, can I get one of those hats with the gold braid thingamabob?"

"Anything you want," Sibylla said, and she wasn't kidding.

A Clinical Case
Alex Winck

Damarco Lycaon Had to be put into a straightjacket. Many may consider this an antiquated and barbaric method, but during the fervor of an outburst, the patient may actually hurt or even kill oneself and others. Sometimes, it´s still necessary to restrict them, at least until a paramedic gets the chance to inject a sedative. Damarco was a particularly agitated patient, grawling, snarling, biting, even attempting to gauge the paramedic´s eyes. Entirely the animal he believed he was.

When Doctor Walter Hooper meets Damarco in his office, the patient´s restless, but controlled. Software analyst, 27, married, no kids. Has a poorly trimmed beard - quite a recent one, given his older pictures - and a unibrow looking like a huge caterpillar resting over his shifty eyes. As the senior doctor in the Landis Clinic, Walter had fifteen years of experience dealing with similar cases. Even so, he had the gut feeling that this would be a tough one.

"Good evening, Mr. Lycaon. Feeling better?"

"By better you mean dope. So yeah, I feel much better now, thank you."

"Please, Mr. Lycaon. It´s important that you understand this. We´re a serious and modern psychiatric clinic, not a looney bin, not Cuckoo´s Nest. You won´t see zombie-like patients limping around in the hallways with dead fish eyes. We use the latest methods of behavioral and occupational therapy. We do use medication, yes, when it´s necessary. Unfortunately, in your case, it was necessary, at that mom—"

"Cut the bullshit. Stop right there. We can argue for years whether daddy loved me or not. And he loved me plenty, just for the record. I can build as many little blocks as you like. The thing here, what matters is you won´t believe me."

"I do believe you, Damarco. I believe everything you see, touch, hear, smell, it´s all entirely real for you. I bel—"

Suddenly, Damarco gets loud and seems to regain some of his agitations. Walter wondered for a second if he was less responsive than expected to the sedative, but decided to let him keep his rant going. The Vistaril they injected in him was usually quite effective.

"I´ll turn into a wolf! I know it! A wolf bit me under the Full Moon. I have the curse. I already feel it running in my veins. The symptoms started. I can hear people drinking and swallowing their coffee in the hallway. I can smell the chicken and cottage cheese croissant you had right before coming here. You need to lock me up in the tightest security spot you can find. Or kill me, even. It´s going to happen. A lot of people will die. Including you."

Even though Damarco sounded like he was quoting from a bunch of bad movies, Walter knew he had to give him the real situation as calmly and sympathetically as possible.

"First, I have to give you credit. your hearing and smelling senses are really outstanding. But I came here in a hurry, I didn´t brush my teeth. My breath still smells. This hallway has an unbelievable echo. You´re not a werewolf, Damarco. You suffer from a pretty rare disorder. It´s called Clinical Lycanthropy. In spite of the name, it doesn´t necessarily mean a wolf. The patient completely believes that they have become, or they´re in the process of turning into an animal. In some cases, a wolf, yes."

Damarco´s eyes were as shifty as ever, his hands nervously caressing the chair´s arms, a boiling feeling of anxiety that he couldn´t find the channel to send from his brain to his body. Not yet.

"The victim even mimics the animal as you were doing just before. They grawl, they get on all fours, they bite, they scratch. But these are all illusions, Damarco. Extremely realistic hallucinations."

For one second, Damarco almost seemed calm, resigned, borderline peaceful.

"What time is it?"

"My cellphone´s recharging. I guess around 7 P.M. Why?"

"Look out the window."

Damarco points to a majestic, impossibly beautiful Full Moon that illuminates the landscape of the forest next to the clinic, almost a second Sun in its brightness.

"Listen. Listen carefully to me. Just because it´s a Full Moon, it doesn´t mean—"

Suddenly, Damarco was grawling again, a deep guttural sound, his teeth fully exposed, his hands tightly clenching the chair´s arms, his eyes devolved back into the one-dimensional, primal rage of the alpha hunter. He leaps and tackles Doctor Walter, incredibly strong for a man of his physical type...

...But still human. No actual transformation whatsoever, merely the physical and mental mutation of his disorder. Luckily for Doctor Walter, he was cautious enough to keep a syringe full of Haldol, a much stronger sedative, in his drawer. He manages to take it before the attack and inject it into Damarco´s arm before he could do any real damage. But the sudden burst of adrenaline not only washed the previous sedative out of his system, it really made Damarco strong enough that his psychotic fury will leave its share of bruises.

Damarco wakes up much later. He has no idea how much time had passed, but he could look at the window and see the Full Moon. He's surprised to see it was a regular room, only his arms and legs were tied to the bed. He thought they were going to put him in one of those padded cells, but he supposes serious, modern psychiatric clinics don´t do that anymore. Yet he knows he's still heavily sedated. Can´t really feel the rage he knew he still had throbbing somewhere in the back of his mind. His thoughts are drowsy, nebulous.

Doctor Walter comes into the room to check on his patient. Damarco can see the little bruises on the doctor´s wrists. He´d actually feel bad for Walter if he could really feel anything properly. The doctor´s talk remains as calm and clinic as ever.

"Good night, Damarco. I can see you´re awake enough for me to talk to you. Good. I told you. You´re not a werewolf. You have a very serious condition. I knew that long before you tackled me."

Suddenly, Damarco´s still able to notice a subtle yet strange switch in Walter´s voice. It has this lower, graver quality to it.

"Not because I´m a skeptical rationalist. Not because monsters are not real. But because it takes a werewolf to know another. You´re not one of us."

Damarco´s heart and mind mean to feel terror, but they were still way too numb for it. All he can do is watch in quiet desperation as Walter goes gleefully, maniacally, through his metamorphosis. His whole body grows long, dark yet glooming hair, his teeth become powerful fangs, his nails erected into claws that could decapitate a man with a single strike, his whole-body twitches, convulses, making nauseating, creaky sounds as it reshapes him completely into an eight-foot colossus of raw power and bloodthirst. His voice, although raspy and cavernous now, still retains the cadence and precision of the doctor's speech pattern.

"The true children of the night are not victims of anything, Mr. Lycaon. We own our destiny way more than you do. You're caged by your bills, your bosses, and governments, your churches, your meaningless social codes. As we run into the night, we're free, pure, and invincible."

Then he shows to Damarco his little present. The savagely severed head of a paramedic, the same one Damarco had almost blinded before. Walter holds it like a hunter posing for a picture with his slain trophy. Damarco finds the strength to ask a question.

"If...If I'm really just a...just a mental patient...how can I know you're real?"

"You can't. Your symptoms indicate that your lycanthropy is the expression of psychotic bursts related to schizophrenia. And you do know what schizophrenia is, don't you? Your senses perceive what isn't really there. Maybe I am real. Maybe I'm not. That is your true curse, Damarco. To lose yourself, your identity, your grasp of reality. Maybe for life."

Walter tosses the head on Damarco's chest like he was throwing a bone to a dog. Damarco stares at the dead eyes for a moment, as if half-expecting the head to start talking. Walter takes a huge leap and breaks through the wall, five stores high. Soon he disappears into the woods, in communion with the wild. The next day, as the doctor, he'd have a thousand prepared explanations for the hole and the beheaded paramedic. Patients rebelling, vandalism, whatever. Anything would fly more than the truth. If any of those things were really there.

Damarco is left alone in his room. Alone deeply inside his disturbed and lost mind.

Devil Dogs
Joanne Magnus
1

"I heard 'em," I told the people around me from my hospital bed, "And I would have killed every one of them if I could. Devil Dogs, that's what they were!"

Ronny Santiago, the local state trooper around where I live, was standing next to my bed put his hand on my shoulder and said, "Ok, Millie, just start from the beginning and tell us what happened."

There was another Spanish or Mexican police officer on the other side of the bed. My Doctor, an Indian man (India Indian, not Native American), or PDA, or whatever he was, was at the end of the bed with some kind of electronic Tablet. I remember the days when Doctors were Doctors and instead of fancy gadgets they had charts. Tubes were sticking out of my arms and it looked like I was pretty beat up. Of course, I never give up anything without a fight and what a fight it was.

"Mrs. Nordstrom," the Doctor asked as he looked at the Tablet toward me, "I am Doctor Mamikunian, let me verify the information on your chart."

"First of all, Doctor, you are a real Doctor, I assume, not one of those PDAs."

"I'm an Intern, Mrs. Nordstrom."

"It's Ms. Nordstrom," I corrected him, "Jesus, what happened to all the real Doctors. Did they all fly off to California to where the big bucks are, working privately for all those celebrities?"

"My apologies, Ms. Nordstrom."

"My husband's been dead about 10 years now. He used to work on oil drilling rigs. He slipped off the rig one day and the company paid me a boatload of money to keep it quiet. Now I live out here in New Mexico."

"So, you are not married to your roommate, Miss Gina Reilly?"

"I ain't Gay if that's what you are trying to say. Not that there's anything wrong with that. No, she's just my roommate. She helps pay for the expenses."

The Doctor lifted his hand to calm Millie down, "Ma'am I wasn't trying to say anything. Gina called the police when she heard the commotion outside and is waiting outside the door. I just want to know if she was a relative."

"She's just my roommate," I explained, "Just cause two women share a house together doesn't make them gay."

"I understand perfectly," the Doctor continued as he looked back at the Tablet, "You are fifty-six years old, you are not on any medications, height five feet six, weight..."

"I could stand to lose a few..." I interrupted.

The doctor turned to the ground and said, "Maybe more than a few."

The policeman with his hand on my shoulder asked, "Millie, could you please tell us what happened in the barn last night?"

"I woke up in the middle of the night. I heard this screech. It didn't sound like an owl or a coyote. My dogs, Yogi and Boo Boo were barking."

One officer was snickering.

"Hey, what's wrong with Yogi and Boo Boo," I said,

"Didn't you watch cartoons when you were a kid? 'Hey, Boo Boo...'"

"My Dad watched those cartoons," the officer commented. The other officer looked at him quizzically and asked, "Do you mean Yoda, from Star Wars?"

"Nope, couple of bears from the sixties, early television cartoons."

"Well, anyway, I thought, there must be something in the chicken coop. Then I heard Yogi and Boo Boo squeal and yelp. Oh, no, not old Yogi and Boo Boo! I ran to the window to look outside. There were at least ten of those little bastard animals running around. Two of them were on Yogi. There were another five or so in the yard."

"Ms. Nordstrom, could you describe the animals that were attacking your dogs? There have been similar attacks in the area." the chubby policeman asked.

"They were little and they looked like hairless Chihuahuas, "I described, "With fangs and red eyes, well their eyes looked red in my flashlight.

"Yogi was spinning around trying to shake them loose; Boo Boo was biting them and flinging them across the yard. Poor things, I chained them to the light post next to the chicken coop. The light was on and I could see them all. Yogi and Boo Boo used to jump the fence in the yard before so I chained them up at night so they don't run off. They would bark if there was a coyote around and I would blast the coyote to kingdom come. I grabbed my shotgun and shot one of the little bastards! Devil dogs, that's what they are! I hit him dead on. It jumped up and flipped over when I hit it. It was dead before it hit the ground.

"I had to help Yogi. Poor thing was tangled up in

the dog chain. I unlocked the dog chain and untangled him while I swatted those demons away from him. Yogi tried to run off of course, but before he did I grabbed one of those little bloodsuckers and ripped it off of him. Little hairless rat it sneered at me with his bloody fangs as I smashed his ugly head into the ground. He ran and I unlocked Boo Boo's chain. He was still fighting those beasts. I shot another one in front of him and told him to, 'run, boy, run!' that's the last I've seen of them."

"Did you see what color these animals or dogs were?" the Chubby policeman asked.

"I couldn't tell what color they were exactly; I think they were brown or black. I heard some more commotion in the chicken coop so I opened the wooden door and went in. There were more of those Devil dogs in there. I flipped the light on by the door and I saw 5 dead chickens lying on the ground on a path through the middle of the chicken coops. There was one of those Bloodsucking animals killing a chicken right in front of me. He was sucking the blood right out of its neck on the ground and doing a little butt dance up in the air like he was having a party. I aimed my shotgun and blew his ass away. The other animals heard this and scurried away except for one in the back of the coop.

"In the back was this, lizard-like horny monster facing me behind a table that was in the back of the coop where I check the eggs from the chickens. Lying on the table was this dead, or at least I thought it was dead, dog or wolf, Thank God it wasn't my dogs; this lizard thing was pulling out the dog's intestines and eating them like spaghetti. Then the dog or wolf howled on the table as this monster ate his insides.

"Well, I reloaded my shotgun and pointed it at the

monster and yelled, 'See you in hell!' I shot at him but I missed. I blew a hole in the side of the chicken coop. That only made the creature angry as it started to come after me with these big claws.

"I clawed my hands up to show everyone. They were scaly claws with black fingernails. Then I started walking backward and trying to reload my shotgun again. I tripped over one of the dead chickens in the aisle just as I got my shotgun loaded and as I fell down I heard the gun go off. That's all I remember until I woke up here."

The chubby Spanish Policeman spoke stifling a laugh, "Ms. Nordstrom, when you discharged your gun you shot whatever was coming at you in the chicken in the face. You blew its head off and now we have the body in the morgue. The dogs or rats that were killing your chickens were gone by the time we got there, which were very shortly after you shot the intruder. Gina called us after she heard the first shot from the barnyard and we were in at your house in about five minutes. We found you in the chicken coop unconscious and brought you here."

"Do you know if Yogi and Boo Boo are okay?" I asked.

"We are still looking for him," the other policeman answered.

The Doctor stated, "We are giving you some antibiotic to stop any infection you may have received from the animal bites you have on your legs, Ms. Nordstrom. We are going to keep you overnight in the hospital for observation, now I think you need some rest. We will tell Gina she can visit you in the morning."

The Doctor and the Policemen left the room and I moved around the covers on my legs. Sure enough, there were black and blue bite marks and puncture marks on my legs from those little bastards! I will get them if it's the last thing I do!" Then I went to sleep.

Outside in the hall, the Policemen talked with the Doctor, "Have you ever heard of something called a Chupacabra?"

"There is no such thing as a Chupacabra. That's an old folktale," the Doctor mocked, "I'm sure the old woman was attacked by a bunch of rats or wild dogs. She shot a panhandler in her barn stealing chickens and she came up with the wild dog story to cover her butt. We have his remains in the morgue."

"I saw the remains," the chubby officer said, "That is some freaky looking panhandler."

2

I woke up early in the morning, and it looked like someone had covered the room with flowers. Oh, surely Gina could not have done all this. It was beautiful. All the pretty yellows and reds! It was like I was sleeping in paradise. I tried to get out of bed but this vine was attached to my arm. I pulled it off my arm and it was such a strange vine covered in red and purple flowers.

I stepped on the floor and felt the warm sunshine through the window. This was amazing! Then I smelled the most wonderful smell coming from the door of the room. It smelled like all of my favorite foods. I opened the door and ventured outside into the hallway. The smell of freshly baked brisket and mashed potatoes just about took my breath away. On top of that was the smell of freshly baked apple pie and, could it be; cheesecake. I filled my lungs with the smell and let out a sigh.

The smell was to the right, so I headed in that direction. It became stronger as I got closer to this one double-door room. I thought it was very strange that nurses and people just stood on the side of the hallway as I walked by. Even the orderly who was nasty to me earlier even jumped out of my way and stood with his back against the wall, but then I remembered the scene in the end of the movie, "Titanic" when all the people stood on the side of the long spiral staircase as the girl made her way up to her meet her beau. I certainly did not expect this kind of treatment, especially when my Health insurance was the most basic type of Health insurance. I was lucky they didn't put me in a hospital ward if they still had such things anymore.

So, I entered the double-door room and I just could not believe my eyes. There was a table stretched out across the room with a banquet of sumptuous foods. At the front end of the table was a brisket that looked like it was slow cooked for ten hours covered with mini onions and next to that was mashed potatoes. There were sweet potatoes, red wine, and sausage and tapioca pudding. At the end of the table, there was my favorite, chocolate cheesecake!

There were Doctors and people in this room. They stepped out of the way for me. That's when I knew this feast was for me and I was famished. I started in on the brisket, and I had a generous glass of wine. I invited the Doctors and orderlies to join me but they had walked out of the room. I hate to admit, I made a bit of a pig out of myself, but it was all so good. I ate every bite. Then I got to the chocolate cheesecake at the end of the table. I put a slice in my mouth when a bunch of people walked into the room. I felt a little guilty having eaten most of the food, but some of the chocolate cheesecake was still there. So, I said, "Come and have some of this wonderful cheesecake!"

3

A young Asian cleaning woman sat trembling on one of the green fabric chairs in the second-floor waiting room in the hospital. She was curled up in the chair with her feet on the chair, her knees bent over her head so when the policeman approached all he could see where the top of the knees of the white nylon pant tightly held together and shaking. She held a Styrofoam cup on upright on her stomach with two hands. In the cup were a tea bag and hot water. She drank half of the tea and every time she tried to drink it her hands shook too bad it was hard not to spill it.

There were chairs on either side of the Asian woman. On the left side of her a policeman sat down and a translator pulled up a chair in front of her.

"I'm Officer Ruiz," the policeman introduced himself, "And this is Ngyen Ho, he's here to translate for you. I understand you have only been in this country a few months and I need to know what exactly happened an hour ago for our report."

Ngyen Ho translated everything the officer said to the cleaning woman, whose name was Sue Yung Lee, Sue understood everything the translator said and began to tell Ngyen Ho what happened. Sue Yung Lee, hysterically spoke to the translator.

Then Ngyen Ho spoke to the officer.

"I was on the second floor working my shift," Ngyen Ho explained, "I had just finished Room 202 and I was in the doorway behind my cart. I wasn't supposed to clean Room 205 until later. There was a sign on the door and on my chart, it was marked for later.

"The door to room 205 opened. I thought that was strange because that side of the hall was for people with IVs. This thing then stood in the doorway."

Sue Yung Lee began to tremble. Her tea began to ripple in her cup on her lap.

The Police officer put his hand on her arm and said, "Please, Miss Lee, this is very important. Take a deep breath and continue."

"I saw this enormous woman," Ngyen translated, "Or what I thought was a woman. She must have weighed three hundred pounds. She stood at the door looking around. She wore a hospital gown that only covered her front. I could see it dangling on the side of her leg. I saw her right arm too. It looked like she had ripped the IV out of her arm and her arm was dripping black blood."

"So, she was facing you?" the policeman asked.

"Yes," Sue Yung Lee answered through the translator, "She turned her head in my direction and I ducked behind my cart. I don't think she saw me. It was as if she was looking for something and wasn't paying attention to me. I saw her face and it was awful. Her eyes were glazed over with milky stars in the middle. Her teeth were greenish, yellow and black liquid was dripping out of her mouth. She had what looked like saliva all over her face and she was white as a ghost.

"Then she made this ungodly moaning sound. It made my skin crawl so badly I closed my eyes and cried and prayed that she wouldn't see me. Then I heard her heading down the hall in the opposite direction toward the morgue. As soon as I could I grabbed the phone on the wall and called security. I could see her fat butt from behind. Her legs were all purple and torn up. It looked like she left a trail of blood and black slime behind her. I'm not touching that stuff!"

"We have a biohazard team to pick up the floor,

Miss Lee," the policeman assured her, "Finish your tea and stay here; we may have some more questions later."

On the way to the morgue was a nurse's station. The nurses were the next people to see Ms. Nordstrom barreling down the hall. These nurses were also in the waiting room cowering in the opposite corner from the maid. Officer Ruiz went over to them next.

"So, you saw Ms. Nordstrom after Sue Yung Lee?" he asked them.

There were two nurses and an orderly sitting together. Each of them had their hands folded in front of them and were bent over. The orderly was a local kid working his way through college and the nurses were RNs who had been at the hospital for years.

"I never saw anything like it," one of the nurses answered officer Ruiz, "I've people lost in the desert for days, drug addicts, people messed up on peyote buttons, but nothing like this. This three-hundred-pound wall of mess blew past the nurses' station on the way to the morgue. Poor Jerry, the orderly saw her coming and flew out of the way before it trampled him."

Jerry nodded in agreement and said, "When I saw her I thought I was going to die right there. I don't think I'll ever get that image out of my mind."

The other nurse, an older woman added, putting her arm around Jerry, "We both dove behind the counter when she came by; I was hoping that Jerry was alright. There was nothing we could do to help him. I thank God you are okay!"

"So, Ms. Nordstrom was headed directly for the morgue?" Officer Ruiz asked.

"Yes," the first nurse answered, "she burst through the double doors to the morgue at the end of the hall."

After the officer was finished with the people at the nurses' station he moved to interview the Coroner and his assistant who were in the morgue when Millie Nordstrom burst in. They were also seated in the waiting room. The Coroner was a short older man and his assistant was a young Indian woman. The older man was holding the Indian woman's hand as the officer came by.

"Dr. Adams," the officer asked, "Please tell us what happened when Ms. Nordstrom came into the morgue."

Dr. Adams began, "My assistant and I were working on three corpses that had come into the morgue from the previous day. We are the county morgue in these parts and we were at various stages of our autopsies. The tables were lined up parallel lengthwise to the double doors. We were at the third table toward the back of the room. I had my back to the doors and my assistant Suri was facing the doors. The doors are normally closed but not locked. They are only locked in the event that the departed carried some dangerous pathogen. In that case, we would just store the body in the freezers on the left wall until a lab in Santa Fe could pick them up. The body of the thing at Ms. Nordstrom's farm was in one of those metal freezers roll out freezers and that was locked. We were preparing to have it transported to Santa Fe because it was so unidentifiable and it needed to go to a better facility.

"Anyway, Suri saw Ms. Nordstrom burst into the room. I heard the noise as Suri looked up and dropped her scalpel. I turned around and looked at the door. I thought one of our bodies had walked out of the freezers! If you could call her human, her face was white and pale. Her eyes were totally glazed over.

There was saliva and green puss dripping out of her mouth.

"She made this ungodly moaning noise when she cleared the door. I've heard many gruesome sound before but this moan made my skin crawl. We stood motionless as 'she' ambled her way to the first table. I thought the best chance we had of getting out of that room alive was to quietly move along the back wall next to the freezers, without her noticing, and slip out the double doors.

It is said creatures like that,"

"Zombies," Suri interrupted.

Officer Ruiz glared at Suri and said, "Now, no one's calling Ms. Nordstrom a Zombie."

"If you had seen her you would not be saying that," Suri answered back.

"Go ahead, Dr. Adams," the Policeman said.

"It is said that creatures like that are simulated by hearing, motion and smell. So, we figured if we were very quiet and careful we might make it out. 'She' ripped open the brains of the first corpse on the first table and had a veritable feast, if you will. 'She' was much too occupied by eating to bother with us, so I took Suri's hand as she crossed the front of the table. We slowly came closer to the door. Then just as we got to the door a metal scalpel dropped on the floor near us. We both held our breath to see if she would turn and attack us. She looked up for a moment and then went back to devouring the corpse. Thank God! Both of us made a mad dash for the door. I hoped the nursing staff had not barricaded us in there, fortunately, they had not. We ran out the door and locked it behind us."

Suri stated, "We not only locked it, we put a wooden plank in the rails of the door to keep it shut."

"It's a good thing those things weren't in front of the door before we got out," Doctor Adams acknowledged, "We would have never made it. I guess they knew we were in there because I had the 'Do Not Enter' sign on. The nursing staff had run away by the time we got out and the SWAT team had arrived as we locked the door. Is it true what I heard from the SWAT team?" "I'll have to ask them," Officer Ruiz answered them.

At that moment one of the members of the SWAT team entered the waiting room and addressed Officer Ruiz, "Everything is secure in the morgue," he said.

Doctor Adams asked the SWAT team member "Is it true what we heard she was doing in there?"

"We opened the doors to the morgue and the walls were covered in blood," he answered the Doctor, "She, if you can call that a 'she' was at the back table. She looked up as we came in. She had a liver hanging out of the end of her mouth from the dead body. She was eating it like it was dessert. We immediately opened fire. I got her with a headshot. She wriggled around a little bit and then fell face first into the cadaver. You've got a big mess in there."

After a few days the Hazmat crew cleaned the morgue and sterilized it, they never did find Ms. Nordstrom's dog, Yogi.

Mystical Phantoms
Amy S. Pacini

A dim sky casts
Death's shadow
Upon the raven path
Blowing an icy wind
As I tread on sepulchral ground
Where peaceful souls lay soundly
In eternal rest
Aloft their subterraneous beds
Detailed epitaphs
Are meticulously inscripted
Upon granite gravestones
Marking their earthly existence
Weeping loved ones gather
In hallowed silence
To grieve the permanent loss
Of mortal departure
Tearstained white roses and lilies
Ornately outline
The perimeter
Of each burial site
Framed photographs
Of beloved spirits
Are carefully placed
At the tomb's base
A golden cross
Is firmly hung
From the top of the headstone

As a blessed remnant
Of God's love and protection
Before departing from
This reverent necropolis
I take another glance
As phantom shadows
Melt into the incorporeal world
Of interminable nirvana
Invincible to death's primal snare.

Love Craft
James Harper

Howie's friends knew right away that he was doomed the moment he clapped eyes on the girl; the classic drop-jaw look of shock on his hangdog face told them that. Howie stood in the hallway, the couch now ignored, gawking at her as she walked toward her apartment.

"Oh crap," Clark said.

"Yeah," Bill agreed.

For a moment no one moved; all four of them standing in the hallway: Howie with his two friends, Clark and Bill, and the girl. In that instant, the silence moved from abrupt to awkward.

She had walked off the elevator as they struggled with Howie's heavy, cumbersome roll-out couch bed, the one Bob had named the Monster for the problems and difficulty it had caused whenever they had to move it. Bob, of course, had a point. The couch required three men to lift, its bulk proving problematic and its size always made the going painful. Regardless, Howie refused to part with it over the years, necessitating its move no matter where or how far he went from one apartment or shared house to another.

Coming off the elevator next to the one that they had just vacated, the girl wore that causal smock dress that one wears on Saturdays when one meant to walk the park in the early morning before the heat of the day to watch the geese and other wildlife make their circuit about the water. Her shoulder-length black hair curled to a point at the top of her back; her eyes, a grey that crossed slate with marble, drank in the scene as they darted about the sprawl; and, she walked with the poise of a kindergarten teacher tiptoeing across a toy-strewn classroom.

Howie looked at her as she took a step into the hall, moving with a slight grin as she negotiated around the obstacle they presented. Then she caught his look. He neither looked away nor stopped his stare. She returned his attention and then smiled. That's when Howie's friends knew he was doomed.

Carrying two boxes, Bob entered the scene off the other elevator, walking into the hallway. Seeing them just standing there staring, he said, "What gives?" The girl blinked then walked into the door next to Howie's new studio.

"Did you hear the thunderclap?" Bill joked.

Bob raised an eyebrow then turned to Clark for help.

Clark nodded toward Howie. "He's smitten."

Bob looked at Howie, still staring, still unmoved, the couch forgotten. "Oh fuck," Bob said.

"Dude, snap out of it," Bill said.

Clark leaned over the couch, pressing his stomach on the bottom front, to wave his hand before Howie's eyes. Howie blinked then grinned the grin of the vapid. He bent to lift the couch.

"Let's get this done," he said.

Bill laughed. "Yeah, make like what just happened never happened. Just try."

Clark grunted as he steered the couch into Howie's new place, slamming into the doorjamb as they pushed through. "It's not like we've never seen that look before."

Howie and the others had spent the afternoon moving him into his new apartment, a lucky find in a grand brownstone just off Capitol Hill near Lincoln Park. The afternoon had gone smoothly, much to Howie's surprised delight, causing few, if any, hang-ups or real hardships. With luck, he was just thinking before the surprise in the hallway, they'd be celebrating before four o'clock.

The three of them, Howie, Bill and Clark, moved the couch to a barren spot in the apartment near the bay windows, an area that served to welcome the morning sun through the large curved arch in the building. The sofa landed with a soft thump.

"Okay, is that it?" Clark asked.

"Think so," Howie said, surveying the room. "Except for a couple of boxes—and some shit I don't think I'm ever going back for—this does it."

He took stock of their effort. The place looked like Dresden after the firebombing: boxes everywhere, clothes spilling out of the closet, possessions spread across the room in disarray. That didn't matter, he thought, it's here, we moved it. He would find a place for everything later. For now, he straightened up by pushing boxes in the corners and against the walls, so that they could get to The Providence.

Then he remembered the girl.

"Where's the beer?" Bill asked.

The crack of a 12-ounce answered his question. Smiling, Bob handed the breathing can to him.

Howie held his hand out from his sides to pronounce, "Time to drink."

Later, at The Providence, four of them sat down at their usual table, one that seated six at a circular booth, a spot reserved for them mostly due to their frequent attendance. Mostly. The Providence itself boasted wood-paneled walls and ornamentation that captured the distinctive feel of a cross between college hangout and derelict dive.

"Beer for all," Bill said in a commanding tone, waving his hand in the air.

Across the room at the bar, Kathy Merrill rolled her eyes. She turned to Jessica Bennett the bartender. "Can I get a tray?" she asked.

"Are those your guys?" Jessica asked as she brought a beer to set on the tray.

"Yeah, you could say that," Kathy said. She reached over the bar to the bowls of pretzels. "They're the dailies."

"Oh, so they're *good* customers."

Kathy met Jessica's look. "You want to know the truth?" she said. "They're really the best." She picked up the tray filled with mugs to walk it over to their table. "Just don't tell them I said that."

"Thanks, Kathy," Howie said as she served the mugs. "We've done yeoman's work today."

"Oh, that's right," she said, "how'd the move go?"

"Brilliant," Howie said. "Just excellent."

"Really?"

"Yeah, no problems at all."

"But that's not all," Clark let out in a singing voice.

Howie blushed. "Shut up."

"No way."

Kathy looked between the two of them.

"You better tell her," Bill said looking at Howie. "Because you know if you don't, you know he will."

"What?" Kathy said.

"Nothing," Howie said, pulling on his beer. "Don't listen to them. They're idiots." He glared at his friends. "Just shut up." "Howie's in love," Clark sang.

Howie's look stabbed at Clark. "Just shut the fuck up," he snapped.

"Okay, okay, forget it," Clark said. "We got more important things to do anyway." He lifted his mug over the table. "Gentleman," he said with practiced pomp, "We must now begin the drinking!"

"The drinking!" they echoed. They all chugged their mugs empty, slamming the glasses to the table in flourish.

"Now, kind lady—" Bob said.

"I know," Kathy said, "more beer."

Bob laughed. "In copious quantities."

"You boys are gonna keep the blood loss to minimal tonight, right?" She blinked then looked around as if noticing for the first time. "Hey, where's Frank?"

"He's got a show," Clark said.

Bill offered: "Don't worry; he's coming straight here when he's done."

"You think he'll bring a clip?"

"If he gets one, I'm sure," Howie said.

"But now," Bob said, "Our poor beers have gone to the beyond. May we please have another?"

"Yes, kind maiden, another?"

"Yes, another."

They all put on puppy-dog faces to show their mock despair at the prospect of their empty beer mugs.

"All right, all right," Kathy said, turning away from the table. "Should have brought a pitcher, to begin with."

Kathy walked over to Jessica at the bar, who had watched the display with a pitcher ready. "You've got to be shitting me," she said.

Kathy smiled. "Nope, it's like this, and more, almost every day."

"Really? And they get away with it?"

"Are you kidding? Not only are they the best customers, they're practically the entertainment."

"People go for that?"

Kathy shrugged. "Mostly. But also, they're really harmless. Most of what they do isn't disruptive. Besides, it's all in good fun."

"Okay," Jessica said, "If you say so."

"You know what?" Kathy said, looking Jessica in the eye, "Your tip today's gonna pay your phone bill."

Later, Frank came in. With shoulder length hair and a beard, wearing a Skinny Puppy tee over jeans, he took his place at the table, reaching for the pitcher of beer before he even sat down.

"How stands the Republic, gentlemen?" he said.

"Safe and secure," they responded as one.

The mug they had left for Frank waited; he grabbed it to fill as Clark asked, "How did the gig go?"

"Well, given that it was a birthday party for some poor teenage schlub living in the high-end burbs of Baltimore and we could only work a strict playlist that included MOR and pop classics and they didn't bother to feed us and they wanted us to stay so we could continue to provide a means for them to publicly humiliate themselves and not a single one of the single females were over the legal age: pretty damn good." "Really?" Howie said.

"Yeah, we got an $800 bonus," Frank said, raising his voice to announce to the room, "Drinks are on me, boys!"

Cheers arose from the others, as they clinked their mugs in congratulations.

Kathy came up to the table. "Hey, Frank."

"Hey, Kath. These feebs giving you trouble?"

"Nothing I can't handle," she said smiling. "You hungry?"

"As a matter of fact," he said, "since I wasn't allowed to eat at the gig, I'm starving. So please, please bring me my usual."

"Coming up. Any you boys need anything else?" she asked. Surveying the damage done to the pitcher, she said: "Besides more beer."

"So how did the move go?" Frank asked.

"Great," Howie said.

"Yeah, fuck that noise," Bill said, lowering his head. "More important: Howie saw a girl." The word girl came out with a twisted sarcasm.

"Oh really?" Frank said.

"Shut the fuck up," Howie said.

"No shit," Clark said. "The young master Howard was thunderstruck, cut to the quick."

"No doubt he's done for," Bob said.

"Fuck all you guys."

Frank shook his head slowly. "Well, Howie, there seems to be a consensus. It looks like you're doomed."

Howie drank more of his beer. "Well fuck you guys till

Tuesday."

"Don't fight it, Howie," Frank said. "It's cool."

"Indeed," Bob said. "The finding of young love is a quest most happily concluded."

"Who said that?" Clark asked.

Bob belched deeply. "Me."

"So, tell me about this young lady," Frank said. "I need deets."

"Look, if you're going to do this, please just slice my throat right here," Howie said.

Ignoring Howie, Bob piled on. "A lass of robust features, her raven hair glowed with warmth as she floated across our view. She exhibited the grace and poise of an elegant creature of socially upward upbringing with a bearing that showed refinement and charm. Her mien exuded style to the degree that our existence grew richer in her presence however momentary its length."

Frank said, "Huh?"

Clark said, "Translation: She wasn't a hideous knuckle dragger."

After they toasted that fact, they drank deep into the night.

The next morning, a Monday, Howie got to work as early as he could manage under the hangover pain he suffered. In spite of repeated roadblocks caused by the unfamiliarity of his new commute, he made it to his downtown office, Hamark

Translations, by 9:02 a.m., well within the traditional window of acceptability. He had come to learn, however, that what had been acceptable in the past could evolve into the unacceptable under the controlling grip of his pedantic boss, Andy Carleton.

Hamark specialized in translation work for the Department of Homeland Security, providing documents in English from a variety of Middle Eastern languages. Because Howie had studied historical Arabic and Aramaic in addition to his major at school, he caught his current project as the only translator available knowledgeable in the content.

He stood at his cubby staring down at his desk, gathering the shreds of his under-caffeinated thoughts to bear against his workload for the day. The bulk of his assignment lay ahead of him since, while he could easily handle the complexity of the language, the weird nature of the work had thrown him off balance. The text, some strange ritual manual entitled *Kitab al Azif* had given Howie headaches in ways he hadn't encountered before. Dating to somewhere in the

215

Eighth Century C.E., the title translated to The Record of The Buzz. He cracked open a 5-Hour.

And why was it called The Buzz? That was very weird indeed for formal Middle Arabic. Like most text from that era and before, nothing was ever written down unless it was very important. The cost and laborious effort of performing the act of writing—not to mention the rare required skill set to carry it off—discouraged any other practice.

Howie knew that it lay just beyond his reach, he felt he stood on the brink of breaking through. Unlike what most lay people think, there's no code, no single Rosetta Stone, in translation. Often for old manuscripts, an author doesn't even remain consistent from one page to another, making the effort in no small way educated guesswork. Translation of very old texts was a more painstaking process involving the translator's skill and his ability to research the words used in their historical context. Howie had been working on *al Azif* for weeks without a breakthrough.

"How's it coming, Phillips?"

The remark broke Howie out of his revelry. Blinking, he turned toward the voice. Andy Carleton stood at his cubby opening, arms crossed, his glare boring through Howie like the look a hundred pound Rottweiler wore uncovering an intruder.

Howie tried to recover. "It—it's good, Andy," he said. "I've got all the preliminary text broken down so now I've only got the heart of the work to go." Then he slipped in an untruth to get Carleton off his back. "I'm definitely meeting deadlines and
should have it ready by the target date."

"You know that's in three weeks," Carleton said.

Howie struggled to not say, "Of course I know the

deadline's in three weeks you pompous, overbearing fuck. Not only do I know how to read a calendar, I've been proficient in calendar reading since I was eight years old which puts me at a sixteen-year advantage to you, you persnicketic worm."

Instead, he said: "Yeah, no problem."

"All right," Carleton said, beginning to move away from Howie's cubby. Howie prayed to whatever gods lay above that he would depart before slipping in the overlord's knife. Then Carleton said, "You better be ready in time." No such luck. Howie took back his prayer.

Pushing away a fiery lake of panic, Howie forced himself to focus on his work for the day. If he could get to the end of the section he currently worked on then he'd make it to a point where the work would be at a manageable degree so he'd have something for Carleton. Then he realized that, in order to do that, he'd have to do extra, he'd have to take the work home. Crap, he thought. He hated to work at home.

He stared at his desk, trying to think about something, anything, that would stave off his anxiety. No use putting this off, he thought; get organized and get this done.

Later, as Howie stood inside the elevator of his new apartment building, he stared glumly at a corner waiting for the doors to close, fingering his thumb drive. While he looked off, lost in thought, his daydream shattered when, as the doors started to close from out in the hall, a voice called "Hold the elevator please!"

Snapping out of it, Howie jerked to reach for the closing doors, managing to insert his hand between them. With a clank of protest, they slid open. When Howie looked up to see whom he rescued, he caught his breath.

It was her. The woman from moving day. She wore a modest dress that clung to her, revealing her structure in such a way so as to compliment her form without the appearance of impropriety. She thanked Howie as she stepped on, moving with a fluidity that spoke of the athletic strength borne of hard training. She carried a large picture frame, whose size put her off balance as she boarded the elevator. They rode in silence for a moment.

He couldn't let the moment pass. He stuck out his hand toward her.

"Howie Phillips," he said.

Still clutching the frame, she moved to touch his hand with hers in an awkward motion. "Oh," she said, wrapping her fingers in his, "Sonia Greene. I'm pleased to meet you, Howie. Welcome to the building. Stop by for a beer when you can."

Howie never remembered how he returned to his apartment, the memory of his actions wiped from his mind. The next he knew, he stood in his living room, satchel on his shoulder, staring at the bay windows that looked at to the street.

He shook his head to clear his thinking. Get to work, slacker, he thought. He had decided to follow the directions in the manuscript, word for word. This way, he thought, once we've discounted the behavior as myth, we can work on why the text held such a grip on the region's consciousness. The text would not have lasted some 1,400 years if no one put stock in it. So, following that reasoning, there must be something to it. But what?

Blood still coursing through his face from his meeting in the elevator, he went about the set up the text had outlined. He pushed back his area rug, revealing the hardwood floor. Then, with chalk, he traced a series of polygons on the wood, a circle, a pentagram and a triangle. Setting candles at the points of each intersection, he lit them. Now the incense, he thought. The text had called for three: frankincense, myrrh and something called cedrus; but hell, if he could find cedrus. Improvising, he decided to go with evergreen.

He took off his clothes. The manuscript dictated that the ritual be performed in the nude, the evocation must have nothing artificial or unloving between the caller and the called upon.

He sat cross-legged in the center of his drawing, laptop balanced on his knees. Thinking he had completed his preparations, he began.

He scrolled through the list of spells he had translated, each with its own specific recipe for words uttered and chants to sing, each its own application. He had planned to go with the spell that granted knowledge, thinking that it would lead the way to the rest of what he needed to know. He thought for a moment about another. Why not go for the love spell? She's next door, you're here. Go for it.

Common sense struck the idea down. As lame as you think you are, he thought, wait. Besides, he told himself, you can always come back to that later.

So, wisdom and information it was, he thought. He sang the chant as required by the text. The tune didn't matter he thought, not that he would have been able to work that out anyway. So, he sang the chant to the tune of Sabbath's "Sweet Leaf," a simple melody that kicked ass. Then he spoke the words from the text. "Arammannggi, Arammannggi, Arammannggi."

Stretching his arms out above his head, he said, "Arannuna, you who bestow wisdom, give to me the knowledge I seek, render me skills to excel in your endeavors and grant me the blessing of your will."

"I pledge the essence of my soul to your behalf, to return to you the equal of that which you grant to me. I will aid you in your quest to restore the arts of the forgotten and strive to follow the path you endorse." Conscious thought had left Howie at this point, he read from his laptop by rote. Good thing too. If he really thought about this shit, he'd be laughing too hard to get through it.

"Oh, Elder Ones, use this, your vessel, to complete the task ahead. Grant unto me the strength to carry out your will and I

shall undertake to achieve the ends you desire." He paused.

Nothing.

That figures. He sat, staring at his wall.

After twenty minutes, he had about given up. He knew his translation was good, he had double checked it himself. So, the words were right. Maybe it was bullshit after all.

One more try, he thought. Standing in the center of his drawing, he thought maybe it wasn't what he said but how he said it. If he repeated the text with feeling if he put something into it, could he expect better results?

I have to believe if I want to get something to happen. The text had been written for believers. He needed to become one himself.

"Arammannggi, Arammannggi, Arammannggi." The words faintly echoed as he spoke. He waited.

Absolute quiet.

Nothing.

Howie moved his butt cheeks off the floor to get blood moving. I'm done, he thought.

Then the air moved. How could that be, he thought. The apartment was sealed; he had closed the windows. Slowly, like a breeze building, the air in the room moved softly, blowing the smoke from the incense from its straight-up rising to a drift to the left.

Howie thought he heard something. What was it? Was he imagining it? A low, soft something. Nearby, not off in the distance but softly, quietly, a burr. A hiss. A hum. The sound held its volume, a low, indistinct thrum in the air. He cocked his head to hear it better: the dull throb of noise sounding everywhere at once. Slowly, it grew in volume.

As the sound swelled, the air moved quicker, rushing through the room. The incense began to twirl in the movement, Howie's skin chilled at the breeze against it.

What had he done?

The candles flickered, almost dimming. Beneath the smell of the incense, beyond the frankincense and myrrh, another odor arose. Howie slowly detected a grower scent of—what? He couldn't identify it at first, he knew the smell but he didn't recognize it. Then he realized.

Decay. Death. He smelled the smell of rot, of flesh in active decomposition.

This smell came to his apartment beneath the incense. Then it rose, filling every inch with the stink. Howie held his hand against his face to cover the smell, sniffing the scent of soap on his fingers against the stench.

As the air in the room moved about, Howie tasted metal, the flat taste of iron like when he drank water from a canteen. His skin rose from the feeling as the air whipped across it, the outer edge of his body rising off of itself.

Then he blacked out.

When he awoke, Howie found himself face down against the hardwood, his skin so flush to the floor that he could smell the lacquer on the wood. When he blinked his eyes open, he felt his lashes scrape its fiber. Slowly, he pulled himself up to a sitting position. As he did, every muscle in his body ached with a pain that felt as though he had been pummeled by hammers, each joint complaining at movement.

Sore and weak, he sat. He shook his head slowly to clear it, regretting it in the same moment, the throbbing in his temple threatened to make him pass out again.

What had he done?

He looked at his hands. His skin was red.

The skin, his fingernails, his palms all were the color of a fire truck, a deep, rich red that at once looked alien and wrong.

Then a wretched sickness overcame him, running through his whole body like a shuddering wave of weakness. He put his hand to his mouth to hold back the bile, dashing to the bathroom before the surge came. He didn't make it. He began to vomit on the floor. He threw up an oozing black liquid, a thick awful fluid that tasted horrible, like vinegar mixed with kerosene. It looked like liquefied asphalt, all black and disgusting. He sank to his knees as he continued to vomit, the sickness coming in a strong wave now, urging his gorge in an ongoing manner so that as he vomited, he needed to do so again and again. His head ached while the rest of his body felt that terrible weakness of body and spirit he felt whenever he had long bouts of barf.

He managed to get to the bathroom. On his knees, he continued to disgorge the black, bile-filled liquid.

For the next hour, he vomited continuously.

Finally, after he had emptied his belly when he felt as if the tank had truly hit empty, he lay on his tile floor clinging to the toilet. He waited for the weakness to pass, for his strength to return. Slowly, it did. His skin, too, returned to normal. After long moments, he felt his limbs and head return to a state where he could move. His head in his hands, he waited for more strength. As that finally came, he stood.

He sat on his couch for long minutes, trying to work out what had happened. Had he actually achieved the promise of *al Azif*? Had he gained command of the Elder Ones?

Only one way to find out before I call it quits, he thought. He checked his research then sat in the circle to call upon Yag lithic Shammosh, the granter of boons. Once summoned, he evoked it to bestow the love of Sonia Greene upon him.

He went over to Sonia's. Knocking on the door, she opened it to greet him with a smile. She wore the same dress, a pattern of green and white; it hung on her as a robe.

"Why, hello, Howie. This is a surprise." She let him in.

"Do you still have any of that beer?"

"Yes, I believe so," she said, crossing into the kitchen to get it. He entered her living room. He listened to the soft music on her sound system, trying to identify the artist, but came up empty.

As he stood in the middle of the room, he smelled then felt her approach from behind, her scent a fresh light morning air. Before he could turn to face her, she had come up to him, gently clasping his hand in hers, she pressed up against him. Without moving he felt her body as she moved her other hand to his chest. In

223

that instant, he realized she no longer wore clothes.

"I've been waiting for you," she said.

The following morning, Howie knocked on Carlton's office door, then entered. "Hey Andy," he said.

"Phillips." He did not even look up from his screen.

"So, Andy. I wanted to check to make sure we're good on the project I'm working on."

"Yeah, yeah. We're good."

"Okay. So, we're clear. I'm working on ordinary translation work of no real importance, just day-to-day communications coming out of Iraq. Right?"

"Right," Carleton said it routinely. He blinked. "Is there anything else? I've got work to do."

"Nope. Nothing. That's all I got. Thanks." He went to leave then remembered the other command.

"One more thing. From now on, my hours will post without interruption, even if you do not actually see me in the office." Carleton stared at his screen. "Right," he said.

"So even if I'm not here, even if you don't actually record any work, my hours will remain the same and the paychecks will

continue to post to my bank account."

"Right."

"As a matter of fact, you will personally see to it that my work is covered by breaking it up and spreading it out among the other translators."

Still staring at his screen, Carleton said, "Right." "Good." Howie left quickly.

Back at his cubby, Howie gathered the items he thought he'd take with him when, in mid-gathering, he realized he neither needed or cared about any of it. All of it, any piece of memorabilia, any item of collectability—such as it was—could now be reproduced with a snap of his fingers, right? He already erased all traces of the manuscript from the Hamark network. He turned away from his desk to leave.

Time for a beer.

At the Providence, he leaned back in the booth, wearing a smile he knew would annoy anyone within its sneering distance. But, he couldn't help it. For the first time in his life, he felt like he controlled his fate like he had something to look forward to.

"Another?" Kathy asked.

Howie blinked. He hadn't even noticed her approach, something quite unlike him.

"Uh, yeah, sure," he said, "Thanks, Kathy."

She leaned over the table, looking him in the eyes as she poured the bottle into his mug. "You didn't get fired today, did you?"

"What? No. Why would you say that?"

"You're here at 11:00 in the morning; we only just opened an hour ago. If I hadn't caught a day shift from Francine, I'd never know it. But here you are."

"No, no, nothing like that," he said. "I just—" He had nothing. Little help, he thought.

"I'm on a remote assignment, working from home on a trial telecommute they're trying out at work."

His mouth worked before his brain knew he spoke. Somehow the excuse he needed had come to him before his mind had concocted the lie. Someone up there—out there—liked him, he thought.

"Oh okay," Kathy said. "That's good cause I'd hate to lose you. As a customer, I mean." She sat at the booth. Howie looked at her, eyebrow raised. He shot a look to the bar beyond her.

"Ah, don't worry. It's early yet. You're my only customer." She smiled as she looked at him. "We haven't had a chance to talk like this in ages."

He looked in her eyes. She was right, they hadn't sat and talked—just sat and talked—for months.

"So, tell me about this remote telecommute, you're working on."

"Well, it has to do with an old Middle Arabic work called *Kitab al Azif*."

Kathy repeated it. "What's that?"

"It's supposed to be an instruction manual for arcane practices of weird rituals."

"Really? And, what is it really?

"I don't know yet. I'm just figuring that part out."

"Remotely."

"Remotely."

"What's it mean? Kitab al Azif."

"It means The Record of the Buzz."

"Got you."

"Sure, sure," he said. He had stopped paying attention. The Elders, or their minions, had bailed him out of a minor jam with only some minimal pleading. He wondered what would happen if—

"Howie?"

Kathy stared at him expectantly.

He shook his head. "Sorry, Kathy. What?"

"Are you hungry? I can get you some lunch."

"Yeah, sure. Sure." As she went to fetch his meal, he slipped back into his thought process.

What would it mean if the denizens, if those who lived in the gulf beyond, if we can call it living, offered to grant his every request, his slightest command? I'm going to have to check this out, he thought.

Sitting at the booth, he focused on the table before him. He held his palms apart the length of the table. He whispered "Kalla bak Nakrimma." A bolt of electricity arced from the left to the right, surging like lightning. He shook his head; the light disappeared. He looked around the room, feeling guilty. Kathy caught his glance. She looked to the floor as he saw her. She hadn't seen anything, he thought.

I better be more careful, he thought. I better do more research to get better at this.

But first, time to visit Sonia again. After lunch, of course.

Later, as Howie lay next to Sonia, he held her as she dozed in his arms. She had met him at his apartment with a broad smile and some very naughty ideas, ones that made him quite pleased in the eight hours that followed. Now, as they basked in the warm afterglow, his thoughts turned back to plan the effort ahead. He'd have to push to the limits of what the Elders could and would provide.

"You do that a lot," she whispered, pulling him closer to her.

"Do what?"

"You sigh the deepest sigh," she said, "As if the world lay on your shoulders. It's as if you have this enormous burden as if the whole of the heavens were atop you."

He hugged her tightly, kissing her forehead. She smiled drawing him closer; he smelled her hair and skin, the scent soft and safe.

At the moment Howie kissed Sonia's forehead, Kathy stood up to get out of her auditorium seat at her World Lit class at GW. Her professor, Dr. Mark Jerome, had just finished the lecture for the final that would come the next week. Two other students stood before him to ask questions about it. Kathy walked to the front row to wait them out.

When her turn came, she remained seated as Dr. Jerome turned to her. He wore a striped Brooks

Brothers dress shirt beneath a blue flannel zip-up sweater with a turned-up collar, its corners pointing upward. "Hello, Ms. Merrill," he said. "How are you tonight, Kathy?"

"I'm great, professor."

"What can I do for you?"

"I have some questions."

He smiled grimly. "Well, that's what I'm here for."

"Have you heard of an ancient work called the *al Azif*?"

"*Al Azif*?" He looked at her quizzically. "It sounds familiar, I think."

"Yeah, it's a very old Persian or Arabic text. I'm not sure its author, but it goes back at least a millennium."

"Okay, that fits. I think I remember something like this. Keep talking: let's see if it will come back to me."

"Well, I don't know if I have much more. Ancient Persian or Middle Arabic, written around 1,000 C.E. It's supposed to be some sort of textbook or manual."

Jerome held his hand up. "Wait. I'm beginning to recall. Very obscure, almost irretrievably so. But I believe I know a resource." He moved to sit at his desk on the dais. He disconnected his PowerPoint then typed some keys. "If I'm getting this right, it's very cool. Exceedingly cool indeed." He leaned over to squint at his laptop. With his hand, he motioned for her to come up behind him.

Kathy walked over to the stage, stepping up to look over Jerome's shoulder. He typed more, then pointed to the screen. "There," he said. "*Al Azif*, the secret to the power of the ages. Definitely Middle Arabic, just at the beginning of the ascent of Islam."

Kathy looked at the web page. Dense text, coupled with frightful pictures, filled the screen.

"How come I couldn't find any of this?" she asked.

"Well, you don't have access to this sort of website. It's available to professional academics only."

Jerome stopped typing. He read aloud, "*Al Azif* is a text written in 738 C.E. by Abdul Alhazred, a writer in Damascus known as 'The Mad Arab.' Kathy stared.

Jerome continued, "Alhazred supposedly learned the secret of the Elder Gods, the Great Old Ones, a race of beings that lived before the dawn of our universe. These powerful gods—there's no better word to describe them—lived in the ages before the dawn of time. When our universe arose, they felt the infringement of their own world, their own realm. They have been combating our kind ever since."

"I don't get it."

"The Elder Ones, the Old Gods, had been banished by the forces that created our universe, exiling them to the edges, the fringes of existence. There, their power is very limited. Abdul Alhazred found a way to open our world to them, to allow them to enter where their power can alter the fabric of our existence. It can change the structure of matter, space and even time."

"Whoa."

"It gets worse."

"Worse?" She blinked. "*Worse?*"

"These Elder Gods are not subject to any restrictions in terms of going and coming and even their very existence goes beyond the pale of what we've come to understand as the laws of physics that govern our universe."

Kathy stared off. She felt a chill.

"Professor, what would happen to someone who read this text? Suppose someone got their hands on this *al Azif*?"

Jerome shrugged. "Well, the work was lost ages ago."

"Well, suppose it's been found? Suppose someone had it now and had translated it?"

Jerome leaned back. "Oh, Kathy, that would be very bad indeed."

Kathy gasped. "Howie." She gathered her things. "Look, Professor, thanks for your help. I really appreciate what you've told me. But I've got to go."

"You want to tell me what's going on?"

She stopped her movement out the door, pausing to stand before her teacher. Looking up at him, she said, "I'd love to but I've got to go now and, to tell you the truth, I really don't know for sure myself."

She ran out of the auditorium to head to Howie's place.

Kathy ran the whole way to the street. Then, in an act she almost never engaged in—because no self-respecting D.C. native does—she hailed a cab. Twenty minutes later, she stood outside Howie's apartment door.

After she knocked on it, she heard Howie's voice say, "It's open." At least, she thought it was Howie's voice; its timbre sounded all wrong.

Kathy pushed the door open with her fingers. She stared openmouthed at the scene awaiting her.

The room was near pitch black as no light seemed to enter from the outside world. Had Howie blacked out the windows, she asked herself. No, the answer came back as her eyes became accustomed to the gloom, the windows had disappeared.

Howie's apartment now occupied a different space, the end closest to the street had melted away to expose the whole side of the room to an empty realm where space itself opened up to an infinite view. Kathy saw an entire alien landscape stretching out from the edge of the apartment, where the hardwood flooring gave way to a vast open area unlike any she had ever seen. She stood at the edge of a gulf. Kathy saw orbs of red and white light careening in arcs against the heavens, exploding into bursts of illumination to render themselves against the darkness.

The landscape itself held no life, not a tree, not a blade of grass, as a barren dirt reached out to the far horizon. The black sand-like ground glistened faintly under the dim light from above.

As Kathy moved forward, her feet slipped slightly as she walked onto a wet surface. It was so dark, she could hardly see her shoes. She squinted as she tried to see where he was in the dark. "Howie?"

"I'm here," the voice came back.

"Where? Howie, what the fuck?"

"Yes. Yes, what the fuck." His voice sounded beaten and exhausted.

Kathy stepped carefully so as to not slip on her ass, her movements slow and measured. She began to see a little better in the dark as she progressed, her eyesight getting used to the dim light available.

Before she knew it, she was on top of him. He sat on the ground a few feet from the gaping opening that emptied into that infinity. In the darkness, his back to her, she could only just make out the object on the floor with him. They were kind of large, but in the dark, couldn't really see.

"Howie, what is going on? What are you doing?"

"Ah, important questions." His voice sounded hammered as if he had been pulling an all-nighter. "But, you know, aren't these questions for all of us? I found out the hard way that the Gulf changes you. It takes back what it gives. It demands from you in equal to what it bestows."

"Cut the crap, man. What's going on?"

"I fucked up, Kathy. I fucked with the primal forces of the universe."

"Howie, I really don't have time—or the patience—for this."

"Of course not. Of course, you don't."

She pulled her lighter, the one every waitress carries, out of her pocket. Holding it over her head like a concert-goer, she thumbed the wheel.

As the flame came to life, she saw Howie clearer. He sat cross-legged on the ground, covered in blood. His face drenched in red and his arms, his chest, he sat wearing only cargo shorts steeped in gore, on a floor flooded with blood. It was the wet Kathy had felt on her feet.

Howie's face was half-eaten to the skull, the bone of his forehead, his cheek, gone altogether. His eye on that side floated loosely in its socket. The eye turned to look at Kathy, its unblinking glare making her skin ignite with cold. A dent in the side of his head warped his face even more. The jaw exposed to his chin, the mandible and teeth showing through the rotting flesh. His hair, mostly gone in a jagged pattern of burnt-out roots, hung, what little still clung to his head, in long strings that fell over his shoulders.

Kathy gasped.

"Yeah, I know," he said. "My world-famous boyish good looks are all gone now."

Kathy looked at the apartment floor. Bodies in various stages of dismemberment littered it. She saw arms, legs and four torsos lying about in different positions. She gasped at the sight. She saw Bob's head lying on its side. And Frank's. Howie held a bone saw in his blood-caked right hand. The saw dripped as he held it.

She whispered, "Howie, wha—" "Yeah," he said.

"I've been kind of busy."

He raised the saw as he moved toward her.

Lanterne: Mix
Linda Jenkinson

Mix
toad's tail,
brown bat's fang into this death mix

Of a Curious Matter in those Tangled Fishing Lines
Kamalendu Nath

Alas... being dragged in this sudden death-grip,
Aghast at the crushing scale rise, all rushes in -

It'd all started with a litter - flying, streaking out a speeding
Car, driven by a 'law', that I was behind, on my way to Conway -
Made me pull over on the shoulder of the deserted *Kangamagus*
Highway, in search of that litter... when just beyond – pristine *Lily Pond* beckoned... I trotted down to its rear shore... tumbled And found myself anchored by a huge trunk – monstrous canopy.

Little did I know what lay in wait – that I'd be sucked in a Void; since no good deed does ever escape - sinner's exploit.

Thin, taught fishing lines, white as cotton twines, glowered on Dangling; hanged from several water-logged brown branches.

In mind's eye flashed our Junk-troop's zeal Collectors be we girls of litter strewn steals!
Haunted by those shameful discards, callousness, destined to

235

Choke this pristine pond raised my hackles... I pulled at a

Tangled line - more - yet more, when in a blistering

Shake came this one loose - to spool and Behold! - lassoed at

Its end lay a horrible pinkish-white scaly being; no more than

Few inches long, glistening fiery scales scorn -

But for those eyes, staring – unblinking and still! I shivered... *Harriet? Wasn't she expecting me...?*

In frenzy untangled another to see what shock is to unfold from this lot -

Only an inch long Live-dead scaly... I was drenched in goosebumps -

Jennifer! Wasn't she missing somewhere upstate New York?

My best friends- I shivered, of these forms? Drawn in...

As if in mocking there went a flying litter at vision's end, out

A speeding car... setting up a ripple; corrupting the pristine...

And as if on cue as suddenly gripped me – a huge *teardrop*

From canopy plopped, my neck across, white, thin, taught

Lasso grip... *vengeance?* I whimpered; gulped for air in choked Screams as I was dragged while shrinking and growing silver scales, fins...

How else could a mocked pond renew its soul pristine?

Carnival Carnage
Samie Sands

God damn 4th of July. It's such a farce!

Every year it's the same old tosh. We have this massive celebration which begins with all the nearby family coming around to ours for a barbeque at lunchtime. This is followed by a good couple of hours with us all pretending not to *totally* hate each other like we do the rest of the year. Then, when all the adults are suitably drunk and things *could* descend into chaos, we pack up and head out to the carnival in the town square.

That bit actually has the potential to be quite fun, if I didn't have to spend the time babysitting my two bratty five-year-old cousins Jack and Jill (nope, not even kidding! Who calls twins such ridiculous names?) and hang about with Daniel. He's the same age as me, but *such* a loser. He loves all sorts of geeky shit and just has absolutely zero social skills. I do *not* know what he does with his time. Luckily, we don't go to the same school. He's far too embarrassing to have around my mates, so I end up spending most of the time trying to avoid everyone I know.

Don't judge me, I actually have a *good* reputation around here, but as we all know, popularity is a fragile thing. Hard to build up, but any little thing can knock you right off the social ladder, straight back down to the bottom. I refuse to have that happen because of my idiot family.

If I'm totally honest, the worst thing of it all is that my bloody mother *always*, without fail, forced me to wear a dress. I have to "Look like a girl for once". She is so God damn old fashioned. People don't wear dresses anymore—that's why jeans were invented for Christ sake! I stare at my unfamiliar reflection and huff, tugging at the hem uncomfortably. This just isn't me in any way. I need this day over with so I can go back to my real life.

Mid-morning brings with it a flurry or grandparents, aunties, uncles, cousins. I can't even begin to keep track. I keep the fake smile plastered across my face, even though inside I am screaming profanities and cringing. The afternoon passes slowly, *very* slowly, but without too much drama. It's surprising really, that all these people can bear to be around each other. After all, they spend the rest of their time bickering over money, child rearing and other pathetic issues. Why must they pretend now? It's so dumb. I'll never understand the politics of adulthood.

The television blares out the political speeches— another 4th July tradition, but I tune out, unable to bear listening. This day is dragging on and I feel so uncomfortable in the swishy, short dress it's unreal. The station finally flickers onto the news, and mum immediately silences it. As I watch the fading black, the inane chatter starts surrounding me again. Why is it that when adults get drunk, they just get louder and more stupid? Seems absolutely ridiculous to me, which is why alcohol has never tempted me.

I finally free myself to shove on some jeans and a plain t-shirt, as we are getting ready to leave for the carnival. The whole facade is embarrassing enough, without being seen in a dress. My parents are suitably out of it now, so I guess they'll never notice. The walk to the carnival is as awful as expected, the twins are screaming top note and running riot around me, and Daniel is blabbering on about Star Trek or Star Wars or something else I don't understand. They're all driving me nuts; I'm just about at the end of my tether. Glancing down at my watch, I can't help but wonder how much longer do I have to suffer this?

Before I know it, the familiar carnival music is blaring out so loud; I know we must only be moments away. I feel a sense of foreboding as I turn the last corner, almost as if I can sense something bad is going to happen. And then predictably, it does. I run smack into Kelly who is lip-locked with Kyle.

I'm too stunned to be humiliated, too angry to move. Kelly is my friend, my *closest* friend. I mean, I've always known that she was untrustworthy, we popular girls normally are, we have to be to survive the jungle of high school, but to do this? She knows how long I have been after Kyle—I have literally liked him forever.

"Bitch!" I spit the accusatory word out before I can regain control of myself before I realize that I am supposed to be incognito. A loud gasp followed by giggling ensures the knowledge that the twins have heard the profanity. I spin around to see them in fits of hysterics, with Daniel blushing brightly. I am too full of rage to think rationally. All I can focus on is a red mist that has descended around me. Kelly and Kyle have pulled apart.

At least they both have the decency to look embarrassed, but the wetness of their lips is too insulting for me to feel any forgiveness.

Angry tears sting my eyes, but I pinch my nose to stop them falling. I refuse to let them have that effect on me. Kelly starts stammering, explaining, but I can't help but notice she doesn't let go of Kyle's hand even once. He keeps a smug grin on his face the entire time. Why do boys enjoy girls fighting over them so much? It's just weird. I don't want to hear *anything* these two have to say, nothing will make their betrayal less painful, this horrible day any better. I instinctively turn and run off, back the way we came. Away from them, from everyone.

Monday at school is going to be *unbearable*. Any sort of drama draws everyone in, especially a bitch fight between two very popular girls—supposed best friends at that! I can't go through all this crap again. I know it sounds old and boring, but now we're so close to graduating, all I want to do is get my head down, try and achieve something so I can actually go to college. I've started to realize how important this whole education thing is *way* too late, I have so much to catch up on. This is the last thing I need.

I suddenly notice voices and footsteps running behind me. I whirl around, expecting an immediate confrontation with Kelly or Kyle, but no. It's just my cousins. The three people I least want to see in the world. "Just...go back." I pant, trying to stop the steady stream falling from my eyes. "I'll be there in a bit. I just need..." After a few seconds of silence, Daniel pulls me down to sit on the ground. The hardness of the floor pulls me back into reality and the tears become sobs that rack through my entire body.

Finally, I'm pulled out of my self-pity stupor by the twin's concerned chatter. I really shouldn't worry these kids; they don't understand the harsh reality of life yet. They have plenty of time to suffer all that I'm going through. I force a weak smile, and even though all I want to do is go home, I suggest going back to the carnival. I know they'll all want to; sitting with a crying girl will not be in any of their wish lists this holiday.

We walk back, me nervously behind the others. I'm frightened I'm going to see *them* again. One heartbreak a night is enough for me. As we turn the dreaded corner, my heart in my mouth, the sight before me is not what I expected.

High flames. Blackness. Grey smoke.

Everything is on fire. What the fuck is happening? Is this arson? I mean, I know I wasn't exactly looking forward to enduring this hell, but I can't imagine anyone going *this* far. I stand frozen as I watch the firemen shoot jets of water onto the flickering flames, creating more smoke and confusion. Where is everyone? What about the rest of my family? There must be an assembly point somewhere. We should go and find them; they're probably all panicking about us. They've got no idea where we are.

Grabbing hold of the others, we run off. We circle the area, looking for anyone and don't manage to stumble across a solitary soul. I start to feel like I can't breathe. I'm not sure if it's the smoke or the panic. What if everyone died in the flames? Is that possible? That means...

No, forget it. That's just an unbearable thought.

I finally find a fireman to ask. He looks at me confused before shrugging his shoulders, talking quickly and frantically at me in a foreign language. Frustrated, I shout after all of the firemen. But they ignore me, starting to leave. Aren't they supposed to make sure we are safe or something? I walk forward into the black and grey smoldering mess. The others follow I can hear their footsteps and breathing behind me. The twins are whispering to each other. I don't know how much they understand about what's happening and I have no idea how to even begin to explain anything.

Nothing. No one.

I turn to Daniel, my confused expression mirrored in his. What do we do? A noise to my left causes me to spin round. Someone to ask, finally. "Hey!" I call out to the shadowy figure as it moves slowly forward. I shield my eyes, trying to get a clearer view. "Hi, um...We just need some..." I trail off as the person becomes clearer. Kelly. That bitch. She looks a bit banged up, possibly burned, but she's walking around, so must be fine. I turn and stalk off in the opposite direction, refusing to deal with her right now.

The others stay close behind me, obviously unable to make any choices for themselves. Much as they're starting to annoy me, I'm more consumed by relief that at least *someone* else is here. I wish we knew where to find everyone else. I've tried ringing mum, but I guess my network is down. Typical. Phones never seem to work when you need them to most.

The silence rings out, deafening in my ears. My sight is restricted to just in front of me. So, when a loud, high pitched scream, full of terror, pierces the air, it induces immediate terror. "Daniel? Jack? Jill?" I question quietly so as not to disturb the obvious mass murder that is about somewhere, trying to bump everyone in this town off. I push forward, reaching in front of me, trying to hold onto one of them. My hands shoot relief through my body as I touch hair. I almost let out a relieved giggle.

The hair is matted and wet, almost like someone has been swimming in the ocean. It must be Jill, she must have done something when I wasn't looking. I move closer, inhaling. The scent of ash and burnt meat makes me gag, fires seriously stink! I pull Jill in close, inexplicably scared. *Growl.* I snap my head down towards the little girl. Why is she doing that? Suddenly a hot radiating pain takes over, starting in my wrist. I want to scream out, but my mouth feels like it has been sewn shut. I want to move, but my feet feel like lead.

When the mist descends from my eyes, I see a sight before me, which makes no immediate sense, but spells danger to my brain all the same. A woman, not a girl, certainly not Jill, who is covered in blood and pus, her clothes all torn, a bone sticking out from her leg, has her teeth sunk into my arm and seems to be relishing the taste.

I tug my arm back ripping off a chunk of skin as it drags against her mouth, and force my legs to run. I try to block out the pain, try not to let it get to me just yet. Isn't shock supposed to set in at some point, taking over everything else? Distracted, I somehow manage to run smack into a tree, the motion sending me flying back to the ground. The radiating agony in the front of my head blacks everything else out for a single moment.

When I finally come back around, I can feel and see a red sticky liquid running down my face. Blood. Well, that's just great. Just another problem to add to the long list. I look around, confused by the eerie atmosphere. Seriously, this seems like some kind of nightmare. If it weren't for the excruciating pain over all of my body, I could almost let myself believe that this hideous day hadn't even begun yet. That I'm still in my bed. Waiting.

I stagger upright, trying to work out what I should do next. My brain is all...fuzzy. I wish there was some around I could ask for help. If I get back to the smoldering embers of the carnival I might be able to find Daniel or the twins. I think back to my reluctance to be seen with them only hours before, now I'm desperate to see a familiar face, especially one of theirs.

I see in the mist ahead of me, moving shapes. It looks like people, but they're moving weirdly. Sort of jerky and very slowly. I speed on, wanting to find someone, wanting to know what happened here. I reach the group. There are eight people here, but they aren't really...human. They're covered in blood and rot and they smell like gone off barbeque meat. What's with these people? I walk up close to them, wanting an answer. One of them snarls and snaps their teeth at me, before sniffing the air and turning away. I get up in one of the girls faces. Her curious eyes follow me and send shivers up my spine. Her irises are completely white. In fact, all of them look like this. I try and speak to them, but am met with low growls and groans.

They circle around me, staring at me, half disgusted, half curious. I'm sure my expression is the same. One of them is dragging a bloody stump behind him where his leg used to be. He doesn't even seem bothered by this. Nor does the girl who has an obvious stab wound in her stomach—that must hurt like hell. She must be all sorts of tough!

Suddenly a gunshot rings out in the distance. As my head snaps around, searching for help, so does all of theirs. Quickly they are ambling away, any interest in me waning. I follow behind, unsure of what else to do. At least they might lead me somewhere safe. Twelve more gunshots ring out, keeping us all on the right track. I wonder what the significance of the thirteen shots is. A boring history lesson flicks into my mind, somehow familiar, but it is gone before any particular memory can click into place.

As we amble, I can feel my body getting heavier, my mind getting more sluggish, my emotions becoming null and void. What is happening to me? The bite mark on my wrist has, somewhere along the line, turned completely and utterly black—what does that mean? I think I need to get to the hospital. I don't panic though like I normally would. In fact, I feel weirdly serene.

A noise distracts my trail of thoughts. I look up to see the group I was following, all knelt to the ground looking at something. I move in closer, curiosity getting the best of me. I quickly see blood splattering everywhere, which confuses and intrigues me equally.

Vomit fills my mouth when I realize exactly what they're doing. They're *eating* someone. Cannibals. That could quite easily have been me. These people are sickoes. Unless, could this be some kind of zombie apocalypse prank? I think I remember someone doing that in the UK a while ago; someone won a few million on the lottery and created a zombie-infested town to trick his mates. Is this what's happening? Then why did I get bitten, that's a bit much, isn't it? Weirdo! Why aren't I in on the prank? I wish I knew for certain because everything is getting a bit much for me now. All I want to do is cry—and that isn't like me at all.

* * *

I feel like I haven't seen anyone for days. I have no idea how long I've been wandering about but my emotions are flicking rapidly between despair and frustration. I need some help. I've got to find Daniel and the twins at least. Then we can all head home to see if we can find the rest of our family. Then I'm going to sleep this shitty day off once and for all. Next year I'm not doing a single thing to celebrate 4th July. I'm staying indoors, locked in my room.

I slump down onto a rock, my body refusing to carry on. I think I must sleep or blackout. I have no idea how long for, but when I awaken, the sight before me pushes my mind to its very limit. A dead body lies at my feet. I push back, eyes flicking around, worrying about my own life. Why would those cannibals have eaten this guy and not me? In my haste to move, I nick my wrists, causing black goo to seep from the wound. Could it be this that stopped them? A newfound gratefulness for the woman that bit me overtakes.

I move away as fast as my ailing body will let me. But as I'm going, something inside me shifts, a new emotion takes over. It's hard to describe, even to myself. It sort of feels like a blinding, blackout rage. Suddenly, I don't want to run anymore. I want to stop, to turn, to fight. I don't though because I know it isn't rational, my brain is at least allowing me that much common sense. I keep running until I come across an unusual, intriguing sight.

People. Hundreds of them, all crying, wrapped in blankets, some burnt, badly hurt. Instead of feeling sad, like I know I should, or happy that I'm no longer alone, I feel a rush of something different. Excitement? Lust? Before I know it, I'm charging forwards, bearing my teeth. I don't care anymore about what is right and wrong, all I want to do is copy the cannibals and feel some flesh against my teeth. It's not hunger driving me, more a desire to cause harm, pain, to inflict fear. I want all the people to be pushed to the brink of despair. I want them to experience emotions they didn't even know they could feel.

A loud scream explodes and people fly in every

direction. I am slower than them, but the fear I inflict stiffens some of them, allowing me to grab hold. Sinking my teeth into tissue at every opportunity, a rush of euphoria running through me every single time, just to chew on it and spit it out. Once I have bitten a person, they become nothing to me. I have no further use for them, so I toss them aside onto the next.

I hear a voice; it's calling out a name. A stirring of recognition inside causes me to stop. Is that...my name? I turn, feeling a sense of déjà vu, of familiarity, blood dripping down my chin. A group of people behind me, all nervously stepping in my direction, chattering incessantly.

My family. I look at them curiously. What are they doing? I edge closer to them and they rile backward, afraid I realize. They don't need to be frightened of me - I know I attacked others, but I love them, I wouldn't do it to them. Good old Daniel bravely comes closer, the twins cowering behind. He's speaking to me, but I am too transfixed on the saliva glistening on his lips to hear any words. His arms outstretched, wishing me forwards. I step, willing myself to play this cool. If I'm ok with Daniel, the others will trust me and accept me again.

I lean into him, nestling into his chest, breathing in his familiar scent. I smile as I eventually pull back, pleased with myself. I have proved that I can do this. It's only when I stare into Daniel's tearful eyes, his open mouth, that the familiar metallic scent of blood wafts into my nostrils. I realize I have a massive chunk of his neck in my mouth. He falls to the floor, the weight of his body too much. The others run away bellowing out screams. I spit the dirty flesh on the ground. That moment was a game changer. Now all I can focus on is my need to devour them all.

* * *

Hours later, everyone in the entire town is either an unfortunate casualty or just another member of the shuffling army that I seem to be leading. I don't know why everyone has turned to me, but I am relishing the power and position. Almost as if it's my destiny to be in charge. I look around and try to grin at the familiar faces I have spent the day with, including many members of my delightful family, but my jaw is slack and destroyed from the battle.

We move forward slowly, but with avid determination. None of us know exactly what happened to our little town carnival this Independence Day, no one is even sure why we're like this. The only thing we collectively know now, is there are no humans left here for us to infect, to recruit. We need to move on; we need to take over the next place. Nothing will stand in our way.

The Witch's Spell
Linda Jenkinson

That heaviness you feel is the witch's spell
cast in the deepest of the night.
You must stave it off,
Never scoff
Elst it give you a nasty bite

The Kodak Troll
Joanne Magnus
1

Jason and Bobby were visiting Bobby's Uncle in Henrietta NY, which is a suburb of Rochester NY. Both were in the tenth grade in Pittsford Sutherland High School. Pittsford was a little further away from Rochester and another suburb. Pittsford was also one of the more affluent suburbs, built on the wealth of the Kodiak Corporation, Bausch and Lomb, Xerox and the University of Rochester. The boys had heard about the subway from their friends and relatives. It was a spooky place! People went in there and didn't come out! That's what made it more interesting!

Jason had a cell phone sticking out of his back pocket, Bobby grabbed it and flung it into the subway.

"You jerk!" Jason screamed, "One of those homeless creeps could have stolen it by now!"

"Go get it or buy a new one!"

"You get it! Bobby, you threw it in there!"

"Alright, we'll both go in, you chicken!"

They walked inside the subway to retrieve Bobby's lost cell phone. As soon as they got inside the subway its blackness enveloped them and the smell was so bad it could knock someone over.

They went up to one homeless man and teased him. He swung at them and the teens ran away deeper into the subway, snickering. He didn't have the cell phone. Bobby had a good throwing arm; they both thought they heard the phone hit the pavement deeper in the subway.

In 1919, the city council of Rochester, New York felt that the canal system that brought Rochester so much prosperity in the 1800's was an eyesore. The Council noticed success of other cities like New York and Chicago and their Subways and decided to build their own. After all, with Rochester's horrible winters, a subway is just the ticket to get to work without plodding thru several inches or feet of snow.

The subway opened in 1927, and it ran from Broad St. to Driving Park Avenue. The busiest times for the subway was during World War II when General Motors was making war supplies and Kodak was making newsreels and films. After the war, General Motors moved to the suburbs and people of Rochester moved out with it. The subway fell into disrepair. It closed on June 30th, 1956. For over fifty years it had been a haven for the homeless so much so that census takers go down there every ten years to get an accurate count of the city of Rochester population.

The abandoned subway became darker as the teens went in further.

"Bobby, call my cell phone and see if we can hear it ring," Jason suggested, "This place is giving me the creeps. If we hear one of the homeless guys has it then I'll just get a new one." "I don't know if I can get a signal," Bobby said.

Bobby called the cell phone. He was lucky, he had not lost reception because of the cement walls of the subway. The phone rang further in the blackness of the subway. The teens wondered if they should go any further.

"Wow, you really threw it far!" Jason commented.

"Too far, maybe, we'd better go!" Bobby cautioned

staring into the darkness, "Come on, your Dad can buy you a new phone."

Jason didn't hear Bobby's caution, he ran right into the darkness to retrieve his phone. He didn't want to have to go to his Dad for a new phone. His Dad would be mad. He would have to tell his Dad where he lost it and he would be in more trouble. Bobby ran after him with his phone on. He used his phone as a flashlight.

"Jason wait up!" he called.

They found the cell phone blinking on the cement floor another hundred feet inside the darkness. Jason quickly grabbed it off the floor and checked it. The phone was in good shape, a little scuffed around the edges, and seemed to be working fine. Bobby caught up to him a moment later.

"Come on, Jason, let's get out of here!"

Jason tried to call home on his phone but they were too deep underground at this point in the abandoned subway and there was no signal. They headed back toward the opening using the phones as flashlights when they saw a figure quickly swish across their path in front of them in the darkness. Both teens stopped in their tracks.

"Did you see that?" Jason choked.

"Come on, let's get out of here!"

The figure stopped in front of the teens, and the smell of urine increased two-fold.

2

The officers radioed in the situation. Something was wrong no doubt. Jason was soaked from head to toe with some kind of mud or slime as well. Within minutes squad cars surrounded the area of the entrance of the abandoned subway. Jason's parents were called along with Bobby's parents and his uncle.

The news crew arrived moments later. A reporter stood in front of the entrance of the subway and the cameras pointed to her.

"This afternoon, two teens, Bobby Snowden and Jason Madison, each from Pittsford Sutherland High School were exploring the abandoned subway near Broad Street when they claim to have encountered what could only be described as an unknown creature lurking in the hallows of the eighty-five-year-old subway. We have one teen here now, Jason Madison. Jason, could you describe exactly what you encountered in the subway tunnel?"

The camera panned over to Jason who was shaking uncontrollably under a gray blanket. He was sitting on a rock outside of the subway. His face was covered in dirt, mud and cement dust. Jason's parents were kneeling beside him. His Dad had his arm around him. Jason's father glared at the news lady as if to say, "leave my son alone, hasn't he been through enough!" But Jason looked up to the camera and spoke. "It's okay Dad really."

"Son, you don't have to answer any questions!"

"If it will help Bobby, I will, please!"

The news lady nodded and Jason began:

"Bobby had thrown my cell phone in the old abandoned subway and we went down to get it. It was really dark and smelly down there."

The News lady asked, "Where there any homeless people down there?"

"There were a couple," Jason answered, "but they didn't bother us. They were asleep against the wall. We got down to where the phone was. It was sitting in the middle of the floor way down deep in the subway. It was blinking and we could see it really well because it was so dark. Anyway, we heard this thing move across the subway behind us. It sounded like a rock rolling across the floor so we decided to hurry up and get out of there. Then this thing stood in front of us, the ugliest thing I had ever seen! It looked like a hairy Hulk."

Jason started to shake and cry but he continued, "It was huge and slimy! We could only see it by the light of our cell phones. It had red, glowing eyes! We could see snot dripping from its nose and mouth! Its teeth looked black. I think it was made out of stone, but there were these huge black hairs coming out of its chest and its arms and on the top of its head. It grabbed Bobby and me. He tried to bring us back into the subway more. We tried to fight it off but it was too strong. Finally, I was able to get my cell phone out and I tried to blind it by flashing a light from my camera into its face. I flashed the light and it seemed to turn into stone for a moment. I was able to get out of its grip and I was trying to help Bobby when it started to come back alive again. I tried to flash it again but the monster knocked my cell phone away and went after me again. My cell phone was smashed. I ran away as fast as I could to get help. Oh, please you have to help Bobby."

The news lady next turned to one of the Rochester policemen, who came to the subway after Jason, got him.

"Could you tell us what happened, when you arrived at the abandoned subway tunnel?" the news lady asked.

"We went down into the subway," the policeman answered, "We found the broken cell phone, but we didn't find any evidence of Bobby Snowden."

"Do you think this could be some kind of hoax?" the news lady asked within earshot of Jason.

Jason yelled, "It's not a hoax! That thing has Bobby!"

"We don't believe it's a hoax," the policeman maintained, we haven't finished our investigation yet and the FBI has been called in. We cannot comment any further."

"Mrs. Snowden," the news lady turned toward Bobby's mother, who was standing nearby, "Do you have anything to say to the person or persons who abducted your son?"

"Please, just let him go," she cried on camera, "Whatever you want, we'll get it for you! Just let my son go!" "This is WHAM news," the lady finished.

Within two hours agents, Marcy Baker and Manny Hiriam arrived on the scene of the abandoned subway tunnel. Manny knew the Bobby Snowden's Uncle from the FBI, they were retired agents. Marcy Baker was now Manny's assistant. Her original partner was killed in West Virginia and Manny, an experienced FBI agent decided to take her on and finish the rest of her training. Rochester was a short flight from New York City. To drive to Rochester would take five hours, at least, depending on traffic. Time was of the essence if they were going to find Bobby Snowden alive. As they got off the plane they saw the Amber alert for Bobby Snowden, missing and endangered.

3

Manny and Marcy walked all the way back to the back wall of the abandoned subway. It was a cinderblock wall that had been put up long ago. The subway, before Rochester, filled it in went on for miles. Filling it in kept the subway from becoming an underground city. They stopped filling it in at the base of the wall.

"Let's go back," Manny said, "I don't see anyone here."

They turned to go back and the creature was standing right behind them

That's where Rodger Snowden found me, seventy years ago, in the old steam tunnels underneath Kodak on Lake Avenue near

Ridge Rd. where I was basking in the steam on a cold January day." The creature pushed a button on the left side wall and the wall. The wall opened ten feet and the creature walked in. The agents followed behind it.

"Your century?" Marcy asked as the agents followed the creature in, still holding tightly to their guns, "Was that the homeless fellow sitting against the wall?"

"Yes," the creature answered, "He scouts out potential dinner choices for me. I let him keep any treasure I find on my meals. I think he goes and sells the stuff I give him for alcohol that I find from various bootleg stashes around the city. It's a working arrangement. I'm known as the Kodak troll, by the way, I try to keep to the shadows as much as I can. I can travel all through the city through the old Kodak steam tunnels and the old abandoned subway. People see trolls and they get their pitchforks and try to kill us when all we want is to be left alone. I enjoy

Rochester. In the winter time, the steam tunnels under Kodak used to keep me nice and warm. Many of them have been shut down because Kodak is pretty much through as a company. That's why I hang out near the subway now. The winters are a little milder here now and the warmth from the Genesee River keeps it above freezing at least. Oh, but I miss the steam tunnels! It was like a sauna in there! I could roam the entire length of the North side of the city practically up to Greece and Lake Ontario!

"I was once human," the troll continued on as he led the agents through various tunnels, "About a century ago. The chemicals and dyes from Kodak and General Motors turned me into my present state. I can turn into stone at will or by being exposed to sunlight. Now, I'm over one hundred years old. I'm

not going to die anytime soon if you call this living!" "This is my only form of heat now," the troll lamented.

"Do you cook your food on this spit?" Manny asked.

"Yes," the Troll answered, "I was just about to tie the boy on when I noticed he was a descendant of Rodger. I was going to say the heck with it and eat him anyway when all the news reporters came by and my century came in to tell me what was going on. The other boy got away because he flashed that light from his camera in my face. The light had the same frequency like sunlight and temporarily turned me into stone. It was brighter than your flashlights. I wonder if Kodak developed the flash. Once I recovered I brought the whelp inside."

"Do you cook them alive?" Marcy asked as she helped Bobby up.

"Oh, yes," the Troll answered, "Gotta make sure my meat is fresh! No one hears them scream down here!

They only suffer for a little while! I'm glad I'm not eating him anyway, he would only

be a snack, no meat on him, and no tasty fat!"

Manny, Marcy, and Bobby gasped in horror.

"Now, I need a favor from you," the Troll demanded, "I need you to go out there and say that this whelp was just hiding in the shadows of the subway and this was all a prank.

The troll quickly got up and took a swing at them and they ran out the opening into the subway and the wall closed behind them.

They had no chance of defeating the Troll now, they had to run.

Selfie
Alex Winck

All right, I admit. I´m one of those d-bags that post pictures of everything on Facebook and Instagram. Pictures of food, ten pics a day of my beautiful little girl, of my dog, and selfies. Shitloads of selfies. I´m worse than hot bimbo chicks about that. Yeah, I know my friends often give a like just to be polite. What can I do, I post it cuz I love it? When I look at my pics, my life suddenly looks like it´s all roses. I forget the fucking bills, wife´s PMS, boss giving me shit, traffic jams...

One day, I notice something quite weird. There´s a selfie of mine that I have no recollection whatsoever of taking. It´s me in front of the large mirror in my bedroom, with my old Kiss t-shirt I love. It´s my usual pose, a little smug grin, trying to pull a George Clooney look. No one shared it, that´s my own post. I didn´t take any new pictures, did I repost an old one and completely forgot about it? But it´s weird that I have a goatee. I never had one before, I only started growing it a few days ago and didn´t take any pic with it yet. Well, it´s just a picture anyway. A lot of people liked it, Nick and Celine say I look better this way... Never mind.

Pretty fucked up day. Bank calls me again to charge my credit card debt. Bought on impulse a Fender Stratocaster. Fucking stupid mid-life crisis. Four classes and I realized I´m not even a three-chord guitar player. Realize I´ll have to embellish a little company cash for me.

Next day, I see the picture again. At first sight looks exactly the same. But I take a second look. I get the feeling that something´s different about my face, but I can´t put my finger on it. The smile looks the same, but it seems like the mouth looks slightly different. But it´s a minimal, practically unnoticeable thing.

Fucking hell shit, boss found out about the scam! Fired and indicted! Some suck up asshole ratted me out. Fuck it, they won´t be able to prove anything, I didn´t even manage to take the money! But now the fucking bank will butt-rape me for all I got and company´ll burn down my rep to the ground.

The next day, to relieve the stress a little, I´ll post this cool pic of my dog stretching in the yard... but then there´s another selfie I know I didn´t take. In this one I have a more open smile, showing a little more teeth. I don´t like to smile like that for pictures, it makes me look, I dunno, kinda devious or something. My friend Gina even points that out in a comment. But what I can´t get out of my head is where do these pics come from? How could I take a selfie, post it and not remember it? Is it some weird prank? Somebody hacked my profile, did a little Photoshop job on my pics and posted them? I decide to write a status. Ask whoever´s doing this to stop, that this is not funny at all, just annoying. This time I delete the photo.

Kelly, my college ex, started to kinda stalk me on Facebook. Talks to me almost every day, but she insists she doesn´t wanna get back together or anything, we just sext a little, she sends me pics of her fine ass, I send pics of my wang. Some time, when I put some of my shit back together and my head cools off a little, I´ll totally hit that.

And there´s the fucking stupid picture again! Now it´s an open smile, and my eyes are a little weird, wide, I never do that. My expression looks increasingly perverse and creepy. Even my dog´s pic looks a little different. He no longer has his tongue out, curved from stretching, he looks stiff, eyes shut, like he´s sleeping, or even... I report to the sites that someone has broken into my account. I´m thinking there´s some lunatic after me. Who the fuck´s doing this?

When I get home, I face a scene that makes all blood run out of my face. My dog, dead, lying at the porch, looking just like the picture. Worse thing is it was my own fault. In the morning, feeling sleepy, I mistook his food for cereal. The cereal had chocolate in it, which is terrible for dogs. There is no doubt anymore. Some maniac is chasing me, tormenting me. Somehow, has even access to my house!

I call the police, ask them to watch over my neighborhood. I wanted to delete my profiles from Facebook and Instagram, but they asked me to keep them because that could give out clues to this sociopath's next move. I remember that day, in the morning, I had taken a pic of my daughter dressed up as Hermione for Halloween. Terrified, I give up posting it.

The next day, it´s with trembling hands I turn on my laptop. I didn´t want to look at my profile. I take a deep breath before I click on it. First thing I see, I expected. My picture again now shadows over my face give my eyes and teeth this macabre look, like I´m a psychopath.

But that´s not what horrifies me. I see the pic I took of my daughter, the same I decided not to post yesterday. She glows and looks semitransparent, just like when characters in the Harry Potter series die and become spirits. I get up in desperation and yell my daughter´s name. I hear nothing and feel my chest tighten in agony. I get into her room and see her lying in bed. She´s wearing the costume. Next to her, a bottle of soda with a scent of almond that´s not from the beverage. It´s cyanide. She´s been poisoned. She wasn´t going out for Halloween anymore after the dog´s death. She was dressed up after she died. Next to the bottle, there´s a note, "with love, Kelly".

I tell the police to go after my ex. I don´t know where she lives now, I haven´t been with her in ten years and she didn´t put her address in her profile. Her IP was from a library computer. Police don´t have a clue to her whereabouts. My wife hates me, says I practically killed our daughter with my own hands. She´ll file for divorce as soon as the funeral´s done.

But what really intrigues me is the damn picture. I didn´t even post the one I had taken; how did she know about it? I decide to ignore the police and delete my profile. I don´t feel like ever looking at another screen, another picture.

Police find Kelly. She cut her wrists and left a note saying she couldn´t stand any longer to suffer over me, not being able to tell how she really felt. She was bipolar, but it never seemed that serious to me. She killed herself the day before my daughter was murdered, so it couldn´t have been her. Then, who? Am I being chased by what, an invisible being, an entity, a demon? What in God´s name is going on?

At the funeral, my cousin Arnold comes blazing at me. he had visited my profile to post a sympathy message. He asks if I lost my mind for good. I have no idea what he´s talking about. Then he shows it to me on his cell phone. My profile is there again, with another picture. In this one, I´m more than macabre, I´m bizarre. My eyes, my teeth are like spots, my face turned into a ghostly blur, a demonic creature.

Visceral hatred possesses me. I run home. I take a knife and coal from the fireplace. I get in front of the mirror. Use the knife to stretch the corners of my mouth, widen my eyelids, I don´t even seem to feel the pain, and coal to darken my face. I see the image of a freak, a monster. I see what I became. Those pictures were indeed a portrait. A portrait of the darkness growing and taking over my life, my soul, getting a life of its own. I point the phone. Take the perfect selfie.

Boo!
Debbie Johnson

October's moving in with its hosts
Ghouls, goblins, witches, warlocks, and ghosts
Pumpkins and gourds show bountiful yields
Scarecrows peer over grain-laden fields
Against harvest, moon thunderclouds roll
Eerie sounds are made by hallowed souls Shadows from unseen creatures are cast In the graveyard, is this night my last?

Heartbreaker
Kevin S. Hall

The town of Cliff Hill was no stranger to the odd bit of scandal over the years. From murders to infidelity and even a little incest, nothing really shocked its core anymore. That is until the She-Beast entered the town.

It was on a cold winter night. Snow had covered the ground quite thick and ice was on the roads. The woman wore a long red cloak covering her head, and in her hands, she carried a basket, but it was not a picnic. She looked like something out of a fairy-tale but this was no innocent human.

Her head was lowered as she came out of the snow-covered forest, standing on top of the hill, looking down at the small town. Tonight, she would feast and be reborn. This was her calling. Her time to shine. For now, though, she waited and looked up at the sound of a car's engine. Her eyes shone a brilliant yellow and she started to growl.

In the dark of the night, it was amazing Danny Millburn had seen the woman at all. Of course, later he wished he hadn't, but right now his main concern was for her. She was lying sprawled out on the road in a long red coat, a small red dress, and red shoes. Even her lipstick was red and she had long flowing red locks. Later people would call her the Red Woman Of Cliff Hill and she would go down as an urban legend.

Right now, Danny was drawn to her dark red

lipstick. Beside her was a picnic basket, seemingly sealed shut. The car screeched to a halt right near her face. He had nearly killed her. He got out and moved cautiously towards her, shaking her gently.

"Ma'am? Ma'am, are you hurt?" No response. He leaned in and checked her pulse. She was still breathing. He lifted her up and carried her into the backseat of the car, laying her down. Danny would take her to the nearest hospital and hoped he was rewarded in some way. He was about to go when he nearly forgot the basket.

Danny looked at it. It was no basket he had ever seen before. So big and with strange carvings on it that looked like heads. There was a latch on it but it seemed safe enough. He lifted it up and placed it in the seat beside him. Then he got into his car, starting the engine. He sped off back down the icy road towards home.

On the way, Danny kept glancing at the basket. It was making him nervous and he didn't know why. He had to keep his eyes on the road. The newscaster was reporting more snow and icy conditions ahead. He continued to look ahead. It was only a few moments later when he started to hear the whispering. At first, it sounded like many voices but then he could clearly hear three women, all sounding lusty.

"Open it, Danny...Look inside, Danny! Join us!"

Danny couldn't resist. He looked away from the road and began to open the latch...

That's when the woman in red jumped up and snarled, bearing her sharp fangs and sniffing with her long snout, her brown, furry hands outstretched with sharp, yellow claws. She grabbed hold of Danny's neck and bit down, causing the car to swerve and slide across the road. Danny screamed as blood oozed out of the large gash on his neck. The woman tore at his chest, ripping the flesh. The car swerved towards a large hill and flipped over, going down the snow-covered hill and tumbling for quite a long way before crashing into a tree.

Later, when the police officers and fire crew arrived and dragged Danny's bloody carcass out, they came across an even gruesome sight. His heart had been removed from a massive bloody hole on his body.

The She-Beast stood high in the woods watching, panting and growling before changing back into the woman she was before. In her hands, she held a still warm, dark, bloody heart. She snapped it with her hands and placed it in the basket. The first of thirteen. She disappeared into the woods and waited for the next one to come along. It wouldn't take very long.

The dark woods made Abigail Brenton very nervous. She was in her early twenties and blonde but definitely not stupid. She may be slim, sexy with big breasts, but she was studying for a Law degree and wanted it so bad she would read and read until the early hours of the morning. This was one such morning where she had overdone it and was returning home. This was the quickest route but it still didn't stop her from being on edge.

A lot of nasty things had happened here, but as long as Abigail stuck to the paths, she would be safe...right? She moved quicker, noticing a fresh batch of snow had started to fall. Would it ever let up? It was the beginning of February but it still felt like the depths of December. That's when she heard the snap of branches.

Abigail stopped, clutching her blue denim jacket around her for protection. She listened again. Only the wind through the trees, an eerie sound at the best of times. She walked on. There it was again, closer this time. There was someone or something moving out there. Abigail peered into the forest.

A woman in a long red coat was approaching her, carrying what looked like a picnic basket. It immediately reminded Abigail of her favorite Grimm's story and she smiled when the woman came near. "Jesus, you scared me," Abigail said, almost laughing. "Are you lost?"

The woman in red looked at her as if she had just been asked a mathematical equation. She stared for a few moments more, not smiling, just looking at Abigail up and down, sniffing the air. This made Abigail even more uncomfortable.

"Okay...I'll be off then..." Shaken a little (the stare had been unblinking, almost animal-like), Abigail turned and walked on at a brisk pace, dying to get out of these awful woods. Maybe the long way around should have been safer after all...

She could hear scampering behind her. Not wanting to look around, Abigail began to run, a lot faster than she had ever done before. She could see the exit of the trees up ahead, panting, her heart beating in her chest. She was going to make it...

Then she felt sharp claws dig into her back and Abigail screamed, falling to the ground with a painful thud. She lay there for a moment and then she tried to scramble away. It was too late. She was dragged backward at an alarming rate through the snow and through the trees. Abigail pulled and pulled and then she broke free!

It was all momentarily of course. Abigail looked around her and tried to get her bearings. She was deeper into the woods this time, and she could hear movement around her, followed by a low growling.

She was being stalked and hunted by something. This was no woman anymore. Abigail tried desperately to stand but her legs were sore and had turned to jelly. One ankle felt twisted too.

Then she saw it. A large wolf but standing upright, with dark shaggy brown fur and large pointed ears and a long snout. Its claws were poised and it was looking at her with large yellow eyes. It wasn't moving, just staring at her. Abigail wasn't stupid. She wasn't about to do any sudden movements. She backed away slowly, crawling along the ground. The wolf walked towards her slowly, sniffing the air, grunting.

Abigail scrambled more quickly, then her hand fell back onto a sharp branch sticking out of the snow and she looked away, crying out in pain. That was her mistake. The She-Beast pounced, lunging at Abigail and ripping her head clean off. It raised a claw and sliced open her stomach, blood and entrails spilling out, the bright red blood staining the shining white snow. The wolf howled in the night, another victim for its collection.

Then the wolf became the woman in red again. Standing there naked, her long red hair covering her breasts, she snapped the heart, placing it inside her basket. "Soon, my children," she whispered. "Soon you will be free."

She picked up her red dress and put it back on along with her red coat. Then, whistling Bad Moon Rising, she disappeared into the forest once again.

Raymond Bell heard the howl and immediately got out his rifle. He had heard stories of wolves out in these woods before but had never ever seen one. He wanted one's head mounted on his cabin wall, just for proof that he had one. He would be the envy of all the hunters in town.

Raymond was a middle-aged man in his forties, a large man with stubble and brown hair and a baseball cap. He wore a thick fur jacket over his black shirt and black jeans. Standing out here in the middle of the woods, he wished he had put on something a bit thicker. He shivered. Even though he was a brave enough man these woods still scared him. Wolf or not, if he didn't come home with something tonight he would be the laughing stock of the entire party come later today.

He started to move deeper into the woods, sniffing the air. There was a beast out there that was for sure. He could smell the damp fur. A bear or coyote maybe? A moose? Nah, it didn't smell like a moose. Raymond checked his gun and it was still fully loaded. He hoped he hit something. Anything.

There was the sound of something moving out there close by. He could hear it clear as day. Raymond moved towards a clearing. There, he saw a woman lying on the ground with long, red hair covering the top of her naked body. She only had on a small pair of frilly panties. Huh. There's something you don't see every day, especially out here. Raymond approached her, gun at his side just in case. It was no animal.

He knelt down, shaking her gently. Her head moved to one side and her hair fell away from her left breast. Raymond suddenly felt a bit horny. He reached down, looking around him. It would be all right...Just a quick touch...He reached out with a stubby hand.

That's when the woman's head turned around and her eyes snapped open, a bright yellow color looking at him menacingly. She started to growl showing sharp fangs. Raymond backed away, horniness gone and fear kicking in. He fell backward to the ground and backed up towards a tree.

She started to change before his very eyes. Her hands grew, stretching fingers and sharp yellow fingernails protruding from them. He watched in horror as dark, brown fur began to sprout from her body, covering her. She grew a long snout and her ears grew larger. Raymond yelped as she began to move closer to him.

"You are a disgusting human being," she snarled, her voice half human, half beast and not of this world. "You will now be mine!"

The She-Beast shoved a hand straight through the chest, grabbing his heart and pulling it out. Amazingly Raymond was still alive but only briefly. Just enough time to watch her turn back into a woman and snap his heart. He slumped back down—dead.

The woman in red laughed and tossed the third heart into her basket. Ten more to go. This was going to be too easy. Yet something would no doubt try to stop her. For now, though she chuckled and waited.

As a shortcut and a way to escape being detected, Andy Warren darted into the woods, laughing. That was a close one. The closest he had ever come to being caught. He was nineteen and had only been in jail twice. One for shoplifting, one for assault. He had been given warnings on both accounts but had gotten away with many more. He had gotten smarter but that had been cutting it fine. He now had a crate of twelve beers in his possession and sat on a wooden stump deep in the woods, opening the first one and drinking long and deep.

He had slick black hair, a baby face complexion and wore a leather jacket with a white t-shirt and low-cut jeans. He was very proud of his look, which was a throwback to the cool 50s and 60s. He would have loved to have been in that time and would have fitted in really well. He'd love to own a Plymouth Fury one day.

He was now on his second can when he heard crying coming from close by. Andy turned to look but saw nothing. Only the early morning light coming through the trees. "Hello?" he called out. No answer. He listened again but no more sound came. He shrugged, figuring it was just the wind and his mind playing tricks and took another sip of beer.

The crying happened again, closer this time. Andy got up and swerved around, dropping his beer and the liquid stained his jeans. Shit. He wiped them with his hands, getting angry. "All right, this isn't funny!" he shouted. "Whoever's out there better come out now! Oh, and you owe me a beer too!"

"Please..." A woman's voice. "Please...I need help, mister. Won't you come and help me?"

Andy peered into the trees and saw a woman lying against a tree with her back to his. She had a long red coat on and red hair. He wasn't afraid, just curious and still a little bit mad. He brushed himself down, ran a hand through his hair and began to move towards her. Maybe if he helped her he would finally go on a date with a beautiful woman. It would surely make up for all the bad ones he had dated in the past.

He stopped by the tree, noticing her hand was bleeding. "Miss? You OK? Do you need a doctor?"

She stopped crying and was now breathing heavily. From where Andy was standing it looked as if she was pleasuring herself. He smiled. "Andy...Andy wish to give me a hand?"

Andy smiled and walked around to face her. Then his smile faded. She had a long snout and was grinning. It was not her hand she was using, but a torn off arm of Raymond's. She cackled and threw the arm to the ground, jumping on Andy and knocking him to the ground. She began ripping at his clothes, tearing at his jeans and pants.

Andy wasn't sure whether to be turned on or afraid. He just lay there, unable to move. She had him pinned down pretty good. Then pain seared through his body and he started to scream. He felt warm blood trickle down his legs. He looked down and saw she had ripped off his penis. She was holding it up to her mouth, sniffing it in disgust. "Hmm..." she scoffed. "I've had bigger." She tossed it into her mouth, swallowing it whole. Then she went to work, digging into Andy's chest and removing his heart, breaking it in two.

A police car cruised up the motorway, unaware of the torture and bloodshed going on in the woods around him. He was just on duty now and Greg Henshaw scanned the outlines of the forest. All seemed quiet. It had been for the past four years – not since the last murder of the Clockwork Killer. Maybe Cliff Hill was finally becoming a safe place to live...

His police car came to a screeching stop. A woman in a red coat was standing before him, carrying a picnic basket and smiling at him. She was a thing of beauty all right. If he wasn't married...Greg stepped out of the car, his gun on his belt along with his stick just in case. He took out a torch and shone it at her. It looked as if she had blood on her lips and hands. She was still smiling at him.

"Evening, officer," she said, looking all innocent.

"Ma'am," Greg said, being polite. "Care to tell me why you are out in the middle of the road? You'll catch your death out here."

"I believe I am lost. I was looking for Cliff Hill you see. I have relatives there and I was planning a nice surprise for them."

Greg smiled. "I'm heading that way myself. Hop in, I'll give you a ride." The woman smiled at him and got into the passenger seat, clutching a basket. Greg hadn't noticed it before. "Want me to take that for you?"

The woman shook her head. No, it's OK. It's part of the surprise.

Greg nodded and got into the car, and they sped off towards town.

When they arrived, Greg let her out. "Can you make your own way from here?"

She nodded. "I think so. Oh, and officer?" He turned to her. "Thanks for your heart."

He looked at her strangely and she lunged for him, scratching his shoulder but Greg was quicker. He shot her in the shoulder making her yelp and draw blood. She growled at him and was about to strike out again when another police car was approaching. She looked at Greg, angry, and scampered off at an alarming rate towards the woods.

Greg tried to fire again but his shoulder hurt like hell. She had really torn into him. The other officer got out of the car and ran up to him. "Jesus, serge, are you OK?"

Greg nodded, feeling a little weak. "Go and get all available units! We have a female suspect, late thirties with long red hair wearing a red coat disappearing into the woods north of motorway 52! Go now! And call me an ambulance will ya!"

Officer Lester Barlow nodded, reaching for his walkie-talkie and repeating the message.

Greg started to feel faint. He then fainted.

He awoke to find himself in ICU, with a drip in his arm and his shoulder bandaged. His wife, Mary, was sat in a chair beside him, looking worried. When she saw he was awake, she looked relieved. Greg smiled weakly, making a cup pouring motion with his hands. Mary nodded and handed him a glass of water.

Greg took it and it soothed his throat. "How...how long have I been out, love," he asked.

She lowered her head, making him feel anxious and afraid. "Three weeks, hon. Three, long weeks."

Greg sat up slowly, wincing at the pain. "No...It only felt like a few minutes. Did they...did they catch that woman?"

Mary shook her head, looking scared. "We can't talk long. She could be listening..."

Greg looked at her. "What do you mean?"

Mary's voice was even shakier than before. "She has killed twelve times now. She needs one more to become Wolf Queen. You are the chosen thirteenth, Greg."

Greg shook his head. "No. No babe, what you are saying is crazy. She is only one woman. She can be stopped..."

Mary shook her head hard. "You don't understand. She is now in control of this town. She needs you and she's waiting for you in the woods. Stop her, Greg. Stop her and this nightmare will come to an end."

Greg discharged himself from the hospital. Everyone was afraid, frightened to do even the slightest thing. Greg wasn't going to let anything else happen to his town. This ended now. Tonight.

He got into his car and headed off towards the forest. It was still snowing outside. Was this part of the curse too? He didn't usually believe in anything superstitious or supernatural, but he did feel scared for the first time in a long time. There was some kind of evil gripping this town in a vice. He could sense it. He had read stories. Werewolf stories. It was just as well he had made several silver bullets a few years ago when there was talk of a monster man roaming the streets every full moon. Of course, it hadn't been real but he had been prepared all the same. Thank God, he hadn't used them then. There were four altogether. He hoped that would be enough.

Greg turned the car off the motorway and up the snow road leading into the forest. The trees were closer together here. He stopped the car next to some fallen logs and knew he had to walk the rest of the way. Getting out, making sure the gun was loaded, he started to walk into the forest. The folk he had talked to had told him of the place where the She-Beast was meant to be hiding and they had said you could not miss it.

They were right.

After a few miles walk, Greg stopped before a hideous sight. Two very large trees with large trunks were twisted together and formed a sort of cave. It was dark in there but it seemed to go into the side of the hill. He couldn't walk any further. This was the place. Feeling a little scared but trying to show his bravery, Greg ventured into the dark opening, flicking on his torch and placing it on his gun.

It stank. There was water drip, dripping from somewhere close by, and the place was littered with skulls. He could hear heavy breathing and growling coming from far away. In what seemed like forever he came across a large picnic basket, the one he had seen all those days ago. Approaching it slowly, Greg undid the strap and lifted it open, shining the torch inside. Twelve broken hearts, black and lifeless. There was room for one more...

A growl again, closer this time. Greg swung around, shining his torch down the uneven path. A tunnel at the far end disappeared around the corner. He could see a large wolf shadow on the wall. "I KNOW YOU ARE THERE, HUMAN," came the low, deep voice. I CAN SMELL YOUR FEAR. COME CLOSER. I HAVE DARK PLANS AHEAD FOR YOU..."

Greg wanted to turn and run, leave this hole and town forever, settle up somewhere new and forget about all of this. But he knew if he did that this beast would still be here. He had to stop it. "Why did you come to my town, bitch? Why did you murder all of those people!"

It growled angrily. Good. He was pleased it was angry. He wanted to make it mad. "I NEEDED TO FEAST TO BE STRONG. SO, I COULD WALK IN THE WORLD AS A BEAST FOREVER AND MAKE A WORLD SO MY CHILDREN COULD LIVE!"

Children?

Greg watched as one small wolf approached him, scampering towards him with yellow eyes and teeth bared. It jumped at him and he fired through the chest with one silver bullet. The creature yelped, crashing against the wall. Still.

Another skidded around the corner, snarling and lunged for his throat. Greg fired again – another clean shot ending its life. He was edging ever closer. The third wolf took him by surprise, coming out of a hole in the cave to his left. He swerved just in time and shot it in the head. It landed on him and he fell to the ground.

The beast laughed, low and deep. "I KNOW YOU HAVE ONE BULLET LEFT, GREG. IS THAT MEANT FOR ME? YOU DESTROYED MY CHILDREN. I

THOUGHT THEY WOULD PUT UP MORE OF A FIGHT. NOW I MUST DESTROY YOU."

Greg shoved the final wolf cub off his body and stood up, shaken but otherwise fine. He rounded the corner and stopped, shaking his head in disbelief in what he was seeing.

Sitting on a throne made of skulls and bloody entrails, was the She-Beast. She was much larger than before, and definitely not a woman. Her fur was now a thick black, her snout long and protruding. Her ears twitched and she was sucking on a long large bone with her now black claws. Her breasts heaved under the dark fur and she looked at him out of big yellow eyes. She laughed again, the sound echoing through the cavern. "LIKE WHAT I'VE DONE WITH THE PLACE?" She mocked. "IT'S NOT QUITE HOME YET. IT'S MISSING SOMETHING..."

Greg pointed the gun at her chest. "You can't be allowed to live! I must destroy you for the sake of this town!"

"HAHAHA.... FOOLISH HUMAN. DO YOU REALLY THINK A SILVER BULLET WILL STOP THE LIKES OF ME? I COULD CRUSH YOU LIKE AN INSECT YOU SMALL MINDED PRICK!"

Greg roared and went for the beast. She stood up, towering above him, and with one hand swiped him against the wall like a fly. Greg crashed against it, pain shooting up his arm.

The beast lumbered towards him and she reached for his throat, grasping a hand around it and started to choke him. Greg pointed a gun at her and it rested on her large, stinking black chest. "DID YOU REALLY THINK YOU COULD STOP ME WITH A PUNY GUN?"

Greg shook his head and smiled. "No," he said. "But

this might." With his other free hand, Greg dropped the torch and plunged it into the beast's chest, ripping its flesh and pulling out its heart. He had surprising strength did Greg, which he hadn't had before.

The She-Beast roared in surprise and pain, staggering backward and clutching her chest. "HOW?... HOW?..." It stammered, before crashing to the ground, still. Dead.

Greg could breathe easily again, coughing hoarsely. He broke the heart between his hands and threw it to the ground. Then he got up slowly, wincing a little at the pain and headed shakily out of the cavern.

The next few days went by without too much incident. Greg set about flattening the two trees and hill, piling more dirt and concrete onto it so nothing could escape or come after the people of Cliff Hill again. He decided to stay and look after them after all and his wife had luckily agreed. Now more than ever they needed him and were so grateful for what he had done. Greg knew that some of the folk here had dark pasts and things that they had done that they regretted, but so had he. As long as they respected the law he would try to uphold it.

It wasn't until the following night that the nightmare would return and try to destroy him again. The dreams had been getting worse. Mary had told him to go and see the doctor but he said they would pass and he would be all right. Greg hardly believed that himself. The nightmare was always of the She-Beast chasing him in the dark woods and he would almost get away...Until she was on top of him, tearing at him.

The nightmare tonight had been different. He was being the point of view of the She-Beast – or that's what he thought. He found himself walking around his house, stalking someone. He would approach the bedroom where Mary was sleeping. She was lying there, all peaceful. He approached her and began tearing into her flesh, and she would wake up screaming as he ripped out her heart.

It was when he turned to look in the mirror that he saw it was him and not the She-Beast that frightened him.

He awoke with a start, sweating. Greg checked the time. It was 3 am. He turned to Mary who was still asleep, He got up quietly and walked towards the bathroom, wincing at the pain still in his shoulder. That had been a nasty scratch he had got...

Oh, my God. How could he have been so stupid? He pulled off the dressing slowly, looking at the deep red scars. Brown fur had begun to sprout through them. No...No, no...He had to get out

of here now before he hurt her... "Greg, honey? What's wrong?"

Greg quickly put the bandage back over his arm and smiled at her weakly. "Nothing, babe. Just a bad dream. Go back to bed. I will join you shortly," he lied.

She nodded, returning to the bedroom, too tired to argue and he was glad for that. Greg took a sip of water and shivered, before slipping off downstairs. He had on trousers but slipped on a shirt from the screen and a jacket and headed out into the night. He needed to get as far away from here as he could. The woods weren't that far. He could make it...

He looked up at the sky. A full moon was high in the air. Greg ran. He could feel himself changing as he did so, his whole body contorting and twisting in so much pain. His snout started to grow. He could feel his ears enlarge. His claws were the worst, shredding through his skin like spears. He tried to get to the forest but his animal instincts were taking over.

He stopped just before the outline of the trees and turned around, scampering across the motorway. That's when the truck hit him. It knocked him flying across the road, skidding along it leaving a bloody trail behind. The truck swerved and nearly came off the road, but the driver was lucky and stopped.

Billy Graham stepped out, rushing towards the body. Jesus, he was sure it had been a wolf, but on closer inspection, it was a man, naked and curled up. What had the crazy fool been doing wandering around in the road in the first place? Billy took off his jacket and covered him. He was still alive but barely.

Greg started to move. "Don't try and move!" cried Billy. I'll call for help!"

Greg reached out a hand, grabbing Billy's. "No..." he croaked. "No time. My gun...Take it..."

Billy noticed a gun lying a bit away from Greg, along with some clothes. He walked towards it and picked it up. "What am I supposed to do, mister? Do you want me to call anyone?"

Greg shook his head. "The gun...Use it on me...End my life...I am suffering...Please..."

Billy shook his head. "I... I can't do that. I won't. They can still save you..."

"No. You saw what I was in the mirror. You know what I will become. Please. Do it now before it's too late..."

Greg pulled Billy's hands down towards his chest. Billy's hands were trembling and as he felt the cold metal on his chest, Greg closed his eyes. "Mister, I can't..."

"Now, Billy. Now. Tell Mary..." Greg squeezed Billy's hands and the gun went off, the last silver bullet entering Greg, ending his life.

Billy collapsed to the ground, sobbing.

Mary noticed the commotion a few hours later, red flashing lights outside her house. She noticed Greg wasn't beside her. Damnit girl, why had she been so stupid? She got out of bed, slipped on her dressing gown and went down to the front door.

There was a knock. "Mary...It's Officer Browning. I am afraid we have some bad news..."

Mary swung open the door, tears already forming in her eyes. "Please, John. Please tell me it's not true..."

John lowered his head and took off his hat. "I am sorry. His body was found on the motorway not too long ago. It looks like a hit and run. We have a patrol out looking for the driver now. Is there anyone we can call? Do you need help with any arrangements?"

Mary collapsed by the door, almost fainting. John caught her, holding her steady. "No...I...Yes. Call Sarah. She will need to know."

John nodded. "Again, I am sorry for your loss. Be strong, Mary. You have lots of friends in town."

Mary smiled and closed the door. She would have to examine the body of course but not right now. She had to go and check on something. Over the past few days, Greg had been working on folklore about the She-Beast. She had read that it needed thirteen hearts to become everlasting but it had failed. However, if Greg ate a heart he would be saved. He could live again and never have to eat another one. She would make sure of it. She would look after him and nobody would ever have to know.

Maybe it was the grief taking over and she must have sounded crazy, but Mary thought it might work. She had to give it a try, even if it was to be with him for one more day. Mary walked into Greg's study and noticed the papers were still on his desk. The computer was still on too—he must have been working on it right until the end.

Mary checked the computer screen. It showed an image of the She-Beast in all her glory. As well as an image of the thirteen hearts, it showed a description of what would happen if you became scratched or bitten by one. Greg had been very lucky. But what if...Mary suddenly felt a small pain on her arm. She winced, scratching at it. No...No, Greg would never have done that...

She really didn't want to but knew she wouldn't rest without having a look. She pulled up her sleeve and gasped at what she saw. Four scratch marks. Greg probably hadn't meant to have done it. It must have been while they were sleeping. This had to end...There had to be a cure to this and she would find it...

Mary left, having a plan but still unsure it would be successful. She gathered her keys and headed to the morgue, taking a knife with her...

Mary arrived there moments later, parking the car outside. It was still early so there wouldn't be many people around. A perfect opportunity for her to carry out her plan. The double doors slid open and she stepped inside, walking up to the security man. "Hi. My husband was brought here. I would like to view the body if I may."

The old man nodded, handing her a form. "Sign here, please. You will need to do this on the way out too."

Mary took the form, scribbled her name and walked briskly to the morgue. This place, always white and sterile, made her feel queasy. She had been here three years ago to see the dead body of her mother, and she hadn't been expecting to come back so soon. She would be glad when this was all over and she could finally have a normal life. If the plan worked that is.

Mary pushed open the white doors, stepping into the dimly lit morgue. There was no one else around, thank God—not yet anyway. She would have to hurry if she was going to do this. She would only be able to stomach it once. Greg's body was still on the table. His leg was tagged and he looked still. At peace. He had just arrived so nothing had been inspected yet. If she was lucky...

Mary approached the body and lifted back the white blanket, noticing the gunshot wound and flinching at the blood. She had been a trained nurse and knew how to cut, but even this made her squirm a little. She put on a pair of gloves and, reaching down, took out the scalpel and began to cut around where Greg's heart would be. She tried not to gag. Throwing up here would be a very bad move.

Carefully, Mary reached inside Greg's stomach and removed the heart, which was beginning to turn black. She looked at it in her bloody gloved hands. She had to do this fast. She brought it to her mouth and bit into it, blood squirting down her chin. She ate it all, feeling vomit forming in her throat, but she was able to keep it down. Then, when she was done, she got out a needle and began to sow the wound back up, cleaning around it carefully. She had to be so careful and not to leave any clues. Once the job was done, she went to the bathroom down the hall to clean herself up. Mary made one final check on the room to make sure everything was just how she left it, then she left and headed towards the exit.

The security man stopped her. Hell, she hadn't checked to see if there was a camera in there. Stupid, stupid woman. It was too late now. It was done—she just hoped it worked. Mary smiled at the man and signed her name again.

He tipped his hat to her. "I'm sorry for your loss."

She nodded. "Thank you."

As she left the man watched her go. His eyes began to glow yellow and he growled...

Mary returned home, got into the kitchen...and threw up. She was surprised it had lasted this long. She was just glad she hadn't done it on the security guard, although it would have been understandable. However, it would have also been evidence, and she could have done without that just now. She felt a little better.

Cleaning up, Mary went to have a hot shower and changed into her loungewear. She would phone in sick today. They probably wouldn't have been expecting her anyway.

It was when she was making a cup of coffee, that the phone rang. She froze. She wasn't expecting anybody...Was it the security guard? Or someone else?...

Mary answered. "Hello?" Her voice sounded croaky, shaky.

"Mrs. Henshaw? It's Officer Browning here. We have just received some very disturbing video footage and wondered if you could come down to the station and discuss it."

Mary felt a large lump in her throat forming and she felt as if she was going to be sick again. "I...I'm kind of busy right now, John. Funeral arrangements to take care of and everything..."

"Please don't make me come down there, Mrs. Henshaw. I don't want to use force but I will if needed. You have one hour."

John had been her friend for years—now he

sounded cold and distant. She didn't blame him. It must have looked horrible what she had done. Maybe if she came clean, then she would be safe...A thought struck her. She would leave town—run away and start a new life somewhere else where no one would know her. No...She would be a fugitive and an outcast. No. She had to go and face whatever punishment was waiting for her.

She changed, pulled on a thick coat and stepped out into the street, glancing around her every now and then. It felt as if she was being watched. The streets were eerily deserted and snow was still on the ground. It had been like this for weeks, ever since the She-Beast had appeared. Mary shivered and stepped into the car, starting up the engine.

"Don't scream. Don't look behind you."

Mary froze. Someone was in the car with her. She could feel his rancid breath on her neck, and felt a brown fur hand land on her shoulder, its sharp claws digging in. "Please...Don't kill me..."

The thing behind her chuckled, low and deep. "I don't wish to kill you. I wish to protect you. I am giving you a gift. The footage the police have. It will destroy you. But they haven't seen it yet. No one has. I have planted a Mind Swap in you and them. When they arrive, they will see ME eat Greg's heart. It's the least I can do for him killing my bitch of a mother. Then you must destroy the tape for good. Do I have your word?"

Mary nodded. She would do anything right about now. "Yes! I promise! But..." She turned but the thing was gone. Shivering, she started up the car and headed off towards the police station.

All went according to plan. The police were convinced that a killer was on the loose hunting hearts—the Heartbreaker they were calling him. Mary tried not to smile but look concerned and upset. She could have been a great actress. She told the police she was getting away for a bit – to clear her head. She would have the funeral, tie up loose ends and start a fresh life somewhere else.

The funeral took place a few days later. Once the service had ended, Mary noticed the security guard standing on top of a grassy hill, looking down at her. He nodded, tipping his hat. His eyes glowed yellow and he smiled, showing sharp teeth. Right before her eyes, he transformed into a wolf and scampered off into the distance.

Mary looked around her. Luckily, she had been the only one to see this. All the other mourners had moved away and were heading into the black cars. So, it had been him that was in the car the other day? A good beast? Was there such a thing? She had to believe so. There had to be some out there to protect her.

Mary smiled and she felt a hand on her shoulder. She jumped. It was Officer Browning. He smiled at her and was ruggedly handsome in the light. "You OK, Mary?" he asked, concerned.

Mary nodded. "I am fine. I'm just thinking long thoughts..."

John hugged her suddenly, taking her a little by surprise but she welcomed it. "I am so sorry about the other day. I didn't mean to come on so strong. I know you would have nothing to do with

Greg's heart."

Mary smiled. "It's OK. Come on. Let's get out of here."

The rest of the week was uneventful. Mary went about sorting out her affairs and putting everything in order. She was ready to leave this town for good but had to stop by somewhere, so she could put her mind firmly at rest.

The site where the She-Beast had fallen had been buried and it was almost impossible to find a way in. But Mary had to try. Just to make sure that she would never come back.

Mary parked the car near the trail and walked the rest of the way, carrying a large chainsaw in her hands. The trees had collapsed down but she still searched around for an opening. There...Hidden beneath rubble, she could just about squeeze through and enter the cavern...

Her body squirmed through it like a large snake, and she slipped into the darkness. The only light was coming from the crack but she had a torch with her, and she flicked it on now. Mary noticed the dead body of the She-Beast. It was black, huge and hairy, with a hideous snout and sharp claws. Mary felt anger towards it for nearly destroying this town.

She moved towards it carefully, knowing that if this was a horror film the creature would jump up at her for one last attack. It never came. Mary got to the head of the beast and turned on the chainsaw. The tool came down on the creature's neck, slicing it clean off, dark blood spraying everywhere and staining the cavern walls. Mary was laughing and crying at the same time. She had been doing this, unaware of a wolf shadow moving towards her, stalking her.

It was one of the wolf cubs. Apparently, it had only been wounded and had been trying to escape for days. It was angry and hungry. When it saw Mary it snarled, scampering towards her.

Mary turned and almost missed. The wolf cub scraped her skin and she cried out in fear and anger.

No! She slammed the chainsaw against the beast and it smashed against the rubble, causing the hole at the top to disappear and more rubble fell down. Mary was now trapped inside. She walked over to the wolf and before it had a chance to get up, she sliced the chainsaw through it. It yelped and collapsed in a pool of blood.

Mary fell to the ground, clutching her other arm. Damn, now how was she going to get out? She had to hurry, not wanting to turn...but she could feel the hairs starting to sprout from her arm and hunger of flesh taking over. She started to growl. She knew there would be no escape now.

Starting to sob, Mary noticed the red coat lying on the ground next to the She-Beast, and a long dark red wig. Mary had to continue this everlasting circle. Her time would come but for now, she must be the next She-Beast. No one would ever find her here.

She would make sure of it.

Mary controlled herself and her eyes turned yellow, the wolf finally taking over.

FROM THE DIARY OF ELSA LYCAN, 5TH MAY 1998.

"This will be the last entry I will make as a human. My right of passage to be the Wolf Goddess is almost complete. I believe my mother to be the cause of my transformation, although there is no proof of this. It seems this is passed through the bloodlines, so it may be true after all.

This will also be my last day at school. I turn 16 today and I believe this is when the wolf will come forth. I have already found hairs in places I never had before...And I feel the sudden hunger for meat. Maybe it's a passing phase. I want to be a good wolf after all and do right by my mother. Maybe if she was still alive she would be pleased I am carrying on the legacy and doing what I was born to do.

I still feel doubt though and I am a little afraid. This is all new to me and with no one to guide me it's going to be incredibly daunting. I am also heavily pregnant and hope that my child does not become a wolf too. I want them to have a normal life and be free of this curse. It would be childish of me to disrespect the legacy though—I believe in doing good and will not harm anyone...I hope.

The hot young security guard on the desk at school may be my ticket out of here. He is only 18 but I am sure we will get on really well. The subject in English today was about werewolves which seemed such a coincidence and well timed. I don't think I will turn out as nasty as one of them though. I really hope not. I need someone to help me through this and to guide me. There must be others out there like me and I will find them and ask them what I must do.

"The path lain before you has many bumps and twists and turns before the end," my mother used to say. "Choose one wisely and it will be your shining light—but choose wrong and it may be the end of you." I hope to do right. I have heard of a town called Cliff Hill which would be a perfect place to go and raise a family. I believe it's the best start for me. I wish my mother and father were still around to watch out for me, but now I am a big girl and can take care of myself I will show them and they will be proud of me.

Well, it's just before nightfall here and the moon is out tonight. I really hope the God's are kind and will look out for me. For whoever finds this and reads this I hope I have done good and set out what was asked of me. Signing off. Elsa. Xx"

Ice Maidens
Stefan Vucak

With a clash of grinding transmission and a snarl from the diesel, the coach swayed as it entered the parking ramp. I squinted through the window, but the glass was smeared with frost, sparkling from the fluorescent strips that hung from power poles outside. The brakes sighed and we squealed to a stop, the whir of air-conditioning suddenly loud.

Across the aisle, a figure stirred beneath a blanket and a head slowly reared up. Someone coughed. A ripple of suppressed mutterings and shifting of cramped bodies ran the length of the coach. The lights come on, suddenly bright and intrusive, and I saw myself reflected in the window.

"Appelton!" the driver growled into the intercom and pried himself out of the seat. "Stopping for twenty minutes only!"

The door hissed as it opened and powder snow swirled into the coach. The driver muttered something as he strode toward the luggage compartment doors. I stood up and groped for my jump bag in the overhead rack.

Pulling up the zipper of my ski jacket, I joined the queue inching its way down the aisle toward the door. I paused on the first step and breathed deeply. The sharp air smelled of snow. Looking at the old diner, I tried to sort out my feelings. How long has it been? Certainly, longer than I cared to remember.

Outside, it snowed gently. The large flakes clung like feathers where they touched. Someone bumped into me and muttered an apology as I stepped off. The figure brushed past me, hurrying toward the diner entrance. The sidewalks were almost deserted. Bent figures moved through thin fog, only to vanish as silently as they appeared.

I turned and looked around, drinking in the sights. It hadn't changed at all. Pete's BP station was still on the corner, a blurred pool of white light cutting through the snow. A car whispered by, trailing a cloud of white exhaust, its parking lights glittering as it vanished down the street. The Wall-Mart store was dark and shadows lay thick around it. A lonely huddled figure hurried on the other side of the street and disappeared into the bright interior of the Kentucky Fried Chicken eatery.

With a stiff hand, I pushed open the diner door and walked in. The air was hot and heavy, a mixture of body odors, smoke and the acid reek of thin beer. Standing there, a small black cat rubbed itself against my leg, looked at me and purred. I grimaced and pushed it away. I have always been wary of cats. Suddenly, I felt alone and lost, wondering where the years have taken me. As I tried to find a familiar face, a finger jabbed my shoulder.

"You getting in or just admiring the scenery?" a strong rasping voice demanded

I turned slowly, stepped aside and my face broke into a grin. "Sorry, bud. Woolgathering."

He looked at me in disgust and shook his head. "Well, gather it someplace else, okay?" He pushed his way through the crowd and vanished in the gloom of coiling cigarette smoke.

I dropped my jump bag beside the door and rubbed

my hands. Maybe coming here wasn't such a great idea after all. I walked to the bar, leaned against it and reached for a bowl of mixed nuts. As I chewed, snatches of conversation washed over me; laughter and shouting drowned in a sea of noise.

"What'll ya have?" a brusque voice jerked me back to reality. The barman wiped the counter with an impatient sweep of a crumpled rag, looking at me with pale washed-out eyes.

"Bourbon," I said. "A double."

As I sipped, I sighed. I was wrong. The place and the people here hadn't changed. I had changed.

The empty tumbler clicked as I placed it gently on the bar. I pushed it away with a flick of my forefinger and walked out, feeling the liquor burn in my belly, tempted to climb back into the coach.

* * *

It had stopped snowing. Through breaking cloud, stars shivered in frosty silence. I pulled up the collar of my ski jacket, and with a grunt, heaved the jump bag over my shoulder. It was late and the street was deserted. A church bell tolled mournfully and the hair on the back of my neck twitched. Icy fingers ran down my spine.

With an impatient jerk, I pulled out my gloves and a postcard fluttered into slush on the sidewalk. I stared at it for a moment before picking it up. I unfolded the stiff cardboard and read the single line. All it said was, 'Come to me now. I need you'. It was signed with his usual scratchy scrawl and I pursed my lips as I unzipped the jacket and slid the card into the breast pocket of my woolen shirt.

Why now, Dad? I've been asking that question all day, but there were no answers. We had a curious relationship, my father and I. I sent him a card at

Christmas and sometimes I remembered his birthday. Since Mother died, he lived alone on The Hill, and from what people said, he rarely came down into town. They said a lot more things besides, few of them flattering, but that was just idle village talk. There had always been something of a mystery regarding The Hill and our place, and folks loved to frighten kids with tales of witches and devils. Remembering the kind of people that lived up there, I often wondered if some of those tales might be true.

Shifting my jump bag to a more comfortable position, I started down the street. The snow crunched and squeaked beneath my feet and my face tingled from the cold. It was a two-hour slog along a steep, winding road to The Hill, but I knew a shortcut. I couldn't see any point in paying a motel good money just to hang around till morning. And besides, the walk would do me good.

The icy sidewalk gave way to a narrow-frozen road and the houses gradually thinned out – black outlines in the night. An occasional yellow circle of light from a power pole scattered brittle shadows. Overhead, a half-moon glowed hard white, streaking patchy clouds with silver, making the frozen fields glitter. The silence lay thick around me, broken only by the regular crunch of my footfalls and my uneven breathing.

After a while, I felt that someone was following me. I even stopped to look back along the road, but there was no one there. Away from the noise and bustle of a big city, I was letting my imagination run wild.

As I walked, I thought I could hear the sound of mincing steps. The more I tried to ignore it the louder they became. I stopped suddenly and whirled, but there was nothing there. This wasn't funny anymore and I chided myself for a fool.

Cold and indifferent, bare birch and oak began to reach toward the road from the blackness of the forest. I started looking for the trail, but it wasn't there, probably lost somewhere beneath the snow. Hands on hips, I stared at the road as it wound its way up, clinging to the edge of the hill.

I checked my bearings, certain the trail should be here. I was puzzled and annoyed that I couldn't find it. I must have walked through here hundreds of times. Snow or not, it was always used – at least it was when I was a kid. Listening to my breathing, I was suddenly cold, a chill that came from within. Shadows moved around me, but when I looked, all was silent and still.

With a sigh, I jumped over a narrow ditch along the road and plowed through the powdery snow that covered the virgin unmarked field. Twenty minutes tops and I would be home.

* * *

It was bright beneath the moon and the air was crisp. The snowline curved gently upward and disappeared among the pines. My legs were beginning to ache, but at least I was on familiar ground. Transformed in summer, filled with clean smells and the buzz of insects, this meadow used to be my playground. I had been happy then, but my heart was lighter then.

Tall pines lined the hill and I walked closer toward them. A branch creaked and there was a flurry of snow, cascading down the branches. I looked around, sensing shadows moving among the trees. I felt a cold touch on my cheek and jerked back. It was only the fur of my ski jacket.

I hurried then, unexpectedly anxious to get to Dad's cottage. The Hill was just beyond the forest ahead of me. I had gotten used to city living and its cloying intimacy. This cold wilderness was suddenly alien and I did not belong anymore.

A soft patter of small footfalls broke the silence behind me and I stopped and turned. The brittle surface of the snow was unbroken and I couldn't see anything. I don't know what I expected, but I waited until my heart slowed before moving on. Foxes and raccoons would be prowling the forest, I told myself.

That was it. Nothing unusual about that, and the animals were light enough not to break the snow's crust.

I didn't believe any of it.

Ice crackled and snapped and the snow squeaked beneath my boots as I pushed my way up the slope. Perhaps I should have spent the night at a motel after all. The coach journey had been long and I was more tired than I cared to admit.

When the footfalls sounded behind me again, I whirled around, my breath loud a white fog in front of me. It was a large cat, coal black, its glowing orange eyes staring at me fixedly. It sat on its hunches and licked its right paw, tail swishing back and forth. It lifted its head, the eyes never leaving mine. It yawned with deliberate dignity and I could hear its rasped purring. I had a moment of fear as I looked into eyes that glowed with open malevolence. Hell, it was just a cat! With a snort, I turned and began walking.

With each step, the pines drew closer, but I couldn't get that cat out of my mind. Every time I paused to listen, there was only silence and my labored breathing. I had a dreaded suspicion it was following me. I wanted to stop and see, but I couldn't bring myself to do it. It was ridiculous, but there was something about that cat that set my teeth on edge.

Stupid!

Then I did stop and stared hard at the wall of the forest ahead. I clenched my teeth, willing myself to turn. When I did turn it was there, staring at me, its tail working in agitation. I crouched and waved, hissing at it. It didn't move. It was almost as though it was laughing at me. I picked up a handful of powdery snow, crunched it into a ball, and threw it. I missed, but as the ball shattered, fragments of snow fell around the cat. It jumped, back arched and spitting, its orange eyes glaring.

There was evil in those eyes and I felt a ripple of apprehension. Then I went pale. Another cat slowly emerged out of the pines. Silent like a black ghost, its red eyes stared at me. The unease I felt was quickly turning to alarm and I hurried away from the damned things. When one of them yowled, ice touched my spine and I shivered.

Pushing my way through the snow, I imagined one of them leaping on me, tearing at me. But that was absurd, of course, wasn't it? Whoever heard of a cat attacking a man? It may have been unreasonable and it probably was, but I knew they were behind me, stalking me.

There was a narrow wagon trail through the forest, cut long ago before my father's time, and I breathed a sigh of relief as I stumbled across one of its furrows. I stopped, turned and felt my face drain.

There were dozens of them, all sitting on the snow, their glowing eyes staring and I stood rooted, unable to move. The apprehension I felt before grew into real panic as I pictured them swarming over me, clawing and biting.

But they just sat there, staring, tails working.

"Man, most mortal," a harsh voice grated beside me

and I yelped in terror and jumped.

Beside me were only trees: pine, oak, and birch. Then I noticed a black figure perched on one of the low oak branches.

"Who are you?" I demanded and harsh laughter echoed around me. The cats began to yowl.

* * *

I have always considered myself religious, but I had long ago ceased believing in the reward of heaven or the pain of hell. As with sin, these were inventions of priests to keep the believers in check. Now, all the childhood horrors instilled into me reared their dark heads as I stood staring at the black shape sitting on the branch. I could just make out the slow lashing of a long tail. There may not be a hell, but there were certainly devils around.

My chest hurt so much, I thought it would burst.

"Why have you sought me now?" I whispered hoarsely, trembling uncontrollably.

"So, you recognize me," the evil creature snorted with derision. "Not at all what you expected is it?" The laugh was nasty and mocking and my skin chilled.

I fought to push back the tide of imagined horrors that waited for me when the demon dragged me into hell.

"Answer me!" the creature shrieked and I gasped.

"But I don't seek you!" I managed to stammer.

Its laughter was the ripping of steel and his tail swished. "Yet you're here. You fear me, mortal. That is good, for you have much to fear," it grated, the sound setting my teeth on edge. "You were told never to walk here at night in peril of your soul. As with other things, you chose to forget or ignore the warning. I demand your answer!" it screamed and the red glow of its eyes held me in horrified captivation as I tried to understand what it had said.

I couldn't recall anyone telling me ever that I couldn't walk here at night. Then, like a window opening, I saw myself sitting beside my father one dreamy afternoon as we gazed together at the forest below us. He clutched the bowl of his pipe, the aromatic smoke pleasant. Then he spoke to me. I was but a boy, restless and not much interested in his tales.

But I did remember his words.

"Our family has held that patch of forest as far back as any of us can remember," he growled, nodding to himself. "It is ours to do as we wish, but only during the day. Only during the day," he had said, nodding solemnly.

I remember how he turned to look down at me, his eyes intense and captivating.

"Never go there at night, boy. Never!" His words were cold and I was afraid. I had played there often, at night too – well, late into the evening anyway.

"Why, father?" I had managed to ask.

"Later, boy. Just remember what I told you."

I had forgotten the warning, and perhaps I was now about to pay the ultimate price. But how could I answer this thing when I didn't understand the question?

A small part of me reared itself in admonition and the burden of my guilt was heavy.

"You have been following me," I said accusingly, greatly daring. But if I was going to lose my soul, I could afford to dare.

"Ah, foolish creature," he sneered and the tail coiled. "I was always there, but when you came tonight, you opened the door to me willingly."

I looked around and the cats were there, licking

their paws, staring at me in anticipation. Their turn may come too. Was that to be my punishment, to be torn forever into pieces by snarling cats?

My soul was in judgment and my omissions were many. I had never strayed along the dark side that lies within all of us, but I knew its shadows. The material lusts had claimed me and I measured success with its coin, ignoring the needs of the spirit. That part of me had withered somewhat, but it was still there – waiting to be nurtured.

When that postcard came, I *could* have stayed away...

"I may have strayed, but you have no claim on me," I said defiantly, the empty achievements of my life tasting bitter in my mouth.

"By answering your father's call, you mean to redeem yourself?" the devil chided.

"I have not finished my work yet," I said lamely.

"Your work?" he mimicked and laughed the tail whipping. "You crave mercy, then?" he roared and one of the cats sprang on my shoulder. I stood rooted, terrified as it bared its fangs and hissed. The smell of death was on it and its eyes burned into mine.

"All I have to do is reach with my hand and you will be mine," the devil hissed, and the cold menace of its voice was a voice from hell.

I may have been half-crazed with fright, but I wasn't about to give myself to that thing.

"You can't –"

The cat on my shoulder snarled and sank its teeth into my neck. I screamed and clawed at the thing, but it jumped away.

Blood flowed warm between my fingers and tears stung my eyes.

"I can't what?" the devil demanded softly.

"You can't touch me," I grated in defiance. "I may be in terror of you and your minions, but I have never walked in your shadow. You and yours be damned!"

It chuckled and its eyes blazed. "Oh, that was good, mortal. Lame, but good. You may not have walked in my shadow, but you touched it nonetheless."

"You tempted me, but I didn't walk it!"

"One day you will, and then you shall be mine for real. You have been warned. If our paths cross again, the terror you now feel will be justified."

A warmth seemed to descend on the forest, a pervasive friendliness. The branch where the dark thing perched was empty. When I turned, the cats were gone. It was a while before I stopped shaking. With tentative steps, I walked to where the cats had sat, but the snow was unbroken, except for my footsteps.

There was a dark stain on the snow and I bent down. It was a fluff of cat hair. A drop of dark blood fell beside it. It was then that I sank into the snow and silently sobbed.

* * *

The coach lurched as it entered the parking ramp and I opened my eyes with a start. Across the aisle, a figure stirred beneath a blanket and a head slowly reared up. The lights come on, suddenly bright and intrusive and I saw myself reflected in the glass of the window.

"Appelton!" the driver growled into the intercom and pried himself out of his seat "Stopping for twenty minutes only!"

The door hissed as it opened and he winced as powder snow swirled around him. I could see his hunched figure fumbling with the luggage compartment doors.

Blinking, I was confused. Had it all been but a dream?

I hurriedly touched my neck, but there was no wound. I opened my hand. In it was a fluff of cat hair. I went cold and started to shake. I swallowed, but it went down hard.

Pulling up the zipper of my ski jacket, I moved down the aisle toward the door. I paused on the first step, breathing deeply of the biting air, trying to sort out my feelings. It was with heavy feet that I descended down the steps. When I looked up, he was there, waiting for me.

"Dad?" I managed to mumble, my throat suddenly tight.

He walked toward me and smiled warmly. When he saw my eyes, he frowned; then nodded slowly.

"Dad, I..."

"It's all right, son. You're here, that's all that matters," he said gruffly and we embraced. He smelled of wood smoke and tobacco. He let me go and patted my back. I followed him to the car, flooded with relief at seeing him. I should have done this much sooner.

He opened the door for me and smiled ruefully. "Don't worry. I didn't heed my father's warning either, boy. Get in. We have much to talk about."

The Wild Pigs
Danny Campbell

On a mountainside, somewhere near Chiang Mai, Thailand, Pati Teyeh, a Siamese Karen chief, tells a traditional story to his friends and family while sitting around a fire in the evening:

"The wild pigs' home was a wonderful place of mountains, crossed with fast running streams. A place for all things wild. Food, though in abundance, took some effort in finding. Roots, fruit, plants, and nuts of all description were to be had by the animals hidden in the jungle. If they were prepared to work at it. That meant long and arduous journeys through the forest daily. Few were as adept at finding food as the wild pigs. Sniffling and snuffling with their wet, twitchy snouts as they trotted along. This lifestyle built them sturdy legs. It was tiring, especially for the piglets trying to keep up. But it meant they were free and independent, which for a pig, an intelligent animal, is perhaps, as important to them as it is for human beings.

For a member of the Karen tribe, hunting a wild pig is as difficult as it is for a wild pig to find food. It requires patience, determination, and ingenuity. wild pigs are incredibly tenacious animals, and extremely sensitive to the presence of danger. While on their gathering patrols, they keep their eyes and ears open. More importantly than that, they use their upturned snouts, nostrils quivering, to sniff the air for scents. Of tiger, of leopard, and of course, of humans. A Karen man name Moo, which funnily enough means pig in Siamese, was contemplating these facts one morning, as he prepared to go pig hunting. As he sat by a small fire in his little baan, he watched his wife roasting bamboo tubes of rice for him to carry into the forest and eat as a meal. It was while watching her turning the blackening tubes over the fire, and smelling the delicious aroma of the herbs, she had mixed with rice and water, that he suddenly had an idea. He said:

'Kob,' which means frog in Siamese, and was her name, 'can you make some more of those to take into the forest today?' she turned to look at him and said:

'What now my dear, are you becoming a greedy man?' Moo smiled, his wizened face creased, and he said:

'Maybe I am. But not for rice. Can you make them look, but more importantly, smell delicious? Imagine that the Hikko and his wife were coming to eat with us.'

The Hikko was the village headman, and as such, Kob felt the challenge to her cooking. After thinking for a moment, she pulled down her cloth bag of seeds and spices, from where it hung on a hook on the bamboo wall. she set to rolling and grinding the seeds and spices in a wooden pestle and mortar until the smell rising from her expert hands caused Moo's mouth to water. when she had finished, and the second batch of rice had been cooked, Moo placed it into his cotton shoulder bag and, resisting the urge to eat them, walked quietly with the rising sun into the jungle.

After walking for quite some time, when he was deep in the jungle, he found the tracks of trotter prints which were numerous and fresh. He chose a spot where the vegetation was clear and emptied the contents of the bamboo pipes onto the ground. then, he walked a short distance away and sat behind the cover of some giant ferns. Slowly chewing his own meal, he watched and waited, hoping his plan would be a success. It was not too long before he heard the rustling and snorting of pigs moving about in the forest scrub. the pigs approached the spot where the rice lay, its aroma carrying high and clear, permeating the humid air. Several wet snouts twitched uncontrollably, as the pigs grunted among themselves.

If it were possible to translate that grunting and squealing conversation between the excited pigs, you can be sure it would have gone something like this;

'What's that smell?' said one.

'Where is it coming from?' said another.

'Let us find out!' said another still. The pigs then moved cautiously through the tangled jungle, until they found the source of the tempting smell.

The pigs could barely contain themselves, as they eyed the fragrant smelling rice. Some of the more impetuous among them were about to pounce upon the food when a voice among them suddenly said:

'Look here! I smell trouble. If you set your snouts properly, you will smell humans.'

This statement caused no small amount of consternation among them, and they began to chatter and jabber excitedly while darting around anxiously. The pig who had caused the drama, the oldest of the lot, again addressed them:

'Let us not be hasty. I have lived in the jungle longer than any of you. Never before has food come to me of its own accord. I do not trust this at all, and in my opinion, we should stick to our habits, as our ancestors did before us.' This caused a huge argument between those who wanted to eat the food and those who thought it best to ignore it.

Eventually, the one group became two, as the rift became a chasm between them, the two sides irreconcilable. The group who would not eat the gift food, led by the old pig, made their way back into the forest, to continue finding food in the old way. The group which stayed behind, became gloating and nasty, shouting after them, things like:

'Ha! You fools, there is more for us then.'

And with that, they set to munching and scrunching, noisily and greedily, devouring the feast before them. From his concealed position behind the giant ferns, Moo, who had been watching the proceedings, smiled a knowing smile and nodded to himself.

The following morning, Moo asked his wife if she would prepare another batch of rice to take into the forest. She asked him:

'What are you doing with this food? For as you know, we could well be eating it ourselves.' Seeing the concerned look upon his wife's face, he said to her:

'Do not worry my love. We shall soon have more than rice to eat.'

Trusting him, she asked no further questions, and again he set off on his walk through the forest. Again, he came to the place of the plentiful trotter tracks, and again he placed the rice on the floor. Only this time, he did not conceal himself behind ferns, but instead, sat in plain view of the food, albeit a respectful distance away.

The pigs who had feasted so splendidly the day before decided they were onto a good thing. Among themselves, they said such things as:

'It was perfectly safe, and so much easier than

looking for food, let's go back and see if there is any more.'

Which is what they did. But when they arrived there, they were shocked and alarmed to see Moo sitting there. However, when they saw the rice sitting there waiting for them, they soon overcame their fear and tucked in any way. This became a regular occurrence, as day after day the pigs returned to the same spot. Even anticipating Moo's arrival. They became fat, lazy, and indifferent, so much so, that they did not care whether Moo was cutting trees and bamboo down around them.

Day by day, a fence was built around them. They did not even notice, apathetic as they were until it was closed, and their world had become very small indeed. Years have passed since that time. In this day, every once in a while, wild pigs pass nearby to the cages which hold their fat cousins. The pigs would grunt among themselves, asking:

'Why are pigs stuck in cages like that?'

If one among them knew the story, he would reply:

'Those pigs are in a cage of their own making.'

At the same time, one of the caged pigs would spy the lean and agile wild pigs, and equally interested, ask about them. If one among the captive pigs knew their history, he would tell it to the others. Then, as they looked through the bamboo bars, they wondered to themselves, what it meant to be free."

Scrambled
June Rachelson-Ospa

ACT 1 SCENE 1

Young woman mid-twenties and her mother are seated at a table in a typical greasy spoon. The waiter enters.

WAITER: Good morning, Ladies. And what can I get for you today?

DAUGHTER: Scrambled eggs, whole-wheat toast, hold the fries. Can I get some lettuce and tomatoes instead?

WAITER: Cost fifty cents extra.

DAUGHTER: Fine.

WAITER: And you ma'am.

MOTHER: Nothin' for me thanks.

DAUGHTER: *(Whispers to her mother)* Mom, order something.

It's on me this time.

MOTHER: Can't.

DAUGHTER: Mom, please.

WAITER: Shall I come back? Give you a few minutes to decide.

DAUGHTER: Give her same as me. And two coffees too.

WAITER: Back in a jiffy.

Waiter exits.

MOTHER: I told you. I don't want anything.

DAUGHTER: Why not, Ma?

MOTHER: Didn't you see him?

DAUGHTER: See him what?

MOTHER: His head.

DAUGHTER: His head? It looked normal to me.

MOTHER: It was green.

DAUGHTER: Green! His head was not green!

MOTHER: Yes. It was green. Bright green and his eyes were. Oh God, his eyes were yellow. Lemon yellow with red specks.

DAUGHTER: Mom, he did not have yellow eyes. Or red specks.

MOTHER: Yes. He did. I know exactly what I saw.

DAUGHTER: What on earth are you talkin' about? That guy looked as normal as you and me. And he was kinda cute, too.

MOTHER: No. He was not cute. And he didn't take your order. He was taking your measurements.

DAUGHTER: Excuse me.

MOTHER: Yes. To see if you'd fit.

DAUGHTER: Fit into what? His arms. I'd like that.

MOTHER: No. Fit in the ship.

DAUGHTER: What ship?

MOTHER: Their ship. I've seen this all before.

DAUGHTER: Maybe I should ask him for a date and he can invite me on his ship. It sounds kinda mysterious and sexy.

MOTHER: I'm not fooling around here.

DAUGHTER: Mom, you're freakin' me out. Please.

Waiter returns and places two coffees on the table.

WAITER: Want cream or milk with your coffees?

DAUGHTER: Cream, please.

WAITER: You got it.

Exits

Daughter reaches for Sweet & Low and rips off top

of packet. Her mother grabs her hand violently.

MOTHER: Don't use that.

DAUGHTER: What?

MOTHER: That stuff. It's poison and all part of the plan.

DAUGHTER: Mom, it's just Sweet & Low. Besides, I think the waiter likes me. He was kinda flirtin' with me.

MOTHER: He's controlling your mind. Gets your guard down. Puts you in a dream state.

DAUGHTER: This is no dream.

MOTHER: You're right. It's a nightmare, and it's starting all over again. Just like when I was out with your father. Shortly after we were married.

DAUGHTER: Mom, maybe we can talk about me and how I wanna get married someday.

MOTHER: We were in a place just like this one. We ate and drank and...

DAUGHTER: Mom, are you listenin' to me.

MOTHER: I blacked out. When I woke up, I was in a ship. My arms and my hands were all tied up.

DAUGHTER: Mom, don't you want me to tie the knot someday?

MOTHER: There were needles. They were poking me and prodding me. Like a piece of meat.

DAUGHTER: Stop mom.

MOTHER: They took samples from every part of my body. I was horrified.

DAUGHTER: Mom, you're scarin' me.

MOTHER: I begged for them to let me go.

DAUGHTER: Maybe we should go now.

She begins to get up. Her mother grabs her arm and yanks her back down.

MOTHER: Sit! I'm talking to you. Then I was back with your father. Like nothing ever happened. He was still sitting in his seat drinking his coffee.

DAUGHTER: Nothing did happen. You were sick. Remember.

Mom begins to roll up her sleeve and points to a mark.

MOTHER: Sick! Look at this. Now I have this mark.

DAUGHTER: Fine. Just forget about my future. Where?

Show me.

Mother points to a specific spot on her arm.

DAUGHTER: That's a beauty mark.

MOTHER: No. It's way too big for a beauty mark.

DAUGHTER: So, it's a mole. Not beautiful. And you should have it removed.

MOTHER: I can't.

DAUGHTER: And why is that?

MOTHER: This is their tracking device. And now they've found me.

DAUGHTER: Mom, have you seen Dr. Cohen lately?

MOTHER: What for?

DAUGHTER: I believe it's time for a visit. It's happening again.

MOTHER: What's happening?

Waiter returns.

WAITER: Here's your cream ladies. Breakfast up in another minute.

DAUGHTER: Umm. Thanks.

Waiter begins to exit and mother grabs his arm.

MOTHER: Not so fast, mister.

WAITER: Need something else, ma'am?

Removes mother's hands.

MOTHER: Don't I know you?

DAUGHTER: Mom!!!!

WAITER: Nope. Don't think so.

MOTHER: I could swear I've seen you before.

DAUGHTER: *(Whispers)*Please don't do...

WAITER: Well, I have done some commercials here and there. Perhaps...

MOTHER: No, that isn't it.

WAITER: Ever go to plays?

MOTHER: No, I haven't seen any lately.

WAITER: I was in one a few months ago. Off, Off, way Off Broadway. But it's a start.

DAUGHTER: Mom, isn't that great for him. Uh, you.

MOTHER: No, that's not it either. I know what you're up to.

WAITER: Yeah. An actor posing as a waiter till I get my big break. I mean this is New York City, where anything can happen.

DAUGHTER: Well, I uh, hope you get one soon.

Bell rings.

WAITER: Oh, that's for me. Back in a few.

DAUGHTER: Everyone in New York seems to be an actor "waiting" to be discovered.

MOTHER: Yes. And now he's discovered me. We are in grave danger.

DAUGHTER: There is nothing grave about him. He's charming.

MOTHER: He's getting ready.

DAUGHTER: Ready for what. This is crazy

MOTHER: I'm telling you.

Daughter starts to pour cream in her coffee and then attempts to take a sip. Her mother grabs her arm and spills some hot coffee on the table.

MOTHER: Don't. Drink. That.

DAUGHTER: Mom, please I need my morning coffee. And you're bein' absolutely ridiculous.

Mother takes the cup out of her Daughter's hand using great force.

MOTHER: Listen. I know about these things.

DAUGHTER: Mom, all I know is that you're havin' one huge hallucination.

MOTHER: I am not.

DAUGHTER: Mom, don't you remember.

MOTHER: Remember what.

DAUGHTER: I hate bringin' this up. I really wanted to have a nice, peaceful breakfast with you.

MOTHER: I wanted that too. But it's impossible now.

DAUGHTER: Why?

MOTHER: Because they found me.

DAUGHTER: You're losin' me here.

MOTHER: I thought. I prayed that they'd leave me alone. Once they have you in their clutches they will never, ever let you go.

DAUGHTER: Mom.

Mother takes her daughter's hands in her own hands.

MOTHER: I am so sorry, honey. I thought I could protect you from them. But no. It was just wishful thinking.

DAUGHTER: I think you've been under a lot of stress lately. That's all. What with losin' your job and everything.

MOTHER: They told me they would be back to take my first offspring. You.

DAUGHTER: Me! Why me?

MOTHER: They did tests. They inserted a special serum into my veins. They wanted to see the effects of the serum on Earthlings.

DAUGHTER: C'mon Ma, you're just makin' this up. Right.

313

MOTHER: Wrong. You are one of the chosen ones.

DAUGHTER: Look, this is totally off the wall. And you're totally off your rocker.

MOTHER: No. This is the truth.

DAUGHTER: Look, let's leave. Forget breakfast.

The daughter opens her bag and throws a twenty-dollar bill on the table.

I can take you someplace else. I know this cute little cafe a few blocks from here and we...

The daughter begins to get up and her mother grabs her and pushes her back into her chair.

MOTHER: It's too late for that sweetheart.

The waiter enters with a green head and yellow eyes with flecks of red.

WAITER: Yes, sweetheart. I'm afraid it is too late.

The daughter looks at the mother.

DAUGHTER: Mom. Do something!!!

MOTHER: Sorry dear.

The waiter brings the daughter to her feet and begins to tie her up.

DAUGHTER: Mom, stop them.

MOTHER: Sorry, dear. I'll be here waiting for you. I promise.

The waiter begins to drag her backstage.

DAUGHTER: *(From backstage.)* No, please let me go. Stop them. Mom. No No.

Then it's silent. The sound of a ship taking off is heard. The mother tears off the top of a Sweet & Low and pours some cream in her coffee. As she begins to take a sip from her cup as the lights slowly fade to black.

The Devil's Therapist
Alex Winck

He was the handsomest man the therapist had ever seen. The kind of beauty that would make happily married women cheat and satisfy the darkest fantasies and whims. And yet she was shaking with nerves as she waited for him to enter her practice. It wasn´t intimidation for his good looks and commanding presence. It was who he was.

"Talk to him as if he were any other patient. Keep that in mind. Never lose control", she reminded herself, and that thought helped her to at least keep her emotions under the surface.

He entered looking impeccably elegant in a tailored black suit. If he were any other man, she´d jump on him and have sex right there on the couch. At first, she half-expected him to wear a red tie just for kicks, but she knows he actually hates that kinda thing.

His handshake is firm and his hands are silky soft.

"Good morning. Still nervous?" he greeted.

"Used to be more. It doesn´t go away, but gets better."

"Perfectly understandable. I´m used to it."

He lied heavily on the couch. His beauty and elegance couldn´t hide the weariness in his expression and his voice.

"You know that line from 'The Usual Suspects', 'The only thing the devil never tried was to convince everybody that he didn´t exist?' I´d change that. I´d

315

say "the only thing the devil never tried was to be himself."

That helped the therapist to calm down. As soon as he begins to talk, shows how vulnerable even someone with such power and authority can be. Now he really was just another patient. For the moment.

"That´s right. Your image. Tell me more about that."

"Do you see horns, goat feet, a tail? All that nonsense was made up by Renaissance artists to discriminate pagan gods. Those jerks make Photoshop look like the standard for accuracy and integrity. I´m the bloody fallen angel, I don´t turn into a werewolf in the Full Moon. Look at the Bible, I´m more of a disembodied voice than anything else. And they were not accurate either. A lot of those cases were schizophrenia, not temptation."

"That´s right, you were saying a lot of things were made up by artists and authors."

"I´m not the king of anything! You read it, those bastards can take the keys from me anytime they want. Like the place would even exist if He didn´t allow it. That whole thing came from that mad fucker John Milton."

It worried her a little that he usually got pretty angry during the sessions. But at least none of it was aimed at her. He was nothing but polite and friendly and grateful to her.

"And that fucking stupid contract thing! Goethe came up with that. Why would I need to buy souls? Hell would make China look like a Malaysian pigmy tribe! If it worked like they show in the movies, most people in this world would live in mansions and fuck supermodels."

Suddenly, he smiled. His smile terrified her way

more than the anger.

"But I do tempt souls. That´s my job, other than that I´m basically a building manager. You know that scene in the cartoons where the guy has a little angel and a little devil version of themselves on each shoulder? That´s truer than pretty much anything in the movies and most of the Bible."

She finally felt brave enough to make a serious, possibly delicate question.

"But there´s something that anguishes you more than any of those issues, isn´t there".

The smile vanished. Now it was an air of melancholy she could almost consider moving.

"It´s this notion. This notion that I´m 'evil incarnate'. That there never was anything good about my existence."

He gazed in the distance. She was tempted to assume he was staring at the clouds, but she already knew that bit is nonsense as well.

"People forget I used to an angel. The most beautiful and powerful of them all. Before the fall, I used to love God more than anything in the universe. More than any mortal ever did. I cried with joy in His presence."

One single tear dropped, he quickly wiped it.

The therapist smiled. That was the most comfortable she ever felt during the session.

"Typical son without a mother. Extremely attached to the father."

"My disgrace was wishing to be exactly like Him. But isn´t that what every loving son wants? That is the natural cycle of life. Parents are gone, the heirs take their place. That´s the destiny He reserves for all parents. But not for Himself, of course. He´ll rule forever, or at least till the universe collapses. He´ll never ever give up power. So, now I´m the damned one, the pariah, hated by all, well, except for some also much-misunderstood followers. And I act as such."

He definitely looked more peaceful at the end of the session, serene at least. He stood up and once again cheerfully shook the therapist´s hand.

"I have to say; these sessions have been really helpful. I´ve heard about this therapy thing for over a century, but always considered it a waste of time."

"It took a long time really. But these days all kinds of people look for psychological help. Even the most unusual ones."

"Absolutely. I´ll highly recommend your work. Thank you very much."

"I thank you for this unique opportunity."

After he left, the therapist was cheerful, excited. "What you know, I´m the devil´s therapist. I´ll become a celebrity, they´ll make books and movies about my work, it will be a revolution for psychotherapy..."

Suddenly, a thought stung her deeply and bluntly slaughtered her good disposition.

"Oh my God! I´m the devil´s therapist! What was I thinking?! Everyone will come after me! Christians, Satanists, skeptical atheists, even other deities, and entities! I won´t have a moment of peace!"

With shaking hands, she got a bottle of water she had in a mini-fridge.

"Worst of them all, my bloody Bible-hugger mom!"

She took a sip of the water as she tried to put herself together. "No, take it easy, think clearly. Think how important that will be for your field, all the knowledge it will bring..."

She was about to take another sip when another thought, even more powerful, took over.

"Knowledge...All I know...All this information will put everyone I know in danger. My family. My kids!"

She went behind her desk. Saw the outlet. Her laptop, her cell phone, her desk lamp, were all connected there.

"I´ll be just like him. A damned one, a pariah, hated by all!" She poured the water on the outlet.

As Satan walked to his Hummer, he took a glance up. A large flame erupted out of a window on the eleventh floor. He smiled.

"I suffer. I really do. But I never lose my touch", he thought gleefully.

The Time Machine
Robert Tozer

They've built a time machine!

They'll tell you I'm crazy, but that doesn't change the fact that they've built one. Why they chose me as a subject, I can only hazard a guess; must be something about my biology that takes well to time travel. But just the same, I'm glad they did. It's an incredible experience, and one I must continue until I get it right.

I hear savage howling coming from one of the other time traveling participants, crying from another, and one whose deranged laughter raises the hairs on the back of my neck. I guess they're not suited for time traveling like I am. They make it near impossible to sleep. But I can't sleep anyway for they'll be coming for me soon.

I was right. Here they are now.

"Don't be stupid, of course, I want to use the time machine again. Maybe I'll make a difference. Maybe *this* time I'll save them. There's no need to show me the way. I could walk there blindfolded at this point."

Okay. I'm all strapped in. They stick a rubber guard with a tube running through it into my mouth. This is to ensure that I don't bite my tongue off during the traveling process.

I should explain here that time travel isn't how they portray it in the movies. It's an extremely painful process. Stop for a moment and try to imagine just how much energy and raw power it takes to rip a hole into space and then transport someone through that portal backward or forward through time.

The machine begins to hum as it warms up.

I hear them begin the countdown. "Three, two, one—"

A blinding light, white hot in its intensity, suddenly stabs my brain. It actually feels as if someone were operating inside my head with a mini blowtorch, butter knife, and dental pick.

I can't speak, can't move, it hurts so much that I can barely think. All I can do is experience the pain and try to wait it out without going crazy. I don't know how much more of this I can stand! It—hurts—so—much! *Ahhhhhhh!*

Suddenly, I'm there.

It's December 16th again. I'm driving home after dining with friends. It was a perfect day—a perfectly happy day. I'm there with my family.

My beautiful wife, Jenny, is sitting beside me. She's currently laughing at one of my jokes. She issues a little nasal snort as she catches her breath. My handsome five-year-old son, Jason, is sitting directly behind me. Jason is best known for giving smart-assed answers without meaning to be rude and brilliant observations that often border on the genius. I can feel this genius now, kicking into the back of my seat as his foot shakes in time to the enchanting voice of Burl Ives singing a number from his Christmas CD. And then there is my precocious nine-year-old going on thirty-year-old daughter, Celeste. In the rearview mirror, I see her enchanting smile in-between her contorting mouth as she belts out verses of the song in a high-pitched, off-keyed voice. She really tries, bless her heart.

I concentrate on the road and almost get lost in the moment. I almost forget that I've traveled close to ten years into the past just to be here. That's when I look up into the rearview again. That's when I see the change. That's when I hear the words. And that's when I know that nothing will change this time too.

Celeste has stopped caterwauling and has become eerily silent. She wears a wide unnatural grin, reminiscent of the *Batman* movie villain *The Joker*. I look over to my wife whose laughter has stopped, and who shares the same gruesome smile as our daughter. Then, I quickly jerk the rearview around. To my horror, I witness that same misshapen countenance on Jason as well. They are all staring straight ahead in a trance. What unnerves me most is their eyes. They seem almost possessed by something alien and are bulging so much that I fear they'll pop out of their sockets.

Suddenly, Celeste makes a wheezing sound and I quickly swing the rearview onto her. Her mouth is inhumanly stretched open, and a sour breath exhales from it. I can actually see it emerge and waft lazily about her for the car has turned absolutely freezing. Without moving her mouth, a dark and evil voice intones, "They are ours now. Your race is doomed. You will never stop us."

Its words turn into white noise as I struggle and fail to apply some sort of logic to this.

Were *they* aliens, demons, some form of malevolence from another dimension?

I knew I had to act. And so, I do what anyone would do in my place.

Approaching through the darkness ahead...an eighteen-wheeler.

I swerve across the yellow line and slam headlong

into the truck. I didn't even get to say goodbye.

Suddenly, I'm back. I failed...again...

I'm trying to reorganize my thoughts and return to the reality of the future. How I survived those many years ago, I don't know. God must have plans for me that I'm unaware of. But I believe those plans include my continued trips to the past to try and save my family. Do something different. Maybe . . . perish with them? I dunno.

They remove my mouth guard and unstrap me from the time machine. I have lost the ability to speak, to move, and have to be lifted onto a stretcher and wheeled to my room where I'll recover and wait impatiently until my next time travel occurrence.

I hear the scientists talking. "I don't understand how they can try to treat this lunatic. You know, he killed his entire family? Claims demons, or some such nonsense, possessed them."

"Well, if this latest treatment doesn't work, Dr. Kriesler has authorized a higher level of electro-shock therapy for his next session."

About the Authors

Robert Tozer

Living in beautiful British Columbia, Canada, Robert Tozer is the author of the upcoming zombie book series, The Dead. You can find out more about him and his other projects through his website, www.thedead.us

Arnaldo Lopez Jr.

Mr. Arnaldo Lopez Jr. was born and raised in Brooklyn, NY, but he has lived in Queens, NY for about 17 years now. He has been employed by NYC Transit for twenty-seven years and is planning to retire in July 2015. He was formerly employed as a dispatcher with the NYPD. Mr. Lopez is also a speaker and trainer, speaking on subjects as diverse as terrorism and customer service. He created the civilian counter-terrorism training program currently in use by New York City Transit and many other major public transportation agencies around the country.
As well as writing, Mr. Lopez is an artist and photographer, having sold several of his works over the years. As a writer he's sold articles to Railway Age magazine, The Daily News magazine, Homeland Defense Journal, and Reptile & Amphibian magazine; scripts to Little Archie and Personality Comics; and short stories

to Neo-Opsis magazine, Lost Souls e-zine, Nth Online magazine, Blood Moon magazine, and various other Sci-Fi and/or horror newsletters and fanzines. He was also the editor of Offworld, a small science fiction magazine that was once chosen as a "Best Bet" by Sci-Fi television.

Arnaldo Lopez feels that the writers that have influenced him the most are—in no particular order— Lawrence Sanders, Ernest Hemmingway, Robert E. Howard, Harry Turtledove, Isaac Asimov, Dean Koontz, James Patterson and Stephen King.

Carey Azzara

Life is not a straight path and Azzara has had many a twist and turns during his life, losing his only sister when he was sixteen and struggling to regain direction. Since then he has accomplished a number of goals such as the pursuit of two graduate degrees, a career in public health, VP of market research, President of a marketing company AtHeath, LLC, raising a family, and rescuing a few dogs. He has published numerous articles, reports, and books. Along the way, he has had experiences that have inspired him to author the short stories in this collection. They say writers write. Azzara writes for the joy of sharing his ideas and stories with you.

June Lundgren

I am a psychic, medium, nurse and author. I am descended from a long line of women with psychic and spiritual gifts. We are of Irish, Scottish and American Indian descent. I was raised by my grandparents for the first five years of my life, my grandmother also had psychic abilities. As a young child, I communicated with animals and angels while living in a secure home with my grandparents. At the age of six, I was taken from my grandparents by my mother. From that time on everything changed, I was no longer encouraged to speak to the animals and my guardians. Over the last twenty years, I have kept notes of my many conversations with those on the other side as well as angels, God and Jesus. I have been writing all my life, but have never felt the need to have my work published until five years ago when those on the other side urged me to write this book to help others understand what the paranormal world is all about.

Over the years I have gathered a lot of information from my conversations with those on the other side. I have been taking and keeping notes for over forty years. It has only been in the last few years that I have felt compelled to put this information in book form so that all can benefit from the information. There was a time when the process seemed almost insurmountable and I almost quit. It was then that I heard God tell me that this was

what I needed to do for him, so I completed the manuscript My website:

www.mysticconnections.org
Books: A mediums guide to the Paranormal, Paranormal Encounters

Anthony V. Pugliese

I am a resident of Harrisburg, PA. I am 54 years old and single with no children. I worked for the Commonwealth of PA from 1987 to 2008 and I am a currently a customer service representative for a small

company in Camp Hill, PA who contracts with medical providers, facilities, and hospitals. My responsibilities include medical bill collections, insurance billing, and customer service. I have no college degrees. My hobbies include antiquing, weird history, paranormal phenomenon, art collection, photography, and of course, writing. I am working on a crime-thriller/horror/Sci-Fi novel, a short story collection and two novellas and have been involved in writing on and off since youth. I have few credits and at this time,
I've only been published in small press magazines and poetry anthologies. My stories center around supernatural elements in our contemporary world, the dark alleys we know are there but avoid and ignore, modern individuals like you and I finding themselves pitted against what they consciously considered myth, legend, folklore, and hokum.
You can find me on Twitter @Apugliese3 and on my Facebook homepage or on my writer's page: www.facebook.com/mymitternaucht. The page is called, The Stoat's Lair. My website of the same name is still under construction.

Amy S. Pacini

Amy S. Pacini resides in Land O Lakes, Florida as a freelance writer at A.S.P. INK and the Poetry Editor for Long Story Short. Her work has been widely published in online ezines, literary journals, and anthologies including Torrid Literature Journal, Lost Tower Publications, Kind Of A Hurricane Press, Page & Spine, Cyclamens And Swords, and All Things Girl. She writes poetry, short stories, personal essays, and motivational quotes. For more information, please visit her website at www.amyspacini.com.

Danny Campbell

Is the author of several books on Southeast Asia, including 'A Tale of Aceh', A Tale about People and a Pipeline', 'How the City Farang Came to Love the Forest and Other Stories', and 'A Siamese Story'. He lives and works in Southwest France, where he is working on a new title set in that country.

Lila L. Pinord

Lila L. Pinord was born and raised in a small Native American fishing village called Queets, a part of the greater Quinault Indian Nation along the coast of Washington State. Because of this, many of her own experiences and knowledge of reservation life- such as myths, legends, and superstitions of her people- are included in her writings. She attended Grays Harbor College in Aberdeen, Washington for a year, got married, then later went on to Peninsula College in Port Angeles, majoring in secretarial. From there, Lila attended Western Washington University and gained a degree in accounting. However, writing has always been her first love, and she continues it in Port Angeles, WA where she lives now. SKYE DANCER was chosen to be featured on the State of Washington Library website in December 2006 under Mysteries of the Northwest. Ms. Pinord is a contributor to 200 AUTHORS and How They Were Published, THE PUBLISHED AUTHOR'S GUIDE TO PROMOTION-Marketing tips by Published Authors, and SHAMELESS SHORTS. Her short story

JOSH DRAKE VIP is included in Gallery of Voices. Her newest book just out on the market is IN TIME, an Urban Fantasy about a young lad who time travels here on earth, trying to find his parents and a place to settle down while at the same time, his mother seeks HIM. It's not available at this time since it's now in the hands of a traditional publisher. Other books are MIN'S MONSTER and EVIL LIVES IN BLUE ROCK. All her books can be found on Amazon, and by asking for them in your favorite bookstore. Website: http://lilalpinord.bravehost.com Email: lilapinord @ yahoo.com

Dave Suscheck Jr.

Dave Suscheck grew up in Erie, Pennsylvania where his passion for reading and writing started at a young age. He has both a Bachelor's degree and Master's degree in English Literature. He attended Mercyhurst University for his undergraduate degree and Gannon University for his graduate degree. An avid reader he is influenced most by the writings of John Connolly and F. Paul Wilson, among a host of other authors. He enjoys the horror genre but reads almost everything.

Linda Jenkinson

Canadian born writer, Linda Jenkinson, has enjoyed writing for different venues, including newspaper and magazine. She was an avid member of Helium Networks where she was valued and rated highly in their 'Creative Writing' opportunities on the site. Poetry writing came rather late but remains high in her affections. She is working on a book about Lake Vampires, so this "spooky" and supernatural theme, presented in the anthology, is right up her writing alley.

L.H. Davis

Laurance H. Davis is a mechanical engineer as well as a writer of fiction. He enjoys designing robots during the day and then sends them on adventures in tales of science fiction at night. Laurance is currently working on two separate space adventure novels and several shorter manuscripts. Although Sci-Fi is his first passion, several of his mainstream short stories have been selected for inclusion in the Aspiring Writers 2014 Winners Anthology. The Florida Writers Association recognized Laurance in 2011 at the Royal Palms Literary Awards with a first place for his novella *The Emporium* and again in 2013 for his novel *Outpost Earth*. The Writers of the Future Contest recognized his work twice in 2008 with Honorable Mentions and again in 2011 as a Semi-finalist. After building and racing cars with SCCA for twenty-years, Laurance hung up his helmet in 2008 and picked up the pen. More information is available on Laurance at LHDavisWriter.com.

Alex Winck

Literary and comic book writer, editor, journalist, translator (English-Portuguese). Born February 16, 1974, in Blumenau, Brazil. Graduated in Social Communication and Journalism. First published work as a fiction writer was the educational comic book Sesinho, with a million copies distributed monthly for free at schools, for nearly 100 issues. Currently edits and writes for the horror, fantasy and sci-fi comic book and short story anthology "Contos do Absurdo" ("Tales From The Absurd"), distributed online for free. Its latest issue had over 26 thousand readers at Issuu. Features brand new comic book stories starring Brazilian horror icon Coffin Joe. It has an entire issue in English (http://www.contosdoabsurdo.com.br/tales-from-theabsurd.html). First printed comic book horror story was published in the "Contos Sinistros" ("Sinister Tales") anthology.

Joanne Magnus

I live in Western New York I enjoy writing fiction and short stories. I wrote a self-published novel called "the Next Pendragon" in 2012 and I'm working on the sequel. I have a dog named Yogi which I borrowed his name for Devil Dogs.

James Harper

A transplanted native in a city full of them, James Harper has worked as a writer and editor in Washington DC for many years. His short story, "Just for One Day," appeared in the anthology Stress City: A Big Book of Fiction by 51 DC Guys, edited by Richard Peabody. He lives in Rockville, Maryland, a suburb north of the District of Columbia, with his daughter and their 90-pound border collie crossbred Pippin. His love for music is only rivaled by his passion for film. But both take a backseat to baseball when there's a Phillies game on.

Kamalendu Nath

Kamalendu Nath, an emeritus professor at Long Island
University, NY, resides in Effingham, New
Hampshire, USA and seeks rhythm in Nature,
including human nature in poems, some of which
have appeared in the *Twisted Tongue*; *The One Three
Eight*; *Vermont Literary Review*; *Thresholds Literary
Journal; Palimpsest; The Aurorean* and in two
anthologies: *The Poets' Guide to New Hampshire*.

Samie Sands

Samie is the author of the *AM13 Outbreak Series;
Lockdown, Forgotten, and Extinct,* published by
Limitless Publishing. She is also a featured Wattpad
writer and has had stories featured in best-selling
anthologies.
http://samiesands.com

Debbie Johnson

Debbie Johnson lives in Nevada, Iowa US with a very
spoiled beagle. She has written two books, 'The
Disability Experience' and 'The Disability Experience
ll', and has been published in several journals. She has
found writing to be therapeutic in dealing with her
physical and mental disabilities. Her website and blog
are www.thedisabilityexperience.vpweb.com.

Kevin S. Hall

Kevin S. Hall is 34, and an up and coming horror
author. He has written a horror anthology called
Thirteen which you can buy online and is currently

beavering away on Thirteen 2 and Thirteen 3. He is also working on a Pet Sematary: The Series, Monster Makers gamebook, and Ravens Edge. He lives in Haddington, East Lothian, Scotland, enjoys anything sci-fi, fantasy, and horror, and loves Doctor Who.

Stefan Vucak

Stefan Vucak is an award-winning author of eight sci-fi novels, including *With Shadow and Thunder*, a 2002 EPPIE finalist. His political thriller *Cry of Eagles* won the coveted 2011 Readers' Favorite silver medal award, and his *All the Evils* was the 2013 prestigious Eric Hoffer contest finalist and Readers' Favorite silver medal winner. *Strike for Honor* won the gold medal. Stefan leveraged a successful career in the Information Technology
industry and applied that discipline to create realistic storylines for his books. When not writing, he is an editor and book reviewer. He lives in Melbourne, Australia.
Website: http://stefanvucak.com
Twitter: @stefanvucak

June Rachelson-Ospa

June is a copywriter, playwright, lyricist, book writer and producer. She is partner with Daniel Neiden in Bozomoon Productions (www.bozomoonshows.com) 1974-1985 June spent over 10 years as an advertising copywriter at Grey Advertising, Ogilvy & Mater, McCaffrey & McCall, Landor Associates. Her clients included Kenner Toys, McDonald's, Burger King. Exxon Arts and more. She created campaigns, headlines, copy, shows and more for her clients. She was a namer for 4 years for Landor Their Welcome to Tourettaville, about Tourette Syndrome, won the Kennedy Center's Very Special Arts Playwright Discovery Award and was performed for Congress at the Kennedy Center in DC: Book -June and Daniel, Lyric- June, Music- Daniel. The musical was adapted from a story written by her then seven-year-old son Jonathan who was diagnosed with TS at age five. June has many years' experience mentoring special need children through YMCA Afterschool Programs, as Academy Director at AMAS Musical Theatre, and with the National

Tourette Syndrome Association. Using musical theatre programs as the vehicle, June has successfully mentored youth with Tourette Syndrome, Asperger's Syndrome, and Obsessive-Compulsive Disorder. See full show on YouTube Tourettaville Live. And also, Tourettaville Cartoon for the animated version. http://juneospa.wix.com/tourettaville

Made in the USA
Middletown, DE
12 March 2022